CARIBBEAN ILLUSION:
A Stranger's Protection

T C Wilson

Copyright © 2024 by T.C. Wilson

Published by Gordian Books, an imprint of Winged Publications

Editor: Cynthia Hickey
Book Design by Winged Publications

All rights reserved. No part of this publication may be reproduced, stored in a retrieval system, or transmitted in any form or by any means—electronic, mechanical, photocopying, recording, or otherwise—without the prior written permission of the publisher. The only exception is brief quotations in printed reviews. Piracy is illegal. Thank you for respecting the hard work of this author.

This book is a work of fiction. Names, characters, Places, incidents, and dialogues are either products of the author's imagination or used fictitiously. Any resemblance to actual persons, living or dead, or events is coincidental.

Fiction and Literature:
Christian Romantic Suspense

ISBN: 978-1-962168-55-7

DEDICATION

To the challenges that made me stronger over the past year and God's grace and blessings

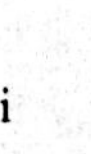

ONE

Tonight is the night…

Maneuvering the boat around the outcroppings of the coral reef under the ebony skies wasn't the brightest idea, but it was a necessary risk. The narrow dock offered little room for errors in judgment. One wrong move or overcorrection signaled certain disaster. It would be too hard to explain the damage to the "borrowed boat." Small waves splashed against the sides as the craft glided up to the slip. He jumped onto the weathered wood planks and tied off the bow and stern before grabbing a tote and heading up the ramp.

Dressed in black fatigues, he crept low toward a thick cluster of trees. His lugged soles pressed into the damp sand, marking his wide gait. Luck accompanied him on this mission; the island's peninsula remained pretty much uninhabited. Predictions of an active hurricane forecast had slashed the tourist population in half. Only the locals felt "seasoned" enough to weather the pummeling of nature's wrath.

He pulled the old metal signaling contraption from his duffle and wondered if this would work. Placing his own life in danger was one thing, but endangering "hers" was another. People were watching him, unknown people. An inability to identify those people forced his decision. Regardless of the outcome, it was too late to turn back now.

Intermittently lifting and closing the lantern's shutter door ushered forth light slivers. Short and long bursts streamed across the water. Time was up. He could no longer afford to remain. Traversing the dark path, he rushed to reboard the boat. Deftly releasing the anchor lines, the vessel veered into the sea's darkness. He prayed the message reached its intended target.

TWO

Dawn broke over the serene waters glistening on the Caribbean sand. The thumping pain of a self-induced headache forced Evan onto the beach earlier than he'd hoped. Wine, women, and Spotify provided the perfect backdrop for little to no sleep. The seven sisters' roaring laughter echoed through the Vitamin Sea's hallways until early morning.

Nursing a cup of "joe," eyeing the breaking waves, Evan was jolted from his solitude by Brent's sudden presence. The bond formed between the two men in Bridgeport months earlier had forged a lifelong friendship.

Brent massaged his temple and offered a raspy "Morning."

"No need to ask if you slept well. Who knew seven females in a house this size could cause such an uproar."

"Definitely, not me. Please tell me Steve and Cooper ARE on their way." Evan prayed for one word: yes.

"They'll arrive this afternoon; we'll have some leverage then. There's strength in numbers." Brent's attempt at spirited optimism fell short.

"Sorry to dispute your theory, buddy, but the women will still maintain the majority."

Both men chuckled and sipped their now-cold coffee.

"Hey, did you notice anything unusual across the way last night?" Brent tossed his head forward, nodding toward the opposing peninsula jutting from the crystal waters.

"Unusual?"

"Light flashes streamed this way from just beyond the treeline around midnight. Rhythmic flashes."

Evan laughed. "Brent, calm those 'spidey' senses down, buddy. It could've been a boat mooring at the docks or the lighthouse keeper making his way for a final check. It's off-season here, and most tourists abandon the place with the arrival of the hurricane season."

Brent rubbed his chin. "Perhaps, but it didn't strike me as normal."

"For our mental sanity, don't breathe a word of this to Leah. We're grossly unprepared for the upheaval your idea might cause. After Bridgeport, you know she would feel compelled to press the issue further."

"Agreed. Our plates are full enough. Whose idea was it anyway to vacation with seven women." Brent's jab struck home, earning him a nudge from Evan's shoulder.

With a slight snicker, the two men turned and headed toward the villa. The cool grains of sand beneath their bare feet offered a final moment of tranquility before encountering the ladies.

~

Amber arose slowly from the luxurious bedding that wrapped every inch of her body in contentment. Yawning, she felt compelled to ensure she wasn't dreaming. The tingling pinch of skin between her fingers produced a squeal of reality. Okay, she wasn't dreaming. She truly was in a luxurious villa for two glorious weeks of pampering.

The nightmare of Bridgeport was behind her and her friends now. Brent and Leah were deliriously happy, and Evan insisted Amber accompany them on a getaway. *Perhaps Evan changed his mind…* Nothing would make her more wildly happy than if Evan felt ready to reclaim bachelorhood, opening the door for new adventures in love. *With me, maybe?* The idea warmed her soul.

Flopping backward onto the pillowy California king,

arms extended above her head, Amber pondered how she could be so lucky. Her best friends surrounded her in this luscious tropical paradise. Plus, she'd managed to secure a hefty amount of time off prior to returning to the stagnant ventilation of airplanes and unruly passengers. Of course, she would pay dearly for convincing the other flight attendants to cover for so long. But who could turn down an all-expenses-paid vacation in a place as luxurious as Evan's Caribbean estate, the Vitamin Sea?

A short tap upon the thick wooden door made Amber beam before she whispered, "Come in."

Leah nudged the door open, peeping into the expansive room. "Well, good morning, you. Feeling okay this glorious sunny day?"

"Oh, Leah, how could I possibly be any better? I feel terrific. I must admit, I hoped you were Evan," she said with a grin. Leah's sharp blue eyes narrowed, "Evan, huh? Now, my feelings are hurt."

"Stop, you know what I mean. Evan seemed to let his guard down during our flight and open up a little. I may stand a chance if I can keep Rhonda away from him."

"Don't stress over it. Rhonda's aware of your feelings for Evan. I have a sneaky suspicion Rhonda will find herself a tan and friendly islander while we are here. Rhonda never lets an opportunity pass her by. Besides, I have my hands too full with your 'delightful' brother to separate you two," Leah giggled. "Enough talk, up and at 'em. We have big plans for the day. I'll see you in a few."

Leah headed for the door, then suddenly stopped midstride. "Amber, I'm glad you came along."

A warm sense of happiness spread over her as she hopped from the bed with a bright smile. "Me too, Leah." With a skip in her step, she rushed to dress, more than a little anxious to hurry downstairs.

THREE

The glorious aroma of freshly baked pastries assaulted her senses as soon as Amber's foot touched the stairway. She generally skipped breakfast, making do with a cup or two of liquid caffeine until noon. But today, exceptions would be made; the overwhelming sight and smell of the smorgasbord before her caused her stomach to rumble. The tablescape featured vases full of fresh tropical blossoms perfectly arranged from end to end while platters of sweet rolls, eggs, bacon, bagels, and fresh fruit filled the gaps. Piping hot brewed coffee, water, and juices lined the kitchen island. Amber giggled,

So, this is what it's like to be exceedingly rich!

She retrieved a dish from the buffet and filled the flowered porcelain plate with a sampling of all the goodies. With steaming coffee in hand, Amber steered toward the noisy dining room. She willed herself not to focus on Evan's location as she scanned the room, but her efforts had just the opposite effect. Her eyes locked on Evan within seconds, and her controlled, radiant smile faltered, sending bright red flushes to her cheeks. Evan's warm, welcoming smile caused her stomach to flip cartwheels when he waved her over. Willing her body to move, Amber inched her way toward the ornate chair beside him. Her clammy fingers loosened their hold as she sat her breakfast dish on the table and slid into the velvet seat. Laughter and plans for the day consumed the women's conversations at the furthest end of the table. Poor Brent remained by Leah's side, agreeing with the ladies when asked a question.

Amber's nervous hands shook as she placed the monogrammed linen napkin over her lap. She reached for her small hot cup and was interrupted by a husky, "Good morning."

Tightening her grip on the fragile china, she smiled, "Good morning to you. That's quite a noisy bunch down there. You'd think they were solving the world's problems," she stated, sneaking in a fortifying sip of coffee.

"They are. Today's excursion involves shopping. Doesn't retail therapy always solve any problem?" Evan chuckled.

"In most cases, I guess it does, even if only on a temporary basis. It certainly can get the endorphins stimulated. And I'm sure this island has magnificent shopping."

Amber peeped over the rim of her cup. "I know I've told you this, but thank you again for inviting me on this dream vacation. After the drama in Bridgeport, I don't think we'll ever be able to repay you for whisking us away to paradise."

"We all needed a little distraction, and 'Vitamin Sea' is the perfect place to shut the world out. Besides, Leah refused to return to work until I made good on the vacation request she canceled during the merger." His broad smile sent a surge of excitement through her.

Evan gently touched Amber's trembling hand resting on her cup. "I'm sorry I was preoccupied with other matters before our arrival. You asked me to open my eyes to my alternatives in Charlotte. Remember? I'm ready to explore that option if you can give me a chance." His soft eyes pleaded for her agreement.

Amber projected her most resilient expression. "Why, Mr. Holcomb, that option may surpass the euphoria of retail therapy." She squeezed his hand, fully contented with his touch.

Their private moment was abruptly interrupted by Brent's command, “Excuse me, are you two even listening?”

Unnoticed by Amber and Evan, Brent had moved to the seat adjacent to Evan.

Amber's loving gaze fell over Brent, “Yes, dear brother, we hear you.”

“Sis, Evan and I need to run errands; we won't be accompanying you ladies today. Can I count on you to help Leah this afternoon?”

Brent’s request sounded more like a command. Amber tilted her head in confusion. “We are just doing a little shopping. I'm unsure what you mean, but you can count on me.” She chuckled.

“Thanks, sis. Evan, you ready?”

Evan slowly pushed his chair away from the table, issuing her a flirtatious wink. “On my way.”

Amber sighed, eyes alight.

That man sure can make a girl's head swim.

~

Brent rushed Evan to the Range Rover parked in the garage, steering him toward the driver's door. His muttered “you drive” demand prompted Evan's quizzical look. Brent’s overhand toss propelled the keys through mid-air into an outstretched hand. As soon as the men were buckled in, Evan gunned the all-terrain vehicle's engine and raced down the cut-stone drive. Shards of loose gravel flew from underneath the chassis. It wasn't until the car slowed at the crossroads that Brent offered an explanation for their urgent departure.

Brent thrust his palm forward toward Evan. “Before you bombard me with questions, I have legitimate reasons for my actions.”

“I don't have any questions. I've learned from our previous adventures never to doubt your intuition. Go ahead, fill me in."

"Remember when I asked you about the activity across the peninsula this morning?"

"Yes, and unfortunately, I still have nothing to add. I never saw the lights."

"I realized something while you were cozying up to my sister at breakfast. I've played the scene over and over my head. Those weren't some random beams floating in the darkness. It was some kind of signal."

"Uh-huh. You sure?" Evan's brow arched.

"99.9 percent. I knew the pattern seemed rhythmic, but it wasn't until breakfast that I realized it was Morse Code. Amber and I would joke around as kids, sending signals to my buddy across the street, pretending we were spies. I haven't seen or used code since the early phases of my military career. But you can be certain someone focused that signal in our direction for a reason."

"Why signal us? As far as anyone knows, we're just tourists. True, I own the house but rarely have time to visit. I know a few locals, that's about it. The caretakers haven't experienced any issues, or they would've told me. So, why me? Or should I say, us?"

"Maybe it wasn't meant for you or me. Think for a moment; we're not the only ones staying at the house."

"Come on, Brent. You mean you think this random signal was for one of the women." Evan ran his fingers through coal-dark hair in disbelief.

"I can't say that for sure, but I know we're going to find out. We have time before Steve and Cooper arrive. Let's check out that area. Who knows, we may find something. I can't just ignore this. Something is off." Concern constricted Brent's features.

"Tell me one thing before we set out on this 'treasure hunt.' Do you have any clue what this mysterious code said?"

"Yeah." Brent swallowed hard. "I think it said, GO

HOME.”

Evan’s shoulders tensed as he stepped on the gas, pushing the pedal to the floor. They stared straight ahead without speaking. Each envisioned their own version of who, what, and why this happened.

FOUR

Leah, Amber, and the group's surrogate "mom," Carol, herded the group into the van. Carol's euphoria over the coming hours of retail therapy spilled into giddiness.

"I simply cannot wait until we get there. You girls know I'm not one to enjoy shopping, but being in this tropical atmosphere has me longing to change my wardrobe up a bit. So, Kimberly, I'll need your expert fashion advice today." Her grin turned contagious.

Everyone but Rhonda shared Carol's enthusiasm. "Carol, you know you'll never wear what you buy again. Unless you're planning another luxurious getaway? Have you changed your mind about finding a new husband?" Rhonda's eyes twinkled with satisfaction, knowing her teasing would incite a comeback from Carol.

"Rhonda, everything isn't always about finding a man. While you can't live without one, I'm content to enjoy my life as it is." Her exasperated huff spoke volumes.

"You know I'm just messing with you, Carol. But your analogy isn't incorrect," Rhonda giggled. "A girl can never have too many male friends."

"Stop the bantering, you two, and let's get moving. We have places to go!" Leah pulled the heavy van door to a close and signaled the driver. In less than five minutes, the van entered the shopper's utopia.

Modest island streets touted talented vendor setups of all shapes and sizes, from the small palm-thatched bamboo roadside huts to the mainstream brick-and-mortar luxury stores. Sparse groups of tourists meandered along the sidewalks clad in faded shorts, flip-flops, and neon shirts. Living on "island time" was a true phenomenon at the remote isle. Time itself held no value for them. Relaxation and enjoyment were the only pursuits in this little corner of paradise.

The driver eased alongside the curb, assisted each lady as she stepped out of the van, and promised to return in a few hours. Carol grabbed Kimberly's hand, tugging her into a vibrant boutique while Suzanne and Rhonda skirted toward the endless array of jewelry stands. Amber casually strolled toward a local artist's shanty, eyes alight with the brilliant hues of the many coastline works of art available for sale while Charlie and Leah stood motionless on the sidewalk. Charlie's quiet mood compelled Leah to question their previous conversation.

Leah smiled, nudging Charlie's foot with her own.

"You seem somewhat preoccupied this morning. Want to talk about it?"

Charlie's startled expression met Leah's genuine smile, "What? Oh, I'm sorry. I don't mean to be."

"You're still thinking about last night, aren't you?"

"Leah, I know what I saw. There's no mistaking the message. But why? Who was the intended recipient? Too many unanswered questions have my reporter instincts in overdrive. Not to mention the message's encrypted meaning - GO HOME."

"Call me crazy, but I choose to believe it was nothing. Brent's intuition is always on par, and he hasn't uttered a word. Could your suspicions be a lingering after-effect from our troubles in Bridgeport?" Leah shrugged, "Just asking."

"I can assure you they're not. I've dealt with much worse when I lived in New York. Something isn't right. What if Brent saw it, too, and didn't want to alarm you?

You know how protective he is toward you." Charlie's voice trembled when she spoke. "Leah, this is real. I assure you."

Filled with uneasiness, Leah responded, "We must keep this from the others for as long as possible. No need to arouse anyone if you're wrong."

Amber strolled over to the two women and leaned in. "What are we whispering about?" she chuckled.

"Oh, nothing important. Did you find a painting you liked?" Leah smiled.

"I did. Come and see it for yourself. And by the way, I don't believe either of you. I'm not blind, you know. The villa's windows offer quite an expansive view of the peninsula in the evenings." Amber's curious smirk gave her away. Leah knew she spoke the truth. Now, there were three – who else had suspicions over the latest unspoken observations? She sighed, acutely aware that Charlie's track record outweighed her doubts.

Amber moved between the two women, linked arms, and offered a calming smile as she ushered them toward her newfound coastal "Rembrandt."

~

Rafe Culliver was a man of few words. A loner at heart, he'd dedicated his life to serving his country. Secret missions, midnight rendezvous, and constant training consumed his days, nights, and anything in between. Being an ace at his job was easy. Guys in his profession shied away from setting down roots - no roots – no trail to follow.

His arrival on the remote island six months ago managed to go unnoticed. Securing the small marina's unassuming "deckhand" job was a breeze. Tie a few nautical rope knots, know the difference between the bow and stern, and it was a done deal. The mundane, repetitious daily rentals of jet skis, small charter boats, and saltwater fishing excursions afforded Rafe the time to analyze other data.

Initially, the endless mounds of tide charts and ledgers meticulously stacked upon the worn mahogany desk remained unnoticed. Any co-worker who took notice would constantly tease the "off-islander" regarding his fascination with the warm, gentle waters or storm patterns. Knowing that no human, only God, could project where storms or catastrophes would strike next, the islanders attributed his obsession to some scientific research program.

Now, things were different. Shadows lurked on the quiet, dimly lit streets, following his every move. Heavy footsteps walked in unison with his own. Daily life posed an internal battle for him. Use his skilled training and end their pursuit, or remain calm and focused on what may come next. Someone had grown suspicious of his "recon" efforts. He understood identifying his adversary would be impossible right now. Instead, he continued his clueless persona of the outsider trying to comprehend the incidents that surrounded him, playing the role of "nerdy newbie" to its full extent. That is until he realized two childhood friends were vacationing in the same tropical sanctuary. All missions required the utmost secrecy. If recognized, more lives than his would be in danger.

Frustrated, he huffed. His mission suddenly encompassed outliers he was unprepared to handle. Pushing the thought into the back recesses of his mind, he began his day. Midnight black coffee, the stronger, the better, and a cool shower ushered in a familiar routine. Caffeinated and refreshed, Rafe balanced the small thread above the threshold, secured the weather-beaten door, and headed to the docks.

~

The three women stood before the watercolor marvels, oohing and aahing over the serenity that met their gaze. Golden beams spilled onto the easel stands, illuminating the canvases and issuing a "buy me" call to the trio.

Amber, Charlie, and Leah bantered back and forth over their top choices. Amber declared artistic perfection in a rendition of crystal bay waters, anchored yachts, and pastel bungalows lining the beach.

"This is it!"

Easing over to the merchant, Amber proclaimed, "That one. I'll take it."

Always willing to strike a bargain, the merchant bartered a "three for one" deal. His refusal to take no for an answer had the women laughing in jest about his skills as they toted their new paintings down the narrow walkway.

Amber's calls to her friends went unheard as the other two ladies continued single-file down the cobblestone path, babbling away, unaware of her absence. Unfazed, Amber stopped, her focus drawn to an exquisite ring sparkling from the storefront display. The piece, perched on the white velvet stand, rendered her breathless. A royal blue, emerald-cut stone glistened atop a wide gold band enhanced by rows of brilliant diamonds. She'd never seen a more magnificent ring. Amber could only imagine the historical tales tied to the luxurious antique accessory.

Captivated by its beauty, Amber blinked, absorbing one last unblemished vision of her second prize of the day. The shiny window reflected images of passers-by that lingered in the glass. Angered initially by their distraction, a sudden rush of recognition of one of those reflections forced a gasp from her lips. Whirling around, she scanned the small group of tourists, searching for his silhouette before the crowd vanished down the lane. Unable to move, she contemplated if her uneasiness was a case of over-imagination or an unwanted reminder of the past. How could a random shadow carry any resemblance to her forgotten childhood friend? Amber squeezed her eyes closed.

No way, it can't be.

The slight touch on her elbow snapped her back to reality. Whipping around to address the person intruding on her thoughts sent her new purchase sailing onto the cobbles. Eyes alight, Amber sighed with relief at her two friends' appearance. Rhonda and Suzanne, stunned, mouths open wide, apologized profusely.

“I'm so sorry, Amber. We thought you heard us calling out to you. We've been trying to catch up with everyone.” Suzanne wrung her hands together.

“Amber, how did you end up way back here? It's quite far from the main street. I'm surprised we ran into you. We were trying a very misguided shortcut back to the van.” Suzzane mumbled.

“Actually,” Rhonda interjected. “I was following the directions of a wildly handsome islander in hopes of crossing his path again.” A slinky smirk played on her voluminous lips.

“No, no, it's fine. You just caught me off guard. This ring mesmerized me.” Amber uttered, pointing to the window's showcase.

Rhonda's face brightened. “That has to be a custom piece. It’s gorgeous. Maybe my sexy islander friend knows the owner. We should ask him, that is, if I ever see him again!”

Ignoring Rhonda's comments, Amber remained fixated on the mysterious silhouette reflection from moments before. Years had passed since she'd seen her childhood friend, Rafe Culliver. In reality, he was Brent's friend. She was the little sister allowed to tag along behind the boys. Rafe always protected and cared for her as a big brother would his baby sister. The image's sandy blonde hair, taunt posturing, and aviator sunglasses produced instant snapshot memories from her high school days. Rafe's rugged, hunky looks had provided him ample female companionship since their teens, but his heart seemed to belong to only one thing – his country. A noisy "hmm" guided her back to the present.

Hands perched on her hips, Rhonda muttered, "Are we going to stand here all day? I'm ready to return to my Shangri-La by the sea, collapse in a comfy pool lounger, and enjoy an ice-cold drink. Buy the ring, or let's move on!" Shifting her weight, she tapped her foot.

"On second thought, don't buy it. Wait and have a man buy it for you. Let's go." With her orders given, Ronda proceeded down the walkway.

Suzanne shrugged and threw her hands in the air before toddling behind Rhonda. Left with no choice but to follow, Amber blew a whisp of hair from her eyes and reluctantly moved in step behind the two ladies with her beloved work of art once again secured under her arm. She couldn't wait to show Brent and Evan her new masterpiece.

Somehow, the three found the correct pathway, placing them only a block away from their assigned pickup point. Trudging toward the van, Amber heard the other "sisters" howling with laughter.

"Lord, Rhonda, you look as though you've walked fifty miles." Leah's cheeks puffed, stifling another eruption.

"I will have you know, Ms. Reynolds, we were given very poor directions. We have been wandering these streets for hours." Rhonda announced as she flopped into her seat, straightened her clothes, and gave an indignant look to anyone with more questions.

Giggles rippled throughout the van, creating an entertaining atmosphere for everyone except Rhonda during the ride back to the house.

FIVE

The Range Rover eased onto the pebble road. Both men sat erect, scanning the narrow drive for anything unusual. Tropical foliage sprouted from the ground, creating an aromatic privacy barrier of colorful blooms. The trail, void of houses or structures, continued the peninsula's length. Evan slowed the vehicle to a stop.

"We have to go the rest of the way on foot. To the best of my memory, just through there lies a drop-off that leads down to an old boat dock." He pointed toward a tight line of trees.

"You sure this is the area directly across from your place?" Brent's skepticism was apparent in his voice.

"This place was once party central for hordes of vacationing teenagers. Bonfires, loud music, and, I assume, lots of beer provided many a night's entertainment. I was awakened more than once by parties here. Trust me. It's the place."

Brent released his seatbelt. "Okay, let's go."

Evan took the lead. Forced to turn sideways to maneuver through the tight path, the men proceeded forward. After several minutes, the trail ended, giving way to a scenic panoramic view. Caribbean blue waters provided a picture vastly different from the overgrown path.

Evan wiped the sweat from his brow. Grinning with satisfaction, he looked at Brent.

"Guess I'm right again," he chuckled, nodding toward Vitamin Sea across the water.

"I stand corrected. There's the dock. Come on." Brent slid his foot to the rough edge. The short three-foot drop was merely a step forward for the two robust men. "Move carefully. I don't want to destroy any evidence that might be here."

"Evidence? How do we know we weren't the stooges in some teenage prank? I remain mystified why anyone would signal us with the words, 'go home.' We're 99 percent sure we don't know anyone here. Most tourists left, and the few people I know besides staff are back in the States. What are the odds our one percent outlier is responsible?" Evan scratched his shadowed jaw stubble, perplexed.

"Can't say, but after our last experience, I've learned not to take anything for granted."

With each step forward, Brent investigated the firm sand while Evan focused on the dock. He trod carefully over to the weathered pieces of sea-worn planking. Rusted nails protruded from the splintered wood dock that extended just past exposed shallow coral outcroppings. Evan speculated the water depth increased to around twenty feet at the dock's end, making it the perfect landing spot for small outboards or jet skis. Seeing the area up close, he understood why teenagers loved the place. The seclusion, calm waters, and endless driftwood supplied everything needed for a beach bonfire.

Sparkling clear waters glistened in the noonday sun. Shadows danced across the shallow ripples forced to shore by the currents. Evan prepared to succumb to his lost cause search when a silver sliver beneath the water caught his attention. The small fragment lodged between a piece of coral and a rusted beer can swayed upward and then back down with each pull of the tides. Crouching down, he shoved his arm beneath the water's surface, extending his fingertips as far as possible. The water depth deceived him; it was much deeper than he'd anticipated. Evan, flat on his stomach, stretched over the dock edge, bending as far as possible, yet the object still eluded his grasp. Frustrated, he rubbed the back of his neck and expelled a few choice words. He released a loud "UGH" that brought Brent over to the dock.

"Should I ask what that was about?" Brent's forehead wrinkled. "I suggested we visit here on a hunch. Of course, I never said we would find something."

"That's where you're wrong, my friend. I may have. I can't reach the darn thing, though. See there." Evan motioned beneath the water. "It couldn't have been there long. There's no rust or corrosion."

"Let a pro handle this." Brent emptied his pockets, tossed his shoes aside, and jumped from the dock's end. Surfacing, he swam over to Evan's mark. "Take notes, my friend!"

Brent inhaled deeply, offered a thumbs up, and dove straight down. His fingers locked around the shiny object on the first try; swift kicks propelled him upward. Breaching the ocean's surface, his broad grin spoke volumes.

"Mission accomplished." A shiny silver chain and clip dangled from his fingertips.

Evan saluted Brent in admiration.

On shore, dripping wet, Brent stood motionless, staring at their newly found prize.

"Well, is it of importance or just another lost trinket?" Evan questioned.

"It's not a trinket. If I am correct, these are very rare. From my understanding, only a dozen exist, and even fewer individuals own one." He pushed wet curls away from his face for a better look. Brent rubbed the object gently, revealing an engraving, "The Brigadier." His mouth gaped.

"Not that look again." Evan reached for the clip. A

closer inspection revealed a flat oval piece of sterling silver. "The Brigadier" etched on one side piqued his curiosity.

"Brent, if it's so rare and what you say is true, what is it doing here? Where have YOU seen this?"

"Several years ago, a buddy of mine was awarded one of these for his black ops services. I've only seen it once. 'The Brigadier' was a code name for their mission. That's all I know. I haven't seen my friend in years. He's a ghost who disappears without warning. You're never really sure if he's alive or dead. These guys live to serve and protect our country. But there's no way this could be his. He'd never part with something so dear."

Evan dried the silver bar on his shirttail and shoved it into his pocket. "I'll hang on to this."

"You wouldn't have a spare towel in the Rover, would you?" Brent brushed his hands over his soggy shirt, slinging drops of water through the air.

"We can check. Question: do you know who else owns one of these?"

"Nope, but we're going to find out." The ring of determination in Brent's words signaled trouble. Evan knew from experience the grit in Brent's tone meant one thing – walking away wasn't an option. Concealing Brent's newfound mission from the ladies would require help, and thankfully, that help was sitting in an airport on the opposite side of the island. That is if Steve and Cooper hadn't boarded a flight back to the States by now.

The two men headed toward a welcome easier path to the trees and car. Brent scaled the rocky rise first. Just behind, Evan raised his heel and bore his weight into the thick clay. Ready to ascend, he angled for a handhold. On his left sat the clear image of a lug sole embedded into the clay. Hurriedly, he yanked out his phone and snapped two photos. He'd share the pictures later. The detour with Brent took much longer than expected. The Rover traveled the dirt pathway at breakneck speed. Steve and Cooper would have a few choice words to offer in response to their delay. *But what else was new?* Evan grinned.

~

Neon beach towels padded the white loungers as the women's bodies absorbed the warmth of the golden sun's rays. The seven ladies laid perfectly aligned along the expansive poolside. Small bamboo umbrella garnishes topped their drinks with fresh pineapple, berries, and cherries. As the conversations flowed about them, Amber took note and listened. Rhonda babbled on and on to Suzanne about the handsome islander who couldn't keep his eyes off her and her quest to see him again before their departure. Leah, Charlie, and Kimberly thumbed through magazines, comparing the latest trends in the pages to the selections in the island's boutiques. On occasion, Carol peered over the top of her book, snatching a quick glimpse of the other ladies before returning to her novel. Amber kept her eyes tightly shut, recounting the day's events under the penetrating warmth of the tropical sun. Luckily, no one noticed her lack of participation. Perhaps they thought she needed a quick nap. Whatever the reason, she was grateful for the peace. Her thoughts wandered from childhood to high school and back to the man's reflection in the square.

Should I tell Brent?

She struggled with the decision since she and Brent never kept secrets from each other. Her thoughts of Rafe Culliver consumed her. She'd hoped to relax and enjoy sunbathing with her friends, but relaxation evaded her.

Could it have been him?

Sure that the island heat must be getting to her, Amber rose from her chair and dove into the pool, splashing cool water onto her friends. Shrieks of surprise echoed about the pool, causing several of the women to follow Amber's lead.

Splashing, laughter, and squeals greeted the men upon their return to "Vitamin Sea." Their broad smiles echoed the joy in their eyes. Cooper turned to Brent, nodding toward the ladies' voices.

"This is what we have been missing! Why did you wait so long to call us." Cooper's cheekbones flushed red. "See ya." Dropping his bags, Cooper tossed, "I'll get those later," and bolted for the veranda.

Steve raised his eyebrows, amused, "On behalf of both of us, I want to thank you again, Evan, for your generous invitation. Things have been rather chaotic since our return to Charlotte. It's been really tough trying to conceal the events surrounding the ribbon cutting and merger. Some tabloids contacted a few emergency responders, offering a fast buck for information. I think we've calmed the rumors for now. Luckily, John took control of things in Bridgeport rather quickly, silencing the gossip mongers."

Evan smiled, "I knew John would come through when needed."

"It appears he and Martha have become fast friends with Troy Marshall. Marshall is now their 'go-to' man. Things appear to be running quite well during your absence." Steve chuckled.

"That's good to hear since we all may need to extend our vacation." Evan declared.

Steve's eyes narrowed. "You won't hear me complaining about staying longer, but I sense the invitation carries a hidden meaning. One of you care to fill me in?"

Leah's pointed finger swaying from side to side forced their conversation to an abrupt halt.

"Uhh, uhh, no way. The last time I saw the three of you huddled up like this, disaster was about to strike. Out with it, Brent Scott! What's going on?" Her arms folded across her waist.

Brent's hand covered his heart in wounded pride.

"What? I haven't done anything. We're discussing our plans for the remainder of the week. We have nothing to hide, do we, Evan?" Brent deflected the conversation to his friend before his willpower faltered.

Steve remained quiet and stepped backward, ready to run.

"Oh, no, you don't, Steve Alexander. I have a sneaky feeling you're just as guilty of something as these two are!"

"Me? I just arrived. I declare on my honor, Leah, I'm unaware of any unscrupulous behavior by these two." He nodded toward his friends.

Evan knew how to curtail Leah's suspicions. "Okay, you caught us."

Brent clutched his throat and coughed.

"If there's one thing I've learned, it's the fact that I can't conceal things from you. Forcing me to tell you will ruin the surprise, but if you insist, here goes … we're extending our stay for a few weeks. Based on the report from Steve, nothing warrants our hasty return to the States. John seems to have the business well in hand. Our absence will give him time to flex his muscles and grow his confidence. I can't think of a better time. How about you?" Evan paused. "What if everyone stays? That's if the ladies can adjust their schedules. I've extended the invitation to Steve and Cooper, also."

"Brent, what do you think? Of course, it's up to you, but I'm not complaining." Leah grinned, batting her long lashes.

Brent released a lengthy exhale as his face returned to its normal color. "Have I ever denied one of your requests?" He pulled Leah into him and lovingly kissed her full lips. "Well, Holcomb, looks like we're staying."

"Perfect, I'm going to tell the ladies!" Filled with happiness, Leah pranced down the hallway.

"Remind me when they hand out awards for the biggest 'bs shooter' to nominate you." Brent touted.

"More importantly, when will you gentlemen enlighten me about why we're truly lengthening our stay?" Steve inquired.

Cooper rushed the men, bouncing from one foot to the other. "Is it true? We're staying another two weeks?" Steve's nod moved the man to a prayerful, "Thank you, Lord."

Sporting a broad grin, Cooper snatched up his bags and waited for directions.

"Up the stairs and to the left. Pick any room." Evan laughed.

"Got it." Cooper climbed the stairs, two at a time, in his haste.

Brent hesitated. "Steve, we may have a slight situation. For now, I think it's best to separate and give the appearance all is well. You and Coop head to the veranda when you both get settled."

"This all sounds rather ominous. It can't be as serious as our last adventure." Steve chuckled and followed Cooper's path up the stairs.

~

Eruptions of laughter and giggles echoed around the pool. Whisperings of an extended stay placed everyone in a joyous mood, except Amber. Evan's arrival went unnoticed. His focus shifted to Amber's forlorn expression the instant he crossed the lanai.

"Hello." He whispered, positioning himself on the rattan chaise beside her.

"Why the sad look? I thought you'd be happy to have another two weeks in paradise." Evan intently examined her solemn expression. Secretly, he'd hoped she longed to be in his company a little longer as he had hers.

Amber raised her head, peered into his captivating eyes, and sighed, "I don't think I can stay. My boss was reluctant to grant my first request. If I ask for two more weeks, I'll be unemployed." The tears she tried not to show dribbled down her cheeks.

Evan's thumbs gently stroked her face, wiping away the moisture. "Hey, I'll have no tears. This trip's supposed to be an escape. I'm not ready for you to return to the States. That is, not if you'd like to spend more time alone getting to know each other better. I certainly do." His sensual lips curved into a sexy smile.

"I'd love that. The house is a little crowded sometimes." She giggled. "But unless a miracle happens, my luggage and I will be on a plane headed to Charlotte three days from now."

"You know, I'm very good at making miracles happen," He promised as his fingers entwined with Amber's.

"Ms. Scott, shall I work a miracle for you?" Evan questioned, leaning into her, their lips only inches apart.

A bashful nod acknowledged her agreement. Amber's innocent smile, dewy eyes, and lush lips pushed him to the edge, unconcerned with the audience surrounding them. Evan bent his head ever so slightly, meeting her lips with his. Soft caressing kisses grazed her upper, then lower lip. Gentle nips tested her willingness to concede. Streaks of fire reignited dormant longings he thought he'd never experience again. His soft moan slowed when he felt her brief hesitance before she responded with an exploration of her own, confirming mutual needs. Loud cheers floated in the distance. Unfazed, Evan tightened his hold. Nothing existed except the need for time to stop… and a little privacy. The unwanted parting of their lips ushered in Amber's groan of disapproval. No longer able to avoid the obnoxious jeering, the two frowned at the captive audience taking in every detail of their encounter.

"Hey buddy, that's my sister!" Brent's friendly grin contradicted his stern words.

Laughter erupted around them when Rhonda interjected, "Let the fun begin! Woohoo." A command declared in true Rhonda fashion.

Steve and Cooper's arrival on the veranda amidst the hullabaloo signaled things in paradise were about to get very interesting.

SIX

Rafe Culliver knew blending with the small group of tourists offered minimal concealment; however, it was his only option. Exasperated that his intel proved accurate, he cursed under his breath. For once, he'd longed to be wrong.

Rafe muttered unheard pleas into the air about him and lowered his head in the hope of hiding beneath the beat-up straw-brimmed hat. Now certain that Amber was indeed staying on the island, he figured Brent must be around somewhere. During their childhood excursions, Amber never left Brent's side. Always the dutiful sister that scurried behind the two boys, she'd served as their gopher, snack maker, and lookout. Her presence aggravated Brent but was a welcome inclusion for Rafe, an only child.

Amber's reflection in the storefront glass caught his attention immediately. There was no mistaking her for another woman. To Rafe, Amber's natural beauty shrouded her with a shield of wholesomeness. From the day he'd met her, he sensed something was unique about Amber. Her braided pigtails bounced to and fro as a kid during their romps about the neighborhood. Little freckles crossed the bridge of her nose, while her long legs in full dash could propel her past even the fastest child on the block. Conjured memories only filled him with regret. Regretful for things he should have said or done. Rafe rubbed his hands briskly from forehead to chin to wash away the thoughts.

You chose your career and country - she has another life now.

Once again, he shoved those memories into the vast recesses of his mind, increasing his stride to reach the docks. The familiar sound of footsteps approaching on his left side spiked his defenses. Today was different. He sensed a lone tracker instead of the usual two or three. He had no time to determine why. The greater the distance between him and Amber, the safer she would be, or so he hoped.

Rafe relied on his endurance training and bolted into a full sprint. He knew those dreaded 6 a.m. workouts in paradise would prove beneficial, and today seemed the day. Acting like he was late for his duties, Rafe jerked open the marina door and yelled, "Hello, everyone." A quick check behind him as he closed the door offered no insight into a pursuer. They'd disappeared, or he'd lost them during the run.

His friend, Paschal, jumped to his feet, arms flailing in fright from the abrupt welcome. "Dude, do you really think offering such a deafening hello was necessary? You're interrupting my afternoon nap time. Besides, I thought you were off today. What brings you to the docks? I can think of better things to do than be here." He grumbled, settling back into the worn leather recliner, dragging his hat over his eyes.

"Ah, Paschal, every hour of the day is your nap time. Unlike you, I like to move around and enjoy the day. I needed to check this week's schedule and see if the storm forecasts have changed. Think we will dodge a bullet?" Rafe prayed the storm turned away from the remote island. His friends needed time to depart, and his mission's completion depended on it.

Paschal eased forward, "Tell me, my friend, why are you so fascinated with the storms that disrupt our peaceful waters? Be an islander for a while. Enjoy the cool breezes, find a shady hammock near the beach, and take a siesta. You're always so keyed up over the charts. Chicks don't like uptight men. Didn't your mom let you play outside when you were younger? Embrace life, man!"

"You have me all wrong. I'm not uptight; I'm voracious. We learn from our past by searching its treasure trove of historical data. Those charts provide more information than you can imagine. Wind speeds, current strength, storm intensity, and shipwrecked boat names are all vital elements to better understand how to increase survivability during the catastrophic events mother nature inflicts upon us. If that makes me a nerd, then I guess I'm a nerd." Rafe turned and wiped the sweat from his brow. He hoped Paschal bought the load of crap he just shoveled on him.

"You're a deep dude, but there's some truth in what you're saying," Paschal agreed. Standing, he straightened his hat. "This place is my home, and I'm all for doing anything I can to keep it safe. I'm joining forces with you. Count me in." He edged toward the day's bulletins and charts with a newfound purpose.

Rafe drummed his fingers on the desk. Apprehension filled his body. His impromptu plan to navigate Paschal's attention anywhere but on his true mission could save the man's life

"Paschal, you will tire easily from staring at endless stacks of charts. Are you sure you want to help?" Rafe exhaled. "What will all your girlfriends say when you cut back on their romantic time."

A brilliant smile beamed from Paschal's lips, "There'll be enough of me to go around. Don't you worry. My ladies will be fine." He reared his shoulders back in pride and returned to the charts.

Left with no alternative, Rafe uttered, "If you're sure and willing to work on your day off, I'll accept your offer. We start tomorrow." Paschal smiled. Rafe was sure of one thing … tonight would be "ladies" night.

"Where are the charters for tomorrow?" Rafe rifled through the mounds of papers scattered about the worn, wood-splintered desk for the listings. "We'll need a boat. Hopefully, there's a small one available."

"Yo, man, heads up," Paschal yelled as he sailed a worn-out clipboard through the air. Rafe's mid-air snatch prevented the board from striking his right temple.

Laughter erupted from his friend. "Dude, you have cat-like reflexes."

Intent on the names listed, Rafe offered no reply. Suddenly, there, written in black ink, was the one person he was unprepared to see. His search of the crinkled yellow pages came to an abrupt halt.

Not possible!

Rafe kneaded his fingers against his neck's clammy skin. Tingles ran down his spine. Anxiety overwhelmed his body. If he didn't play his cards right, disaster would strike long before he anticipated it. Tomorrow's undercurrents would pose a problem in more ways than one.

The daylight hours gave way to a glorious sunset without notice during Rafe's intensive search through the hordes of shipwreck logs. Thankfully, his efforts offered the location of one wreck he felt sure had escaped detection from other marauders. His childhood obsession with pirates and treasure prepared him for this mission. Ages of pirates' plunderous ships blanketed the ocean floor — some worthless relics, victims of spawned storms, outmatched by the sea's ferocious tidal waves. Others suffered the wrath of cannon fire and lost battles on the open seas, bested by skilled scavengers. But Rafe's treasure hunt involved a modern-day vessel lost long after the days of pirates' booty. Her cargo was so valuable the "manifest" never even mentioned the contents.

Paschal's return to the office drew Rafe's attention. "All boats are anchored and refueled, and the jet skis are washed and ready. So, let's get out of here. I don't know about you, but I have a big night planned." Paschal removed his straw-brimmed headpiece, rubbed his hands together, and smoothed the coal-black strands of hair away from his brow. With a grin, he tugged on his shirt collar in affirmation of his "cool" factor and turned to Rafe. "My fan club awaits." Arm extended in a wave of goodbye, Paschal headed toward the door. "See ya in the morning, dude."

Rafe laughed. "Don't worry. I'll lock up."

Tired and hungry, Rafe flipped off the lights, eased the door closed, and twisted the knob for a final check. Confident the office was secure, he checked his watch. It was past time for a bite of food at his favorite hangout. The old dock planking moaned under the pressure of his footsteps, producing a familiar creak with each step. That is, until those creaking noises multiplied tenfold from the additional weight of someone behind him.

Nevertheless, Rafe's sense of urgency remained minimal. He assumed that tonight would be like any other night. His "friends" would follow behind, skulk in the shadows, and ensure he ventured straight home. However, on this moonlit night, the word "assume" would spark a profound change in how he'd conduct his mission from here on out.

The sudden, powerful grip on his arm triggered instinctive defensive maneuvers that placed Rafe and his attacker face to face. Slim in stature, the man exhibited a surprising amount of upper body strength for his size. Glazed, mission-driven eyes stared into Rafe's. Undeterred by Rafe's quick actions, the man blinked, determined to achieve the superior hold. An upper thrust sailed past Rafe's head, prompting an elusive turnabout that resulted in the sudden snap of the man's shoulder. Wails of pain filled the air. A second assailant emerged from the darkness as if he sensed his partner's defeat.

A thick, sweaty bicep seized Rafe from behind,

applying a stranglehold around his neck. A fast hop and his swift kick to the first attacker's upper body propelled the man face-first onto the dock. Rafe gasped for air before slamming an elbow into the man's chunky midsection. Struggling to breathe, the second attacker doubled over and cursed. Back for more, the slim assailant dragged himself to his feet and leaped forward. Rafe drew a deep breath and launched a right upper hook to his jaw. The man bellowed in pain again before falling to the ground. Both men struggled to return to an upright position. Each hurled insults and accusations at the other for failure to subdue their target, forgetting about Rafe. Prepared for another round, Rafe stood firm.

Suddenly, bursts of laughter floated on the air when a group of intoxicated partygoers stumbled onto the marina gangway. In fear of detection, the two goons scurried into the night, uttering vows to return and finish their task.

Rafe massaged his bruised throat. His eyes darted from left to right in search of his assailants, but he sensed they were long gone. Theories of the men's identities swirled in his head.

What just happened?

Something had escaped his detection, leaving him vulnerable. His assailants were amateurs. Professionals would have provided a greater challenge and possibly succeeded in their quest – capture or murder. Neither option appealed to him for understandable reasons. Nevertheless, he remained thankful that the inebriated group approached when they did.

"Hey, mister, can you tell me where the Savannah Jane's docked?" The lanky twenty-something tourist's words slurred into multiple drawn-out syllables.

Rafe rubbed the muscles in his neck. "Down the docks and to the left. You'll see it anchored in the second slip." One eyebrow raised, questioning, "Having a party tonight?"

"Our final hurrah before we leave tomorrow. Wanna come with?" offered a tanned blonde coed. "We're headed to the peninsula's bonfire beach. You know where it is?"

Bonfire Beach!

Rafe knew the area too well. "No one's leaving this dock for bonfire beach unless you have someone a little less, let's say, 'happy' that can handle the boat. That area can be tricky during low tide." Prepared for a debate, Rafe waited. "And by the way, who offered you the use of the SJ?"

A deep throaty proclamation emerged from the group, "I've got it, sir." Moving from the rear of the group stood a clean-cut, fit male, most likely the only sober person in the group by Rafe's detection.

"I'll drive the boat and make sure everyone's careful. I have some navigation experience in these waters, and we don't plan to be out that long. I have permission from a friend to use the Savannah Jane." He lifted the keys in the air, driving his promise home.

Rafe smiled and reflected on his early twenties and the mischief he used to get into.

"I'm going to hold you to your word. I'll check on the Savannah Jane bright and early tomorrow to ensure her safe return to the docks. Don't let me down." His stern stare fostered a quick response.

"Yes, sir. I understand. You can count on me." Then, issuing directions, the boat driver herded the bunch toward Savannah Jane's slip.

With a fatherly nod, Rafe turned and headed down the gangway with a grin, sure the house across the peninsula would also be having a late night. *Perhaps they would cancel their charter tomorrow.* The prospect crossed his mind as he rubbed his achy joints and headed home.

SEVEN

The tropical sunrise splashed bright golden hues along the seafoam-covered water's edge. Amber's toe tapped at the small waves that inched closer with each break of the surf. Her thoughts drifted toward Evan.

Was yesterday a dream?

The slow drag of an index finger across her lips assured her it was no dream. Her lips still tingled from Evan's touch. Reminded of her silly, superstitious childhood wish, she smiled softly. Could a wishing well coin toss have created the events surrounding her now? Only time would tell. She stifled a giggle. Superstition or not, there would be no complaining from her. Her heart longed to be loved, truly loved.

Apparent from their first meeting at Lebeau's restaurant, Evan Holcomb conjured emotions within her that resembled fairytales of "one true love." Butterflies filled her stomach every time her eyes met his. With his broad gladiator frame and spellbinding gaze, Evan's allure could pierce any girl's armor. Unfortunately, her defense mechanisms had melted from the first moment her eyes met his mesmerizing gaze on a sidewalk in Baton Rouge many weeks ago. Happy this excursion offered her the time needed to help Evan see that love awaited him, and their lengthy kiss by the pool marked a promising start.

A string of quick taps upon her shoulder alerted Amber to Charlie's presence.

Startled, Amber exclaimed, “Morning! Sleep well?”

“No.” Charlie snapped. The clench of her teeth underscored her obvious disapproval. “Someone had a grand time last night across the way.”

“Yes, I think they did,” Amber replied, sensing Charlie's displeasure with the party antics.

“How about you? Did you sleep?”

“No, not really. I was too preoccupied.”

“That’s understandable.” Charlie’s mouth formed a thin smile. “I know I would be.”

Amber’s eyes creased before she stuck out her tongue. “Oh, stop. I heard enough out of my brother last night. Can I help that I’m irresistible?” Laughing, she gave a swift kick of the surf, accidentally spraying Charlie and her glasses with salt water. “Whoops!”

Saltwater droplets covered Charlie’s glasses from Amber’s swift kick of the surf. Laughter erupted from both women.

“Okay, I deserved that one.” Charlie squinted, wiping her eyes and frames clean. “But in all seriousness, you haven’t noticed anything strange on the peninsula, have you?”

“Define strange…” Amber laughed.

“All my reporter instincts tell me this island has a secret to tell, and I’m determined to find out what it is. My gut’s never been wrong. Something on this island is amiss. I feel it. First, the mysterious light flashes, and now a sudden extended stay just as Steve and Cooper arrive. My hunch is the men know more than they’re saying.”

Amber chewed on her bottom lip, glancing away because she, too, felt something on the island wasn’t right. And if Charlie had suspicions, the odds were not in their favor.

“You have noticed something!” A pointed finger conveyed Charlie’s speculation. “I wasn’t sure at first, but you’ve just confirmed it. Amber, you’re a terrible liar.

Don't ever try it with Evan."

Amber puffed her cheeks. Charlie's perceptive, intuitive moments had saved them in Bridgeport—no reason to doubt her now. She twirled a strand of hair through her fingers and wondered how Charlie knew her so well after only a few short months of friendship. Amber hastily analyzed her options. In fact, Charlie seemed to be the only one she could confide in. Brent wasn't a viable alternative. He would try to convince her that she'd imagined it. After all, Rafe Culliver hadn't contacted them for over six years. With the decision made, Amber determined Charlie would become her confidante.

"Okay, maybe I have. When I separated from you and Leah on our shopping trip, I thought I saw someone from my very distant past. Everything in me says it was him, but I can't figure out why he would be on this island."

"Why would who be here?"

Amber hesitated, remembering how painful it was to say his name and remember his rejection. "I guess that information might help. His name is Rafe Culliver. He was a childhood friend of Brent's and mine before he and Brent joined the military together straight out of high school. Rafe dedicated his life to serving and found his niche in special forces, and you know Brent's path. Strangely enough, we haven't seen or spoken with him in at least six years, possibly more. Yet, while in the market, I saw either his or his doppelganger's reflection in the window. There's no chance he's vacationing on the same island, right?" She asked dubiously.

"And you say your friend, Rafe, was in special forces? Those guys come in, do their job, and disappear like the morning mist." Charlie's angelic face changed expressions in an "ah ha" moment. "Mmm…I think it could very well have been your long-lost friend in the cobblestone market. Someone with M Code expertise sent that signal. He has the training, probably the equipment, and definitely the knowledge of your whereabouts if needed."

Amber chewed on her fingernail. "This is crazy. Why us? Why here?"

Charlie's eyes narrowed in thought. "Just how close were you and Brent to Rafe Culliver? Any romantic interest between you two?"

"Wait a minute. You don't think Rafe was trying to warn us of some impending doom, do you?" Avoiding Charlie's romantic involvement question, Amber paced back and forth through the white foamy surf, unwilling to divulge the deeper feelings she'd once had for Rafe.

"You said he's skilled. This island does offer a perfect trajectory to some interesting locations. Who's to say he's not here for other reasons?" Charlie's shoulders lifted in a shrug. "Besides, you never answered. Did the two of you share a romantic connection?"

Charlie's questions flooded her brain with vivid memories and fresh pain. Feelings she'd fought hard to shove from her heart, yet they crept back in from their hiding place. And feelings she wasn't ready to share with Charlie.

Rhonda's loud whistle startled Amber, causing her to jump, grateful for the interruption. Her anxious wave acknowledged Rhonda's summons before noting trouble stood within inches of her. Clearly, Charlie, with her ultra-keen reporter instincts, suspected there was much more to her and Rafe than friendship, but Amber couldn't think of that. And she sure couldn't lie. Charlie had told her that.

She could only heed Rhonda's call quickly. "Race you," Amber said with a teasing smile, challenging her friend as she bolted toward the villa because she refused to allow Charlie's questions to drag her back into the pits of misery.

~

Brow crimped in thought, Evan watched the two

women curiously through the great-room window. Charlie and Amber raced up the boardwalk, finally linking arm in arm. Cryptic smiles adorned their faces as if concealing a secret when they reentered the house. Before either of them could close the door, Rhonda thrust cups of steaming coffee in their hands and stifled a yawn.

"You're welcome, don't mention it." She moaned and stumbled back toward the kitchen.

Evan smiled. Neither woman appeared to be in the mood to tangle with Rhonda this morning. Their lips pursed tightly in protest, and yet, somehow, snippets of laughter still managed to escape. Following the familiar sounds of silverware clinking against china and endless chatter, the women screeched to a halt at the doorway, each backing up a few steps when they encountered Evan wedged in the door, blocking their way. A smile slid across his face as he surveyed Amber from head to toe. His pulse always accelerated whenever she was near.

Evan had wedged his sizeable frame in the doorway, blocking the women's pathway to breakfast.

Why would I ever feel this woman wasn't right for me?

Initially, he'd fooled himself into thinking she was too much like her brother. Thank God that proved to be the case. If his inkling of pursuing a serious relationship with Amber held fast, she would need all the grit and determination she could muster. His fishbowl life required the presence of a strong, positive personality by his side. The daily grind of being a notable entrepreneur and celebrity remained a challenge that would never change. Columnists constantly jockeyed for the latest news on the world's youngest manufacturing millionaire. Intrusive camera lenses and false rumors were old news to him, but that life would require adjustments for Amber. No matter how badly he wanted her, and he did, she needed to be aware of the consequences of her choice - a conversation he'd save for later.

Aware his probing gaze produced a flush of embarrassment in her cheeks, Evan shifted out of the way, interlocking his fingers with Amber's.

"Excuse me, Charlie, can I have a minute alone with your cohort?" Offering a smile, he dragged her into the study down the hall before Charlie could even answer.

"Sure, be my guest," Charlie replied, a snark in her tone.

His swift kick slammed the study door behind them. He smiled again at Amber's stunned expression as he secured the lock. Privacy was a rare and prized commodity around the villa, and he refused to waste the opportunity. Taking her by surprise, he drew her into his arms and brushed a strand of hair over her shoulder.

Innocent eyes met his, breaking down the barrier between them, and with a groan lodged in his throat, he took her mouth with his. Concealing the bashful smile that had only seconds ago adorned them. Desire coursed through his veins and assaulted his senses when her soft lips molded to his, communicating a yearning all her own. His groan escaped into her mouth, all but devouring her as he drew her deeper into his world. Standing on her tiptoes, she pressed in, and in one fluid motion, he swallowed her up in his arms and carried her to the sofa, his lips never leaving hers. Filled with the passion this woman ignited in him, Evan gently laid her on the couch and eased in beside her. Her attraction to him was unmistakable, given her flushed cheeks and pink lips swollen from his kisses. Her wide-eyed, innocent look now took on a dazed, smokey quality, telling him she desired him as much as he did her. He tenderly cupped her face in his hands, staring into her eyes in wonder. How could he be so lucky to find the perfect woman for him? He swallowed hard as he studied her face.

This woman is more than I deserve.

Reaching forward, Amber guided him back to her moistened kiss, dispelling any doubts he may have for the moment, spiraling them deeper into a trance. Barriers built from years of hurt and pain seemed to collapse around them, and both relinquished their plight to the other for rescue. Drawing back, he traced his fingers along her cheek before caressing her lips again, deepening the kiss. Heat spread over him when her body melted against his, and a soft moan parted from her lips, signal flares went off in Evan's brain. They were on the cusp of no return, and he couldn't let that happen. Reluctantly, he raised up and tenderly brushed the tousled strands of hair from her face. Their ragged breathing confirmed that they needed to slow down. But when her arms locked around his neck to guide him back, Evan questioned his intent to end their unexpected tryst… until a light knock on the door reinforced his decision.

"Anyone in there?" Carol called. "Hey, does anyone know why the study door is locked?" The simple question launched a hush over the kitchen as all chatter ceased.

Amber shot up on the sofa, eyes wide with panic. A low chuckle left Evan's lips as he gave her hand a reassuring squeeze.

"Yes, Carol. I'll be out in a moment."

"Ah, Evan, it's you." Carol stammered. "No problem. I can grab a new book for the pool later."

The faint "pitter-patter" of footsteps on the cool limestone sounded while Evan evaluated Amber's flaming cheeks, his smile mischievous as he tilted her chin up with his fingertip.

"You *do* know we are grown consenting adults, right?" His gaze softened. "And I wouldn't have allowed it to go further, Amber, so there's no need for embarrassment." His gaze softened.

Her cheeks fused to a deeper scalet. "Of course, I know that, Evan Holcomb." Amber cleared her throat and rushed to the door, obviously uncomfortable over the awkwardness. "It's just… oh, whatever!"

"Wait." Evan strode over to her to stop her retreat. "Don't be upset, please, although I must admit, you're cute when you get flustered." Turning her around to face him head-on with a gleam in his eye. "There's no need for embarrassment, although you and I both know Carol is forming her own opinion about this right now, which is the least of your worries since she's, no doubt, sharing her suspicions with the women."

Peeping up at him, Amber blew a curl from her eye and smoothed her blouse. "No doubt, which means we probably should join the group now."

"No, ma'am." He drew her close with a lazy grin. "Not until I finish what we came in here for."

Laying a quick kiss on her nose, he anchored firm hands on each of her shoulders. "Ms. Scott, would you accompany me on an excursion today? I've taken the liberty of reserving a boat for us at the marina. The chef will pack us a basket, and we'll spend the day sunning, swimming, and enjoying life. That is if you're willing, of course."

Mouth gaping, Amber blinked before a hoarse whisper passed her lips. "Uh…It would be my pleasure, Mr. Holcomb."

"Good." He briefly brushed his lips against hers. "I think we should talk with the chef and make our selections. After all, a man can become quite ravenous on the open water all day." He said with a wink, sending another broiling red hue to her cheeks. Reaching around her, he opened the door, and the quick click of the lock brought all six women to attention as he opened the door. Obviously, much sooner than they anticipated, judging from the sheepish smiles and nervous scattering that ensued when the couple exited the room.

Ignoring them with a calm smile, Evan steered Amber

by while the six women backed against the walls with nowhere to run, staring blankly at the flooring.

"Told you!" Evan whispered into Amber's ear, his hand pressed on the small of her back. "We'll just have to deal with it later." He gave a nod over his shoulder. "And them."

~

Evan chuckled and squeezed through the flabbergasted group en route to the chef's kitchen with Amber in tow. A devious wink to her "sisters," and off they went.

Now out of earshot, the couple produced a rousing round of laughter from the women. Rhonda indulgently flipped her blonde locks over her shoulder, uttering. "Well, doesn't that take the cake! Suzanne, we have a job to do."

"No, no, I know you too well, Rhonda. Those words mean there's a male involved. There are four other people here you can draft as your 'wing woman.' Not me. How about Carol? She's unattached."

Carol's mouth pruned into puckered lips of denial. "Oh no. Hold on. I might be unattached, but it's by choice. I'm not searching for a man. I'm perfectly content with my life."

Leah's interjection put the group on pause, "Why don't we gather the other men and make a day of it in the market? I'm sure they would love to accompany us. All in favor, say aye."

A mumbled "aye" sealed Rhonda's agreement. "That's fine. My islander was in the market the first day we met."

"Everyone else in favor?" Leah's question, followed by the rumble of "aye," meant the men had a new agenda for the day.

"ETD – one hour. Hustle, ladies!" Leah chuckled and headed to secure Brent's agreement, well aware that a difficult task awaited her.

EIGHT

His temples throbbed with a fury, cymbals clashing together in unison in his head. Rafe grabbed the feather-filled pillow and bent it over his head, fighting the tinge of pain that rocketed through his arm. Fragmented fight scenes flashed in his memory. Every ounce of reasoning told him he was closing in on the individuals responsible for the top-secret security breach. *Funny, the laugh's on them.* As much as he believed the search was narrowing, he lacked specifics. The escalation in aggression he experienced last night with his "shadows" spoke volumes. Someone suspected he held the key, and they were willing to risk exposure to discover the truth. Rafe knew that his fate could've taken a different turn without the young tourists' arrival. Hopefully, they made good on their promise to return the boat safely.

He placed his bare feet on the cool flooring and rolled his bruised neck in circles, hoping to alleviate some stiffness as he wandered to the shower. The hot steam worked wonders for his head and achy body. Refreshed, he swallowed a couple of ibuprofen, dressed, and headed out, coffee in hand. Rafe closed the door and placed the small thread in its usual location. He could no longer postpone the inevitable. He had fifteen minutes to reach the marina and contend with a lifetime of mistakes. Maybe a brisk walk would miraculously fill his mouth with the words to say.

Today will not be easy.

Paschal was on the job bright and early. True to his promise, he looked rested and prepared for work.

"Hey, dude. You're moving a little slow today. You didn't have some late-night adventures of your own, did you?" He grinned.

Rafe saw no need to speculate on Paschal's activities last night. He already knew the answer. "I'm sure nothing to compare to your evening."

"A man can't hide his sex appeal. What can I say, women like ole Paschal."

"Yeah, yeah. I'm going to check on the Savannah Jane for a second. I'll be right back."

"Okay, why the SJ?" Paschal questioned. "No one ever uses that boat."

"I'll fill you in later." Rafe started a slow trot to the slip.

Prayers answered.

The boat glistened in the early morning sunlight. Reflections on the water offered Rafe a mirrored glimpse as he scoured the hull for damages that proved nonexistent. The boat moaned, rubbing against the bumpers when he boarded for a closer inspection. All decking sparkled like glass. Freshly polished railings guided his steps into the cabin: no empty cans, no coolers, nothing. The interior was as pristine as the exterior. Rafe raised his head in pride and chuckled—chalk one up for the nice guy. The kid held true to his promise.

With one foot squared on the steps, Rafe's final once-over sent an uncomfortable sensation up his spine, prompting his return down the stairs. Despite the cleanliness, something seemed amiss. What had stirred his intuition? Further inspection confirmed his suspicions.

The small slip of paper had escaped notice on his initial walk-through. Tattered, barely visible edges sat wedged between the captain's chair and console edge.

Keenly aware it was no leftover piece of party trash, Rafe's curiosity peaked. A slight twist revealed written in pencil, list style:

- mission backup
- continue search
- Brigadier

Rafe gulped hard. His throat tightened. Backup? His Commander clearly felt the need to send in reinforcement, but who? Whoever it was, made no matter, not after last night's skirmish. Being confident the individual possessed the necessary skills to help when called upon was enough for him.

Rafe tucked the small white slip in his back pocket, cleared the boat, and hurried to the marina office. With any luck, he'd make it before Evan Holcomb arrived. His hand twitched as he turned the tarnished doorknob. Beads of sweat dripped from his brow. Were they from the heat or fear? *Probably both.*

Paschal's smiling face greeted him along with two others, except one carried no smile. Instead, the girl he'd left many years ago stood there motionless in a state of shock.

"Hey, man, your charters arrived early," Paschal said. "Rafe, meet Evan Holcomb and Amber Scott. He lives across from Bonfire Beach," pointing to Evan with a toothy grin. "Pretty cool, huh? I love that beach."

Evan's extended hand offered a firm shake. "Thanks for readying the boat for us today."

Rafe's eyes shifted from Amber to Evan. "Yeah, sure. We'll walk down together to ensure you have everything you need." He skipped a beat before addressing Amber.

"Nice to meet you, Ms. Scott. The weather should be perfect for you today." Rafe stammered.

Amber barely spoke as she reached for the safety of Evan's hand. "Good. Sunshine is good."

Evan's body tensed. His large frame moved

protectively in front of Amber. “Could you take us down to our vessel now?”

“Yeah. Follow me.” Rafe knew Holcomb sensed Amber’s uneasiness.

Small talk evaded them during the walk to the boat slip. After a thorough rundown of safety measures, equipment, and the like, Rafe questioned Evan, “Do you feel comfortable taking the boat out alone? I’m here to ensure our charters meet certain standards. I could accompany you on your excursion today. Island currents can be tricky.”

Rafe awaited the firestorm that his statement undoubtedly would provoke.

“Don’t concern yourself, Mr. Culliver. I have more than enough sailing experience to ensure your vessel is returned safely by day’s end.” Evan’s chest broadened as he once again clasped Amber’s hand.

“It’s not the vessel’s safety I wish to protect—human lives trump material things. And I would never want anything to happen to Ms. Scott. Or you either, of course.” Rafe struggled to break the hold Amber’s closeness held on him.

“Again, thank you, but we’ll manage. Can you cast us off? We’ll see you this afternoon.” Evan guided Amber onto the boat, passed her the overflowing lunch basket, and untied the stern before jumping onto the decking.

“Just remember the emergency radio channel is 908 should you need it.” One last look at Amber made Rafe grumble under his breath over past mistakes. Different choices would’ve placed him – not Evan - sailing crystal waters with Amber.

“I doubt we’ll need it, but thanks for the heads-up.”

Rafe gave the boat a shove, pushing it and Amber out of his life. Again.

~

Amber’s focus remained transfixed on the marina

until it was nothing but a speck in the distance. She was thankful Evan was too busy navigating the shallow reef to question her change in demeanor. She prepared herself for the onslaught of questions that awaited her when they safely anchored. Evan knew her too well. His interest peaked the moment she saw Rafe. Unfortunately, Charlie's analogy haunted her once more. Not only was she a terrible liar, she'd never been able to hide her emotions with any success. He'd want answers, and she would need to provide them.

Do I tell him the truth?

"Hey," Evan called.

"Oops, sorry. What do you need me to do?"

"For starters, check the anchor line when I drop it. Then, tell me, what's going on with you?" His words struck a chord, leaving her with seconds to decide – truth or half-truth.

A weak reply left her lips, "Okay."

With the boat secured, Amber readied the chef's delicious meal. Surprisingly, her stomach rumbled with hunger. The stressful encounter with Rafe had left her feeling both ill and ravenous at once. Nibbling on something might ease the discomfort she felt in her gut. Besides, she couldn't answer Evan's questions if her mouth remained full. Unfortunately, the glimmer in his eye told her she wouldn't consume a bite. Not now, anyway.

"Well, this looks delectable," Evan said, easing his body down atop the rainbow-striped cushion beside her. His hulky form filled the small space as his tanned leg brushed against hers, sending ripples of excitement through her body. A nervous smile cloaked her enthusiasm.

Evan laughed, "Do I make you that nervous?"

"I'm not nervous." Amber spouted.

"Is it me or the thought of explaining how you know Rafe Culliver that has you all wound up?" His questioning eyes examined her.

Now in the "hot seat," unsure of her next step, Amber twirled a strand of hair between her fingers. "I'm not sure what you mean."

"Don't play coy with me. You know perfectly well what I mean." Evan leaned closer. "You realize you're even more attractive when you try to conceal things from me."

Feeling as though Evan knew all her secrets, without truly knowing any of them, she lowered her head in defeat before Evan's finger lifted her chin upward. Her timid eyes leveled into his soft gaze. The feel of Evan's lips gently brushing against hers offered a promise of understanding.

"That innocent act didn't work in Bridgeport, and it won't work now." Evan's tone softened. "You want to tell me the truth, or should we continue with our lunch? Your decision."

Her internal instinct to remain quiet won the battle, fueling her hesitant response. "Would it be okay if, for now, we have lunch and enjoy the day?"

"Of course." Evan's grimace contradicted his statement.

A tinge of guilt prompted Amber's soft caress of Evan's cheek. Her palm stroked his sun-kissed skin as she inched closer. Slim feminine fingers circled his upper and lower lip with a touch light as a feather, tracing a path to joy. Immersed in the depth of his accepting gaze, Amber tenderly brushed his lips with hers. Unable to withstand the need to convince him there was no reason for concern, her breathy capture of his mouth produced his throaty growl. Evan yielded to her fiery quest as he accepted every degree of heat her lips delivered. Emboldened by the sun's warm embrace on their skin, Amber relaxed into further euphoria.

The boat drifted to and fro with the sea's swells clanging the sail clips against the tall mast, luring her deeper into romantic bliss with the rhythmic sounds and motions. Locked in Evan's arms, Amber had longed for the moment when they would finally be alone with no one to interrupt. She never dreamed the getaway invitation would place her in the atmosphere surrounding her.

Evan's hypnotic kisses moved her to another dimension. Sensations of delight cascaded about her - thoughts of whether their relationship could progress further floated through her mind like butterflies on a summer day. Yet, her heart, wounded beyond measure in the past, also made her question,

Would Evan commit to one woman? Rafe hadn't.

The notion brought tears to her eyes. Small droplets trickled down her cheek, leaving a salty, wet trail.

Evan's slow withdrawal from her lips signaled he'd noticed.

"What's this?" he asked, reaching for a napkin. "Is something wrong? Is it something I did?" The sincerity of his concern for her well-being made her heart sore.

"Can you at least give me a hint?" Evan smiled, drying her tears with the soft cloth.

Her cheeks flushed red, reluctant to answer at first. "It's you."

"Me!"

Amber offered a bashful nod. Her faint voice was barely audible. "Yes. You see, I've had my heart shattered into tiny pieces before. The pain was so overwhelming I put up walls to protect myself that I swore would never come down. And then, you entered the picture. Ughh. I wouldn't be in this position if Leah had chosen you instead of Brent."

Evan dabbed another teardrop and listened intently.

"But that didn't happen, did it?" she whispered. "And while I'm very thankful she made a different choice, I've started removing bricks from those walls because of you. Now, I'm second-guessing if that's the right decision." Her eyelashes, heavy with moisture, fluttered.

"Amber, are you asking me if that decision was a

mistake?"

"I guess so. Do you see 'this' moving forward?" A bent finger waved between them. "You're the most eligible bachelor in Charlotte, for goodness' sake. Could you ever be happy with just one woman?"

His tranquil blue eyes cast a spell on her, making her head spin.

"I've expressed my feelings to you before. I'm ready." He snuggled her close to him. "You have captivated me since we arrived. Every moment we are alone strengthens my feelings for you."

Too frightened to believe his words, Amber squirmed about on the cushion, reached for a fruit skewer, and began nibbling on the edge.

Evan's rousing roar of laughter shocked her so, the skewer launched from her hand and flew across the deck in surprise. Her embarrassed gasp initiated another deep chuckle.

She raised her chin, a hint of defiance creeping into her voice, "I fail to see what is so funny."

"You, my dear. You."

"You nearly gave me a heart attack with your thunderous laughter. I was unaware confessing my feelings would be so hilarious." She huffed.

Evan grabbed her in a bear hug and kissed her head.

"I'm starved." He chuckled and reached for the overflowing platter of tropical delights beside her.

Amber stomped her foot in exasperation when Evan paused to avoid further discussion and planted a playful nip upon her lips.

Their relaxing meal, coupled with a small bit of wine, quickly diminished her frustration with him. Evan Holcomb wasn't a man you remained upset with for very long. He was a force of masculinity, charisma, compassion, and intellect rolled into one magnificent body. She couldn't imagine any female in her right mind that would turn Evan down – no matter the request.

The distant hum of a boat motor interrupted their solitude. Of no concern initially, Evan's command of "stay here" sent waves of apprehension over her. Amber propped on her elbows, straining to gain a better view. A beefy, athletic-looking male captained the craft as it approached from the starboard side. His slim companion wore a tattered cap that accompanied an unfriendly expression.

"How can I help you, gentlemen?" Evan questioned, leaning over the boat railing.

His authoritative tone brought Amber to her feet. Evan was uncomfortable, which told her their visit wasn't a welcome one. She squatted down, grabbed the paring knife from the basket, and shoved it into her pocket. Having no clue what good it would do, she felt ample preparation never hurt anyone.

"Help," growled the man. "We don't need help."

His soured-faced companion replied. "We prefer answers."

"An answer requires a question, and since we've never met, that nullifies the need. Are you gentlemen with the local law enforcement or the Coast Guard?"

Both men scrubbed their jaw. "Us, law enforcement? Definitely not."

Evan widened his stance. "Perhaps you have the wrong boat, then."

"You anchored in a very remote place. Why? Engine trouble?" The boat driver asked.

"I don't think that's your concern. It's a big ocean. I'm sure you gentlemen can find another suitable location for your – business." His fists tightened at his sides.

Amber crossed the deck and eased up behind Evan. "What seems to be the problem, dear?" She squeezed his shoulders and planted a kiss on his cheek. "Oh, we have guests."

"Slim" grinned, "I'm betting it's not engine trouble,

bro. I think we'll come aboard now." In an instant, his hand clenched the deck cleat, rope in tow.

"I don't think so." Evan's swift strike crushed the man's fingers underneath his foot. "Slim" released a thunderous scream and withdrew quickly, or so he tried.

Amber clung to Evan's shirttail. His movements were hers. He slid his hand behind him, protectively pushing her backward. A swift grab into her pocket produced the knife, which she slipped into his grasp.

"I suggest you two move along." His shoe lifted slowly from the cleat.

Wails of anguish accompanied by a deep bellow. "Maybe we were wrong," the bulky man said as he guided the thin man back to his seat.

"You win for now. But we'll see you again," wafted through the air as the boat sped away.

Amber and Evan watched in silence until the boat reflected on the distant horizon.

His gentle touch nudged Amber's hand open where he laid the small knife.

A tiny smile creased her lips. "I thought it might help."

"It may have." He smiled. "Fortunately, they backed down. Never place yourself in danger like that again. When I ask you to stay somewhere, there's a reason. Promise me you won't move next time. Besides trouble, I have no clue who or what those two were looking for. YOUR appearance only heightened their plans to board." His concern superseded the curt tone in his voice.

"I can try. No promises, though," Amber said softly. "Ask Brent; I've never been very compliant when being told what to do. Even as a kid, I followed him everywhere. He'd get quite angry. You remind me of him right now." She bit her lip, holding another laugh at bay.

Aware her playful sassiness had riled Evan when he yanked her into his arms and melded his lips to hers. His fears were evident as he devoured her lips with a passion meant to convey everything his absence of words did not. Amber buried her hands deep into his hair, saturating her core with the taste of his being.

Evan Holcomb weakened her inhibitions. No longer could she worry about removing bricks from her defenses; she struggled now to prevent the entire wall from crumbling. Lifting her lips to slow their path, Amber faintly brushed her nose against his, seizing the opportunity she'd waited for.

"Evan, I would never do anything to hurt you. You know that, right?" She asked, a little afraid to hear his answer.

"I know that, little one. Nor I, you."

Her lengthy sigh preceded her confession. "There are a few things you don't know about me."

"Why the gloomy disposition? I can't imagine it's all that bad. Relax, and save your confessions for another time. Let's enjoy the rest of our day. I've had enough surprises today." His warm smile initiated a spontaneous peck on the tip of her nose. Amber giggled. *Lord, I'm in trouble.*

NINE

"Be Back Soon." The small sign would only buy them half a day at best.

"Where are we headed, dude? It's a big ocean out there." Paschal asked.

"There's a place close to the cliffs I want to check. Navigation issues have historically plagued ships in those waters for years. Seems like a great place to start."

"Whatever you say." Paschal grabbed their backpacks and headed toward the door. "So, which boat are we 'borrowing' today?" He laughed.

"The Savannah Jane," Rafe replied with a thin smile.

"What's up with the Savannah Jane? You've mentioned it twice. Is there something I don't know?" His friend's brow wrinkled in question. "Besides, that boat never gets used."

Paschal's never-ending curiosity presented a problem Rafe would need to contend with, just not today. "That's the very reason we're taking it, buddy. Let's go. We don't have much time."

The two men snatched up the remaining gear and hustled out the door. Rafe planned their departure shortly after Amber's and steered the SJ toward the cliffs. Paschal's constant jabbering enlightened Rafe more than he ever dreamed. Most importantly, Rafe learned that Evan and Amber intended to anchor dangerously close to his "sweet spot." Was it dumb luck on Holcomb's part? Rafe couldn't be sure. He only knew Amber's safety trumped everything else.

The Savannah Jane cruised along the cliff wall, dropping anchor well out of sight. Evan's charter floated in the distance, a mere speck from Rafe's vantage point. Their proximity, Rafe assumed, would be the last thing on Evan's mind - regrettably.

"Ole Paschal is ready for some treasure hunting." He rubbed his weathered hands together with anticipation.

"Don't get over-excited. We may not find anything."

"Who's to say we won't, though? Where do we start?" His optimism refreshed Rafe's attitude.

"We'll run some checks with the drone first. Then, as soon as the lines are set, we go live."

Paschal checked and rechecked the leads' fastening and lowered the device into the glossed waters. The small prop on its rear sputtered to life, propelling it beneath the surface. All the majesty of the underwater menagerie appeared on the vivid screen. Sea anemones swayed in motion with the undercurrents while clownfish weaved through their protective extensions. Fascinated by the sights, Paschal smiled, talking to the fish as though they were children playing in a park.

Rafe's attention remained diverted elsewhere. Their excursion was merely a futile attempt to further Paschal's belief in their quest and allowed him to maintain a watchful eye on his favorite charter. Visions of Amber danced across his mind. Her freckles had faded, replaced by maturity and beauty. A natural beauty that he recognized from years past. Regrets flooded through him. How could he have allowed her to slip away? He had been the one who chose to become a stranger, not her.

Unable to stifle the internal cry for details any longer, he dug the long-range binoculars from his pack.

Paschal rounded the starboard, water bottle in hand. "Whew, it's a hot one." He chugged down the cool liquid, crushed the bottle, and chunked it into a bin. "Any luck with those things?"

"Not really. I suppose I was wrong about the cliffs." Paschal's perception of his defeat related to their research when, in actuality, Rafe's glum mood centered around one woman.

"Don't get down, dude. It's our first day. We'll have more opportunities." His quick slap on Rafe's shoulder signified promises of better days.

"Thanks, Paschal. Let me know if anything interesting shows."

"That I can do." With a quick adjustment of his sun-filled brim, Paschal rushed away.

Rafe eased the ocular lens over his long, dark eyelashes, their tips touching the glass, obscuring his view. He refocused and steadied the cylinder frames.

All his logical reasoning shouted, "No way," as he blinked, centering in on the rented charter. The small skiff's occupants floating alongside shared a strong resemblance to his attackers. Their mannerisms and stature matched to a "t." Witnessing the men's aggressive posturing, Rafe watched in horror. Anger raged within him from his inability to intercede. He lowered the binoculars and rubbed his brow. Indecision toyed with his rationale. In the end, he conceded defeat, aware he could only watch.

He abruptly raised the binoculars. Evan appeared to hold his own with the two unwanted guests. Within minutes of their arrival, the skiff sped off. Rafe released a controlled exhale. Good for Holcomb. Amber appeared to be out of harm's way for now, although concerns remained. The addition of two more lives to his protection list placed a heavy strain on his success.

Why didn't the signal work?

With no time for error or to play bodyguard to unsuspecting tourists, Rafe knew what he must do. His old friend's happiness paled in comparison to the alternatives.

"Hey, Paschal, prepare to wrap for the day. Old Mr. Jenkins will be making the rounds soon. Heaven forbid he discovers we ducked out and on the Savannah Jane, no less." Rafe stressed.

"You ain't wrong, dude. Lines coming in."

Savannah Jane's speed outmatched any other vessel in the marina, yet guests never chose the boat as a day charter. She was often overlooked or written off as an old relic compared to the newer, sleeker boats. SJ's lack of rental income continually kept the boat docked. Still, she held a sacred place in the marina owner's heart. Jenkins never elaborated on why, just that he'd never replace her. God help them if Jenkins ever discovered Rafe and Paschal used his prized possession for their excursion. Or that he allowed a group of twenty-somethings aboard.

The boat glided into the slip in the nick of time. Jenkins pulled into the marina on schedule. The two men hustled toward the office, yanking the "out" sign from its post just as Mr. Jenkins turned the doorknob. Paschal plopped into the worn, rickety chair and sighed.

Jenkins' taut, erect form entered the office with a brief wave of acknowledgment. "Good day."

Rafe issued his usual response, "Good day, sir. How's your day?"

"Fine, my boy. Just fine. The air is a tad heavy. We may see a bit of rain today."

"We feel a change in pressure, too, sir. Don't we, Paschal?"

"Boy, do we!" Paschal skimmed his wrinkled bandanna across his sweaty forehead.

"Has anyone rented my beloved Savannah Jane lately?" Jenkins questioned.

"Rented? I can't say they have, sir. I was just at the slip. She remains ready to board if you want to take her into open water."

Jenkins lifted his hand and adjusted his captain's hat

in pride. "In my younger days, I've captained the military's largest vessels, but my Savannah Jane is like no other. I miss my Savannah Jane dearly. We had some good times on that boat. Unfortunately, she left me ten years ago."

Rafe noticed a swell of tears in the senior's eyes. Jenkins' sorrow over his loss tugged on his heart every time the senior dwelled on the subject.

"I'm sorry, sir. It hasn't been easy for you, I know."

"Uhmmm. I'm making it just fine." The older man's shoulders stiffened. "Military life is not easy. We do what we must, Rafe. Well, you two seem to have things under control. Until tomorrow." A dip of his hat and swift turn moved Mr. Jenkins out the door before Rafe could comment. Jenkins' words, surprisingly accurate, weighed on Rafe.

"Dude, that was too close for me. Can we use a different boat next time?" Sweat beads clung to Paschal's brow.

"Suggestion noted and approved." Rafe chuckled. " I don't know about you, but I'm ready for lunch."

"I'll go. You got it yesterday. Same ole, same ole?" Paschal jumped from his seat. "Back in a few."

Rafe plopped onto the hard stool and lowered his head to the table. If a swift punch of the wooden surface would help, he'd gladly offer up a few knuckles as collateral. Fortunately, experience had taught him better.

Amber's charter would dock at day's end, and he'd be face to face with her again. His stomach churned at the thought. Unfulfilled promises and lingering regrets battered his senses. Why had he let other people convince him that his life path had no place for love?

Unwilling to wallow in misery, he exhaled and devised tonight's plan. Rafe prayed his old friend would be happy to see him and not slug him.

TEN

Evan docked the boat with skilled precision. Amber sat in awe, watching this gorgeous man exhibit one more of his hidden talents. He'd proved quite capable of protecting himself back in Bridgeport, but witnessing his skills firsthand today boosted her sense of security to a higher plane. They'd shoved the event with the two strangers aside and reveled in being alone. Lively conversation, easy laughter, warm sunshine, and passionate kisses carried her into a world of happiness. Evan fulfilled his promise. It was an unforgettable day. She leaned into the soft cushion, closed her eyes, and recounted her blessings. Amber's smile, so broad, caused her cheeks to ache. Evan's suntanned fingers slowly glided down her shoulder.

"Ms. Scott, are you ready?" He questioned, interlocking his hand with hers.

"No, Mr. Holcomb, I'm not, but I'm afraid we have little choice."

She rose slowly and cocooned her arms around his neck. "I guess it's back to the Vitamin Sea. I never dreamed I'd be reluctant to return to the lap of luxury." She giggled. "But, if I'm being honest, I feel the villa will be a bit crowded for me now." Rising to her toes, Amber rained one more long and pleasurable kiss upon his lips. Evan eased away from her grasp and inhaled as if to catch his breath.

"A few more of those, and I'll buy you whatever kind

of watercraft you desire, madam." He teased.

"Oh, silly, I don't need a boat, just you."

"That you already have." His tight squeeze prompted another round of laughter.

Hand in hand, they strolled to the marina office all smiles. It wasn't until Amber glanced to her left that she noticed Rafe's solemn stare. Panicked, she yanked her hand free and fidgeted with her collar.

Evan's brow furrowed in a shocked response that spurred her rapid reply.

"We should probably hurry. Everyone might begin to worry." Amber hastily walked ahead, basket swinging wildly in hand from her fast pace.

Rafe emerged from the shaded slip and muttered. "How was your day? Was everything satisfactory?"

"Um, yes, we had a great time," Evan responded with a sly smile. "Thank you for your attention to detail. I had all a man could ask for – sunny skies, solitude, and a beautiful woman by my side.

"Yes, she is beautiful. You're a lucky man." His disparity was apparent.

"I agree with you wholeheartedly. May I ask a question, if you don't mind?"

The air between them thickened with apprehension. "Of course," Rafe replied with a nervous uptick.

"Are these waters, perchance, patrolled by private security officers, maybe hired by locals to keep tourists in check."

Rafe stroked his chin, eyes squinted. "I've never seen anyone 'patrolling' the water except the Coast Guard, and they rarely interact with rental occupants unless a craft looks suspicious or issues a distress call. Why?"

"Amber and I had a strange encounter earlier, and our visitors were not CG — quite the opposite, I think."

"Could it have been locals throwing their weight around?"

"You might say that," Evan grumbled. "Thanks for the information."

"No problem. FYI, we've never had a problem before."

"There's a first time for everything," Evan replied sarcastically. "Have a good one," he called.

Rafe's disgruntled reply of "Yeah, you too" followed Evan up the marina walkway.

Amber observed Rafe and Evan's interaction from the office window and desperately tried to read their lips. Impossible … She shifted her focus to concentrate on body language. Her assessment caused more anxiety, not less. Each man stood erect, eye to eye, hands clenched by their side, all telltale signs of a testosterone battle. Lord, have mercy. Her only reassurance, if there was any, was the brevity of the conversation. She prayed Rafe wouldn't utter a word about their past and that Evan wasn't in tune with their uneasiness.

Or was he?

Pushed to the edge by the thought, the unknown evoked a sudden spell of dizziness. Amber reached for the chair arm, not sure her bottom would hit its mark. Instead, her misjudgment placed her square on the office floor, both legs sprawled in front of her, picnic basket still upright.

Paschal rushed to her aid. "Oh, wow, you okay?" His firm grip guided her upward and maneuvered her onto the chair. She found herself unable to speak.

"Maybe you had a little too much sun today, miss." He blotted a damp cloth on her forehead. "It can be tough to adjust to these intense rays. I'm sure you'll be fine after a few minutes. You should sit still." His hand rested on her shoulder.

Amber stared into the distance, barely blinking, seeing a lifetime of what-ifs and whys.

Paschal snapped his fingers in the air. "Yo, miss, hello?!" His concern escalated with Evan's arrival.

“What happened?”

“Don’t know, dude. One minute, she's looking out the window, perfectly fine, and the next, she’s on the floor.”

Evan’s wide gait closed the distance between them in mere seconds. “Amber, Amber, look at me.”

Nothing. A gentle shake followed. No response. Evan brushed the sun-quenched golden-brown strands from her face, leaned in, and placed a delicate kiss upon full lips, still plump from their day together.

Languishing in the sweetness, Amber climbed toward the rock before her and clung to its security, where she longed to remain. Evan’s gentle release ushered forth her return to clarity.

“What happened?” she whispered.

“Well, I’m not sure. It seems you gave Paschal quite a fright.” Evan indicated with a nod.

“He’s not lying, miss.” Paschal anxiously fanned his straw hat back and forth.

“I’m so very sorry,” she said and slowly bent her elbows to stand.

“Oh, no.” Evan’s quick whisk had her cradled in his arms within a second.

“I can walk.”

“Sure, you can, but I like you right where you are.” He smiled. “Paschal, could you grab the door?”

“No worries, dude.” Paschal reached for the knob just as Rafe turned the handle from the outside.

“Amber? What happened? Are you okay?” Concern marred Rafe’s features.

“She’s fine. I’ve got it.” Evan barked, swinging her legs through the door’s threshold. “Thanks, Paschal.”

Amber gazed over Evan's shoulder back at the marina office. Rafe’s forlorn expression flooded her with memories of that day, long ago. A day she’d removed from her mind.

Why is he here? Why?

ELEVEN

The sun dipped slowly, sinking into the majestic waters; another glorious day moved to an end.

Leah had somehow managed to keep Brent, Steve, and Cooper entertained the entire day. The trio cheerfully accompanied the ladies in and out of one boutique after another. Of course, she had a little help from Carol and Kimberly. Cooper's attentiveness to Carol made Leah smile. Carol's multiple purchases lay strewn across Cooper's arm as they covered the market block after block. As for Steve, he never complained once while in Kimberly's company. The smell of romance lingered in the air, making Leah giggle.

A familiar grasp and tight squeeze of her waist put a broad, loving smile on her face.

"Can we please find a quiet restaurant and have a nice dinner? I've been more than cooperative today, Ms. Reynolds. Which, by the way, I think deserves a reward." Brent's flirtatious wink never grew old.

"You have my deepest gratitude, sir. I'm not the only one who's happy. Look at them. They've had a wonderful time, too," motioning toward their four friends.

"I see. I am a little stunned at how well this worked out. You women have magical charms." He smiled and planted a proud kiss on her lips.

"I promise you, tomorrow, the men can plan the day. Sound fair?" Leah teased, snuggling into Brent's embrace.

"Anything we want?" A mischievous smile slid across his face.

"Anything you want. As long as we get to tag along."

"It's a deal." Brent chuckled. "Prepare yourself. We men have a vivid imagination."

"I think I'm already aware of that." Leah bestowed a toe-curling kiss on his lips. She never wanted him to forget how much she loved him.

Refreshed by her joy, Leah enthusiastically offered, "How about we stay in town as you suggested for dinner? There's no need to rush back to Vitamin Sea. Let's try the local cuisine and give the chef a break."

"Here, here. I vote for that." Carol's brilliant smile and agreement surprised everyone except Cooper.

"Shouldn't we fill the others in on our plan? I presume Evan and Amber are back by now. And where are Charlie, Rhonda, and Suzanne?" Carol questioned.

"Brent, try to reach Evan, and I'll call Charlie."

Almost on cue, Leah's phone rang. Charlie and the other two "sisters" loved the idea. With a meeting location secured, Leah urged Brent to call Evan with a poke in the ribs.

"Okay, I'm calling." He laughed, rubbing his rib cage.

~

Evan walked in silence. His arms filled with the very essence of loveliness. Amber's head cradled into his shoulder.

"Can you stand a moment? I need to get the keys?"

Amber's weak "um hum" made his heart ache as he eased her feet onto the asphalt. Readied for her possible collapse, he held tightly to her waist. He dug through one pocket with his free hand, searching for the Rover's remote. No luck.

"Can you check my back pocket? I've got you." Arms tight, he turned.

Hesitantly, she lifted the pocket placket and withdrew the remote. A quick button press, and the chirp sounded. Evan eased Amber carefully onto the cool leather seat. A breathy "I am sorry" caressed his ear as he reached across her for the seatbelt. Tears welled in both their eyes.

"Why are you sorry? I shouldn't have kept you in the sun so long. Paschal is right. The rays are more intense here." He rubbed his thumb along the high cheekbone that accentuated her charm.

"Besides, there's no reason to cry. I don't think it was on your "to-do" list today." He laughed.

"No, but I never planned to be in this position. EVER." She stressed.

Evan's heart lurched. She was in pain, and her pain caused him greater pain. Years ago, he'd felt a tidal wave of pain that mimicked this moment. His parent's death crippled him. Water pooled in his eyes. The anguish his siblings experienced was mirrored once again before him in Amber's eyes. Why? His guttural instinct drew him back to one reason: Rafe.

But why?

Amber wiped a dangling tear from her lashes. "I told you there are some things you don't know about me."

"Yes, you did. But now is not the time to discuss it. First, you need some food and then rest. Agreed?" He stared into blue pools of uneasiness.

Her brief head movement at least meant she comprehended his requests. As he walked around to the driver's seat, the gravel beneath his shoes crunched, breaking into softer, smaller pieces with each step. Was this to be the fate of his heart? To be broken into bits. No, he vowed. He would do anything in his power to prevent it.

Quietness enveloped them before the ignition sputtered and clicked. Scratching his head in curiosity, Evan pushed the console's start button again - small grinds emitted from the hood. Another attempt produced the same result.

"What's wrong?" Amber's voice crackled.

"I'm not sure. Let me look. Don't worry." He patted her hand and moved toward the front of the vehicle.

A pop of the Rover's hood instantly revealed the problem — tattered edges of cabling hung from the battery. Fury flowed throughout his veins, elevating his heart rate. Rolling the cables through his fingertips, he cursed. His tantrum was interrupted by the unwanted phone call that buzzed nonstop.

"Hello!" he barked at whoever was unlucky enough to be calling him right now.

"Evan?"

"Yeah, what, Brent?" Irritation flowed from his lips.

"You good, buddy?"

"Not really."

"Where's Amber?" Brent's tone elevated in concern.

"She's fine now. Look, Brent, I may have a situation here. Can you or Steve come pick us up at the marina? The Rover won't start."

"Fine. Now? What? Someone will be there in five minutes. We're staying in the market for dinner, so we are close. Sit tight. I'm on my way."

"Thanks. I'll call for a tow while we wait." Aggravation hummed through the phone.

"Evan, take care of my sister."

"It's covered. See you in a few."

Evan returned to Amber's car door and lifted the handle. He clasped her hand and stroked her palm with his thumb.

"It seems we have a bit of car trouble. The battery is dead. Brent's on his way. How do you feel about dinner in the market? Everyone's eating in the square tonight."

"That would be nice. My stomach is rumbling a little."

"The square it is. Are you feeling any better?"

“For now.” She whispered.

Evan slid his hand up her neck, drawing her in for protection. Tranquil blue eyes searched her soul as he peered into them, offering comfort and safety before his lips claimed hers. Round and round tumbled his heart with every second their lips melted together. He felt her relax; she would have stayed there forever, and he enjoyed that idea. His step backward separated their hold.

“Brent’s here.” He murmured.

A loud squeal preceded Brent’s arrival. Hot tires and a speedy turn indicated he’d made the trip in less than five minutes. Evan shook his head. His earlier attempt to control Brent’s assumptions hadn’t worked. Brent slammed the car into park, flung open the door, and nudged Evan away from his sister.

A plethora of questions shaped themselves into one word. “Amber?”

“Oh, Brent, I’m fine. I got a little overheated earlier. It wasn’t a life or death situation.”

“Holcomb?” Brent hissed.

Evan perceived using his last name was intended to evoke a sense of brotherly intimidation.

Evan shot back. “Scott,” he said, but he couldn’t keep from chuckling.

“Will you two please cut it out? This is ridiculous.” Amber huffed.

“Whatever…we’ll talk later.” Her brother promised.

“You done with the big brother thing?” Evan asked. “I need to show you the problem.”

Brent pointed his finger toward his baby sister, “Wait here.”

The two men walked over to the vehicle’s engine. Evan stayed quiet. His intuitive friend noticed the frayed cables in an instant.

“This is no accident.”

“Nope. Someone knew we drove this car. Let’s be

thankful it was only the battery. A brake fluid leak might have placed us at the bottom of a ravine." Evan's face reddened with anger.

"Guess that signal a couple of nights ago WAS meant for us. What do you make of it?"

"Someone feels we are a threat, but a threat to whom or what, I have no clue."

"We may not have much time to figure it out." Brent lifted the raveled cables. "I never thought I'd back down from a threat. My sister, Leah, everyone's in danger as long as we stay. We just put Bridgeport behind us."

"We can't leave," Evan ordered.

"Give me one valid reason because I can't think of one right now."

"Our quiet little getaway wasn't so quiet. A couple of shady gents felt the need to try to board our boat earlier today without explanation."

"What, the …." Brent's cheeks puffed, fists balled.

"I handled it. Maybe our boat resembled another, but if the two truly wanted to escalate the situation, I would've had a fight on my hands. Luckily, they chose to leave."

"And I'm just now hearing about this. Number one, Steve, Cooper, and I could've been spared a day of endless shopping. Two, ever think you may have needed a little help out there, buddy?"

"I had help." Evan smiled. "Your sister is extremely resourceful. She came to my aid with a weapon in hand."

"My sister? What kind of weapon?"

Evan burst into laughter. "A paring knife."

"Really." Brent snickered. "Okay, then. At least she was willing to fight for you. Guess she cares for you more than I realized."

"That's encouraging. I'm not complaining." Evan grinned. "In all seriousness, the two took an issue with where we anchored the boat. They didn't elaborate. Amber's appearance only increased their motivation to board, and I don't need to tell you why." Evan groaned. "By the way, did your sister ever stay put in childhood when told to?"

"Not one of her better traits." Brent smiled.

"Found that one out earlier."

The horn's ear-piercing screech evoked a loud yell from both men. Evan slammed the Rover's hood closed and viewed what may be the love of his life, pointing at her watch from the van.

"Guys, come on," Amber called.

Brent threw up a thumb and laughed. "Better you than me, buddy. I have my hands full with Leah."

"We need to get with Steve and Cooper over dinner. Separate tables tonight."

"Agreed."

Unaware of the curious eyes that watched in silence, Evan and Brent moved toward the van. One last glance at the Rover's tag gave Evan cause for alarm. Rafe hoisted a bait bucket and nodded.

~

Brent checked his phone once more. Five texts from Leah in ten minutes meant she was concerned or, worse, suspicious. They'd regret it if she sensed anything out of the norm.

"We might want to speed things up. Leah's blowing my phone up with texts, and we all know what will happen if she thinks we're keeping something from her."

"Unfortunately, yes," Evan mumbled.

"I'll calm her down when we arrive. There's nothing to get riled over. A dead battery and too much sun are hardly cause for concern."

Amber's robotic reply troubled him deeply. Brent watched Amber through a brother's eyes. His baby sister meant the world to him. Protecting her in their younger years came naturally. More often than not, they ran in the same circles of friends. All the guys had younger siblings.

Amber was the only one they'd allow to tag along. His friends often paid more attention to her than their planned agenda. She discouraged most of them, with one exception… that exception left his baby sister miserable and brokenhearted. The siblings could read each other like a book, and Amber's pages were crumpled and torn. Unwilling to jump to judgment on her behalf, he would await Evan's explanation.

Brent's phone vibrated in the cup holder. "Who wants to talk to her?" Neither Evan nor Amber volunteered.

"Chickens." His quick grab and crisp "hello" released Leah's barrage of high-pitched questions. Each ear roared from the vocal assault.

"Leah, Leah. We're in the parking lot. Everything's fine. See you in a minute. Love you."

Brent pressed the glowing red icon, stroked his chin, and inhaled.

"Amber, talk to her. You women speak a different language. None of us want to suffer Leah's grilling."

The trio drifted toward the restaurant. Evan tucked Amber's small hand into his. Her radiant smile caught Brent's attention, creating a brilliant smile of his own. Rowdy tones of laughter billowed from the tin-roofed structure.

With a moan, Brent faked a smile, "Game faces, people."

"Well, it's about time. Tore up the Rover, huh, Holcomb?" Cooper teased, nestled in a cane bottom chair next to Carol.

"I'm not sure what happened, but at least we made it," Brent interjected.

Leah patted the seat next to her with a wink. "I'm glad you're finally here."

"Yeah, me too. So, you missed me?" His lips engulfed hers, savoring their fullness. The moist kiss, enhanced with a tasty tropical flare, had Brent licking his lips.

“Pineapple?”

“Yes, sir, with a touch of love and mango. Would you like one?” The twirling straw between her slender fingers escalated his desire.

“I’ll take a couple more of those later, please.” Leah frowned at his answer, ready to protest. “Don’t be mad,” he continued, “but the guys are going to huddle over there.”

Her pouty sigh signaled trouble. The dimly lit corner table of choice set off alarm bells.

He knew it.

“Why?” Her eyebrows arched.

“Didn’t you say the guys are in charge of the outing tomorrow?”

“Yes…”

“Then we need to decide what we want to do. We can’t focus with that going on.” Rhonda’s loud giggling invaded their conversation.

“You did promise.” Brent coaxed.

“Oh, for heaven’s sake. Okay.” Leah pursed her lips. “One request…”

“Anything for the love of my life.” Brent prayed he could fulfill her request.

“At least make it fun for everyone. I haven’t informed the ladies yet.”

“Deal.” He planted a kiss on her forehead and followed the other guys toward the dark corner.

His gaze remained on Leah as the men approached the dingy table filled with queso-covered dishes. Guilt consumed him. Bridgeport had taught them one thing: the truth always prevails. An intense level of trust saved their lives a few short months ago. Yet, Brent found himself in a situation that required uncomfortable secrecy. Rapping knuckles on the stained table spurred curious looks from his friends.

Cooper shoved the dirty plates into a pile.” Can

someone enlighten me? I was kinda fond of my other seating arrangement."

"I second that notion. You're both acting rather odd." Steve replied.

"Where do I start?" Exasperated, Brent continued. "Remember when you arrived? I said we needed to talk. Until now, I'd dismissed strange occurrences as nonsense, but Evan's call for a ride blew that theory out of the water." He struggled with what to say next.

"What Brent's alluding to started 24 hours after our arrival. We spotted a mysterious light beacon aimed toward the Vitamin Sea on our first night. Curious, we searched the area and found some interesting things before you arrived. Like this?" Evan tilted his phone. In plain sight sat the image of a boot's sole.

"How'd I miss that?" Brent questioned.

"You crossed over to the other side of the ridge. Markings look familiar?"

Steve's interest was piqued. "Those are military-grade. Not something I would expect to see on this island, but hardly damning evidence of some conspiracy theory."

"True, very true, my friend. However, this little jewel, embedded amongst the coral beneath the dock, tells me differently." The dangling silver clip Brent dug from his rear pocket swayed before Steve.

"Read the engraving."

"This can't be an original," Steve flipped the piece back and forth, examining the texture and weight. "Brent, you know as well as I do there are only a few of these in existence. The odds of an original embedded in coral on this island are a million to one."

"But you must admit it appears to be legitimate. I've seen one up close and personal. That's the real thing, I assure you. The question is, who does it belong to? And why were they here?"

Cooper scrubbed his fingers over a day-old beard in

awe. “Seems to me, y'all are all riled up over a vacationer’s lost trinket. It doesn’t look that important if you ask me.”

“Well, Coop, you’re wrong. This ‘trinket’ represents the success of a classified mission that saved countless lives. Ten individuals received this commendation. Their assignment remains top secret to this day. The subtle design of the medal is intentional. You see insignificance because that’s what you’re supposed to see.”

“Uh-huh, okay,” skepticism rang from Cooper’s words.

“He’s right,” Steve said. “I’ve heard the stories. I must admit I’ve always thought they were fabrications.”

“Back to the matter at hand.” Evan groaned. “Brent, you and Steve seem knowledgeable about its origin, but that doesn’t solve our problem.” Evan folded his hands, silenced by the arrival of their server.

“Excuse me, mon. Need to clear the table.” A quick swipe emptied the table of dishes. The petite waitress’s hasty surface scrub left the smell of lemon cleaner. “Back later to take your order, OK? We’re pretty busy. You good?” Her flirtatious smile lingered on Steve.

“We’re good. Thank you.” He chuckled; her inquisitive eyes locked with his as she sashayed back to the kitchen.

“Romeo.” Cooper slapped Steve’s shoulder.

“What else? The look on your faces says there’s more.” Steve’s gaze turned to Brent.

“The battery wasn’t dead on the Rover when I went to pick up Evan and Amber. The cable ends were cut into by someone between their arrival and return to the marina.”

“There’s more,” Evan signed heavily. “Two, let’s say, unsavory characters decided to visit our boat today. They seemed solely focused on our reason for anchoring in that location.”

“Privateers? Fortune hunters?” Steve asked.

“Not sure. The men had the muscle and advantage to

do whatever they wanted. Something kept them from it."

"What if…." His phone's familiar ringtone interrupted Brent's comment. Turning, expecting to see Leah's phone raised in the air beckoning his answer, Brent saw her engrossed in conversation with the other women. Consistent ringing returned his attention to the caller.

"Yeah."

"BRENT. We need to talk." Disbelief shook his body. *No way*, he thought.

"Hold on! I'll be right back." His deep tone required no further explanation. Evan, Cooper, and Steve remained silent.

Leah's curious look, followed by his okay sign, cleared the way as he hurried outside.

"Rafe?"

Heavy breathing preceded a throaty "Yeah."

"Man, I thought you were dead." Brent pulled his hand through his curls in disbelief.

"You know me better than that. I won't die that easily."

"I'd ask you where you are, but that would get me nowhere. A better question is, why the call?"

"I thought you'd already know where I am. I take it Amber hasn't told you." Rafe mumbled.

"Amber hasn't told me what? The last time she said your name, I held ice packs to her tear-stained, swollen eyes. I want to believe we are still friends even after everything that's happened. At the same time, that doesn't mean I won't break your legs if you hurt my sister again."

Rafe stammered, "I saw her today at the marina. Look, I can't explain. Take my word for it. You need to get your vacay buddies off this island, stat."

"That sounds ominous."

"I'm trying to protect you and Amber. They will come after anyone remotely important to me. Brent, get Amber and leave now."

"We're in that much danger? We haven't seen or talked to you in years. How would anyone know about our past relationship? Wait, never mind, I know."

"Believe me; it won't be long if they don't already know."

"I'm here with some pretty powerful people. Maybe we can help you."

"Appreciate it, buddy; you can't help. Leave. Now." His words flowed through gritted teeth.

Rafe's orders required compliance, not questions. Brent knew he was testing his old friend's patience.

"They're not an easy group to boss around. I'll see what I can do, although I won't promise anything." Brent could feel his friend's anger surge as the line went silent.

"By the way, I have something that belongs to you." Brent touted.

"What might that be?" Brent heard a deep inhale and assumed Rafe longed for the one word he was unwilling to say – Amber.

Calmly, Brent answered, "Your *Brigadier* medal."

Rafe's grumbles and tension filled the air, followed by an irate "I'll keep in touch" before the line went dead.

Brent reentered the cantina, perplexed by Amber's lack of honesty with him. Questioning eyes met his. This time, it was his sister's, not Leah's. He would have to deal with her later. Hurt by Amber's actions, he turned his attention elsewhere and returned to his buddies.

"Gentlemen, we have a serious problem on our hands."

Interrupted once again by their vivacious waitress, each man held his tongue. Brent's grim expression led them to one conclusion – TROUBLE was afoot.

TWELVE

The veins in his neck protruded, exposing deep blue pulsations. Anger racked his body. Bothered that he had let his fury get the best of him, Rafe mumbled under his breath. Not one but two matters gave rise to the rage he felt. His prized possession lay in hands other than his own. When and where he misplaced it remained a mystery. Secondly, he knew his friend well enough to discern that he would not leave. At least not right away.

Rafe leaned against the rough wood post and stared into the cantina across the street. Questions whirled through his mind. No longer willing to speculate on the outcome of his untimely call, he pulled the battered hat brim lower, shoved his hands deep into ripped, worn jeans, and made his way over to the hangout's front door. Steel drums riffed through aged black speakers plastered above a makeshift stage. One of the island's favorite hangouts for karaoke, Rafe was ever so grateful that tonight was not one of those nights. He settled onto the closest bar stool, head down.

"Hey, mon, what'll it be?" The spunky little server delivered a smile. "Nice to see ya tonight. Don't usually see ya in here during the week. Must be a rough week."

"You have no idea. Just give me the usual. I'm not very hungry."

"Good thing for that, mon. We wouldn't be able to fill ya if ya were." She tossed and disappeared through the kitchen's swinging door.

Her familiar laugh rang in his ears, alerting Rafe she was nearby. Maybe too close. With all the background noise, how could her voice be the only one he heard? Rafe winced from the sharp pain stabbing his chest. Convinced he'd recovered from the misery of leaving, the truth ensnared his heart in deep regret. Bitterness overcame his sense of logic. One slight glimpse of her would ease the hurt. Rafe straightened, shifting the stool closer to the sticky wood surface. His purpose for hiding in plain sight was fallacious, sure that the notion would only inflict more heartache. Deep down, he wanted Amber to see him and long to be with him, all the while knowing any contact between the two would only result in more pain. Eyes lifted, seeking a moment of satisfaction revealed a dangerous outcome. Motionless, Amber sat fixated on the bar. For a brief second, he relived the passion they previously shared through her spellbinding stare.

"Hey, here ya go. Just the way you like it." His waitress shoved the aromatic smoking plate in front of him, plunking silverware beside his drink.

The clang of silver broke his focus. Rafe's startled jerk sent liquid flying; ice cubes sailed across the bar top. Quick action by the waitress kept the glass from hitting the floor.

"Little edgy tonight?" Intrigued by his actions, the server patted his shoulder. "No worries, mon." Her loud " I got it" returned everything to normal. Loud chatter spilled throughout the room.

Unfortunately, three people were now keenly aware of his presence, and those were just the ones he knew about. Elbow bent, Rafe cupped his forehead in disbelief.

This is what happens. It's why I left. I can't think clearly around her.

"Hey, dude. It wasn't all that bad. You only made a total mess of the bar." Paschal chuckled.

Relieved to see his co-worker, a meager "thanks for

the support" greeted Paschal.

"I didn't know you were coming here tonight. We could've come together, dude."

"Thanks for the invite, but I didn't know I was either."

"Since you're here, want me to introduce you to some of my sexy friends."

"Uh, no thanks, that's kinda what started the catastrophe you walked in on."

"Oh, saw someone you liked, huh? Which one? I may know her." Paschal surveyed the room's occupants. "Dude, there's our charter guest from earlier today." His pointed finger led Rafe's eyes to the source of his despair.

Rafe's sudden slap on Paschal's hand brought forth a loud "ow."

"Why…?"

"I saw her. No need to point." Rafe barked.

"Now I get it. That chick makes you nervous or something. Is she the reason for your weird behavior at the marina? She is quite lovely. But alas, she has a very capable companion in Mr. Holcomb. They looked pretty happy together, dude. Let's find you someone else."

Paschal resumed his inspection of the cantina. His startled "oh no" spelled trouble. Rafe shook his head. Next time, he would go home. If given a choice, he preferred to tangle with his shadow friends versus the melodrama of the night. At least those two served as a suitable outlet for his pent-up aggression.

"Do I even want to know, Paschal? More than one of your girlfriends in attendance tonight?" Rafe moaned, chin propped on his hand.

"Not my girlfriend, per se. At least not yet." He grinned. "See our charter guest; what was her name? Amber, right?"

"I told you. I saw her earlier."

"I met the tall blonde one chair over the other day in

the market."

"Seriously?" *And the web becomes more entangled...* Rafe's head started to pound.

"For real. Rhonda is her name. She was lost and needed directions. Too bad I was late for work. We had an instant connection. It's fate, Dude." Paschal grinned.

Disaster nipped at Rafe's heels. He knew the mission was a challenge when he accepted the task. However, he never prepared for a cataclysmic event. Underlying circumstances stoked the fire more each day.

"Paschal, how will your female friends feel about you playing the field with tourists? You're going to create a firestorm, buddy." Rafe's grim look gave way to caution.

"Didn't consider that one. Could be worth it, though." His lips curved in a smile.

"Tread cautiously, my friend. Women will cause your downfall." Rafe longed to interject, "I know from experience." Mouth closed, he gave Paschal a weak salute and headed for the door. Sleep would evade him again tonight unless his shadows started a rematch.

~

Amber stopped listening to Rhonda's relentless chatter when the tanned lady-killer sat down on the bar stool. Her attention diverted to the six-foot, rugged frame that stole her heart years ago. Unable to look away, she patted the cheap linen napkin across her forehead. Beads of sweat saturated the cloth's creases. Clean-cut golden locks of hair peeped from under the straw hat. Taut biceps inched his shirt sleeve up, strained by the pull of muscles. Still every bit the mysterious officer, he sent butterflies crisscrossing through her abdomen. Shock and anger had consumed her during their first interaction. Unwilling to give him the satisfaction of knowing the turmoil he stirred within her, she remained silent and unfazed. Somehow, she felt not making eye contact at the marina would save her. Save her from what exactly she didn't know. All the pain was locked tightly in a box, submerged in the deep chambers of her heart, until today.

Amber swallowed hard, awkwardly trying to appear oblivious to his presence. If her luck held out, Rafe would never spot her in the crowded room. Unable to comply, she lowered her head. How could she remain unflustered after the man she would've given her life for randomly shows up ten years later? The longer her thoughts lingered on Rafe, the more her body began to tremble uncontrollably. A soft touch to her forearm sent a frightened gasp to her lips.

"Huh!"

Charlie jumped in surprise. "Amber, I didn't mean to scare you."

"It's fine. I'm a little uneasy tonight." Amber's chin quivered.

"A little? I'd say a lot. Want to share?" Charlie's caring smile reminded Amber of their earlier conversation on the beach.

"I have to trust someone, right? You see, you were right earlier, Rafe Culliver…" Her explanation stopped mid-sentence when a loud commotion at the bar drew everyone's attention. Rafe stood helpless as ice cubes flew in every direction.

"And I thought I was clumsy." Carol laughed. "I'd hate to be him right now. I've embarrassed myself like that. No one wants every eye in the room on you. Poor guy."

Rhonda flipped her lengthy blonde strands over her shoulder. "I beg to differ, Carol. I welcome all eyes in the room on me." She announced, straightening in her chair.

Amber sunk her body lower. Her uncomfortable attempt to hide drew Charlie's attention.

"That's him, isn't it?"

"Your uncanny investigative abilities scare me, Charlie. Yes, it is." Amber patted her brow once more.

"I'm good at what I do." She laughed, trying to ease Amber's discomfort. "And, for anyone trained to take notice, he looks every bit the part. Some things you can't hide under old hats and sloppy jeans."

"I guess not," Amber replied in a whisper.

"Any idea why he's here?"

Amber's throat constricted, unable to speak, weak shoulders gave a short rise and fall.

"Thanks to the indiscreet finger-pointing of his friend, he now knows you're here."

Amber's sharp inhale caught Rhonda's attention, drawing her eyes to the same area that captivated Amber.

"Well, I'll be. Suzanne, look who's pointing in our direction. He's seen me!"

"Rhonda, the room's full. How do you know he's pointing at you? Besides, he may be pointing out his wife."

Five of the women burst into roaring laughter while Amber focused on not passing out, fanning the napkin over her clammy skin.

"I just know." Rhonda chimed and began to stand.

"Rhonda, sit down. Wait to see what he does. You think there's no wife. Keyword: think." Suzzanne clasped her elbow, pulling her back onto the hard seat.

"Oh, alright. I'll wait a few minutes. I must admit the man with him isn't exactly loose change. I could also spend a few hours getting to know him better." A provocative gleam covered her eyes.

Amber's heart lurched. Was there any man Rhonda didn't want to get to know better? Evan, now Rafe. The first held her in his arms earlier today. The second man had discarded her after she'd offered him everything.

"Can we just finish our meal and leave?" Amber moaned. Quietly praying Rafe would depart before them.

Transfixed by his alluring stare, Amber's knees weakened when she felt another pair of eyes upon her. She stiffened. Evan's somber expression spoke to her from the room's far corner. Her fantasy getaway had manifested into a nightmare in less than 72 hours, prompting a heavy sigh.

The ride back should be fun!

THIRTEEN

Brent longed for a peaceful, enjoyable night, but that was not to be for him or his sister tonight. He somehow managed to dodge every question Leah threw at him on the ride home, changing the subject more often than not. Thank the Lord she was too sleepy to argue when they returned to Vitamin Sea. Her delicious, loving kiss of tropical fruit was the last he saw of her as she bounded up the stairs, promising to see him in the morning.

The orange glow encapsulating the sky arrived way too early for his liking. A fast shower and shave provided him the time he needed to speak with Amber before the others awoke. If his assumptions were correct, she would be deep in thought somewhere.

His knuckles softly rolled across the mahogany door. Several knocks later, no response. Brent placed his ear closer and strained to hear movement – nothing. A fight to quell his fears rose within him. The cold doorknob turned too easily. Brent whispered, “Amber?”

Fluffy bed covers neatly folded back showed no sign of use. Brent moved to her bathroom, expecting to hear the shower’s spray, yet silence surrounded him. Puzzled, he scratched his head and made one final check. Visible through the sun-streaked window, Amber sat perched on the shoreline, knees drawn close to her, her head lowered in her hands. The heartbreaking image brought a tear to his eye. Brent knew a hefty round of tears accompanied his sister's posturing. Shame overwhelmed him. Consumed with anger over her "untold secret," he never considered the anguish and pain that most likely assaulted her heart.

Guilt-ridden, Brent scaled the stairs and bounded out the door. He ran full stride to apologize and support his baby sister.

His abrupt halt sent sand granules flying through the air. "Hey."

Tear-swollen eyes greeted him as Amber brushed the sand from her legs. "Hey, back."

"Look, I considered your lack of honesty a personal attack when I shouldn't have."

Amber's puzzled expression urged his complete confession.

"I know about Rafe. I know you saw him at the marina. I also know he was at the bar last night."

"But how? Evan?" Amber patted her fingertips to moist cheeks, drying her tears.

"No. Evan would never betray your confidence. He cares for you too much."

Her faint smile reassured him he was steering the conversation in the right direction.

"Rafe called me last night before he came to the cantina. He assumed you'd told me about seeing him. While that's the least of my concerns now, I need you to promise no more secrets."

"I … I promise."

The two sealed their promise with an age-old children's "pinky" promise and a loving smile.

Brent exhaled. "With that behind us, we need to focus. Rafe's certain if we stay here, our lives are in danger. He couldn't elaborate. I am sure of one thing. He still cares deeply for you. I could hear it in his voice. The last thing I think he wants is for you to be in trouble again because of him."

"I have so many questions." She sniffled and wiped

away tears.

"I wish I could answer them, sis, but I can't. He only stressed that we can't stay on this island."

"We're a team, Brent. We always have been – you for me, me for you. What do you want to do? I know what I prefer." Her voice trailed.

"We stay and figure this out. No matter the past, Rafe remains our friend. And I have a feeling he's going to need help. Can you handle it? Seeing you like this kills me."

"My heart shattered into bits a long time ago. How many more times can he break it? I agree, though. We can't leave a friend. I'll survive as long as the people I care about survive with me."

Amber jumped to her feet and tightly hugged her brother.

"I thought you might say that. Evan deserves to hear the truth, sis."

"I know. I'll tell him today and pray he understands. What about Leah?"

"She'll know, just not this morning. The men decided last night we are all going fishing today. Think that marina can provide a charter big enough for everyone?"

"There's only one way to find out." Amber's expression returned to the radiant smile he preferred.

The duo trudged up the dune and headed for the villa. Brent felt at peace for the moment, although he knew the feeling would be fleeting. With every instinct within him elevated, he felt certain chaos would place a stranglehold on their lives once again.

~

Leah and Evan stood side by side, peering out the expansive breakfast room windows. Each witnessed the siblings' interaction on the tranquil beachfront, afraid to vocalize their opinions.

Unable to remain silent, Leah sighed heavily, "We suffer the same fate. I'm in love with a man who intrigues me to the core. I can never predict what's going to happen next. And you, dear friend, are in love with the female version. Whether you wish to admit it or not."

"Not." A gulp of coffee loaded his mouth.

"That answer wasn't the least bit convincing. You should probably come up with a better one." Brows raised. "Don't forget I've been in your shoes. When a Scott gets in your blood, you may as well concede defeat." Her eyes fixated on the two figures seated in the sand.

"It's that obvious?"

"That and more." She laughed.

"They do have a knack for monopolizing your thoughts."

"Yes, and your actions. The misfortune is that you become so in tune with their nature that a person knows when the other is hiding something. The funny thing is… I can also tell when you are too." Her curious smirk awaited a response.

"Wait a minute. How did the conversation turn to me?"

"Because when I delve into Brent's thoughts, I often find you're thrown into the mix somewhere."

"Now, Leah, you know that's not always true." Evan fidgeted with his collar.

"More often than not, though."

Her focus was relentless. "I won't be coerced into confirming anything. The best way to find your answers is by talking to Brent."

"Bro-code, huh? Rest assured. No matter how much I love both of you. I will find out the truth."

"Here's your chance." He nodded.

Amber and Brent's surprised faces greeted the two as Brent closed the door.

Leah's fingers tightly gripped the porcelain cup in determination. "You two are up bright and early. Evan and I were just discussing how touched we are watching you on the beach."

Amber threw an arm around Brent's shoulder. "Isn't sibling love grand!"

"Oh yes, grand indeed. Funny, it looked like your sibling love' was suffering a little setback. What do you think, Evan?

"All families have quarrels now and again. They look fine to me."

Leah stifled a chuckle when she saw Evan look in every direction except Brent's.

"Evan's right. You've never seen me fight with Amber. We love each other to our core. Don't we, sis?"

"Most of the time." She replied.

"No, really, it's true, Leah." Amber nodded. "Brent was telling me about his plans for the day. I understand we have the pleasure of fishing with the men. I'm not a big fan of the sport, but he pleaded his case and won." Amber tossed a hand to each side and sighed.

"You three are terrible liars. It's only a matter of time before I discover what you're hiding. As for fishing, my parents used to take me all the time. I love it. We'll put this discussion on the back burner until tonight. But rest assured, tonight we talk." Leah's penetrating stare fell on each of them.

"Great." Brent clapped his hands. "Since you love fishing, you can tell the remaining 'sisters' what we're doing. Evan and I will round up Steve and Cooper." He pressed his lips tightly to hers, allowing Leah no time to disagree, and ran out the door.

Amber, left to bear the brunt of Leah's skepticism, offered a weak smile. "I'll gather the women in the study. Prepare for Rhonda's quibbling and maybe Carol's. They don't seem like the seaworthy type, and I should know." Amber leaned and clutched her stomach, simulating nausea. Her soft giggle hung in the air.

Leah turned back to the window, taking in the

majestic setting. *This island has certainly offered its share of enjoyment. What else does the tropical paradise have in store?*

Cold as ice, her coffee clung to the sides of her mouth. Ewww. She'd never been a fan of iced coffee. It was about as bad as the load of bull she'd been fed by the guilty trio. Opposed to further negativity, she shoved her disapproval to the back of her mind and headed to the study.

Leah crossed the threshold to an uproar of murmuring and complaints. Her cheery "good morning" wasn't reciprocated.

"What's good about sitting in the middle of the ocean throwing dead fish overboard to catch live fish?" Disdain filled the air. Rhonda angled her head in defiance.

"You know I love you, Leah, but the excursion sounds smelly and gross. I don't do well with unpleasant odors." Carol's palm flew to her mouth.

"Suzanne, Kimberly, what about you two? I won't ask any of you to do something you find repugnant. I thought it might be fun."

The two women replied, "I'm in."

"It beats shopping all day again," Suzanne said, nodding to Kimberly.

"True. All I do in the States is design, market, and shop. I'm happy to go fishing." Kimberly's eyebrows rose. "Did you say all the men are coming along…?"

Leah wanted to laugh. "They definitely will be on board. It was their idea."

Carol perked up, straightening in her chair. "Well, I suppose if everyone else is going, I might be able to handle the smell for a few hours."

"Really. Rhonda, that only leaves you. Sure you won't come along?"

Brent poked his head in. "Speed it up, ladies. Paschal says our boat leaves the marina in one hour." Leaving one last "hurry, please" between them.

"Paschal, huh? Maybe I will go. He might be cute." Rhonda answered.

Amber anxiously stroked her throat the instant Brent said Paschal's name. Leah's eyes widened. Brent's charter choice wasn't by accident. She knew that now. Today, she would catch more than fish.

FOURTEEN

Self-doubt and worry tormented Rafe. Had he made the right decision to call Brent? His episode in the cantina ended in disaster. His impromptu stop was only made worthwhile by the sight of Amber. Her allure stoked flames within him from years gone by. Visions of starry nights locked in her embrace plagued him. Her moist, warm lips, covering his, controlled his dreams. What a cruel joke fate played on him. Her presence here changed the entire mission. His orders must come first, not Amber's safety. Somehow, he needed to combine the two. It was the "how" that concerned him.

Years of training and the well-practiced task of shoving her into the dark recesses of his mind drew him back to the present, along with sopping wet shoes. The heavy rubber hose had sprayed water on the same spot for so long puddles formed around him.

What else can happen today?

Rafe rushed to the shutoff valve, stopping the continuous spray, and pulled the long black line across the planking. Loud whistles interrupted his pity party. Paschal's frantic hand motions beckoned his presence. He dropped the hose and ran.

"What?"

"Dude, we have a problem. One of Evan Holcomb's friends wants to book a fishing charter for eleven people, like now." The flimsy yellow Post-it note waved in his hand.

“Some guy named Brent Scott wants to charter. He must be here on vacation with Holcomb. Eleven, dude, that’s a lot of people. What boat do we use?” Panic consumed Paschal and Rafe simultaneously.

“Seems we have no choice but to find a boat. Old Man Jenkins will be happy about the revenue. He won’t, however, be too keen that we have to use the Savannah Jane.” Rafe replied grimly.

“Again? We barely made it back on time the other day. That’s his pride and joy. I’m not going to lie, dude; I’m scared to use that boat.” Paschal said, shaking his head in worry.

“This time, we have ‘paying guests’ on our side.”

“You’re right. It still makes me nervous, though. Jenkins will kill us if anything happens to that boat.”

“Then, we better make sure nothing does,” Rafe cautioned.

Paschal anchored his hat, drawing the chin string tight, and reared his shoulders back. “I’ll head down and stock the wells. You better find someone to make lunch for this bunch, dude, and us.” He grinned and disappeared out the door.

Rafe grumbled under his breath. Amber’s attendance on another charter wasn’t something he’d anticipated or wanted. Not only would she be on board, but so would his best friend. Regrets flooded his body again. Deep-seated feelings of betrayal consumed him. He and Brent had helped each other through boot camp. Brent thought career path differences directed their parting, completely unaware of the true reason for Rafe’s sudden departure. That fact remained a secret between him and Amber. God help them if he allowed himself to fall under her spell again. He had enough trouble.

Vehicle doors slamming drew him to the window. Time was up. Brent, Amber, and the group from the cantina casually strolled toward the marina door. A final glimpse of Amber released endorphins that rifled throughout his body. Holcomb wasn't by her side. He led the others through the parking lot. Hope grabbed his heart and squeezed.

The bell's familiar jingle rattled upon their entry. Rafe moved to a stack of maps, hoping it gave the semblance of preparation. Red pen and chart plotter in hand, he tossed a mundane "Morning."

Evan replied, "Morning. Brent Scott made a reservation for a fishing charter for our group today. Is everything in order?"

Rafe perceived Evan's territorial tone served as a warning. Unable to control the sarcastic smile that covered his lips, Rafe stood toe to toe with Evan, stifling a laugh. "It's ready, although I should warn you, the seas offshore are building. It may be a bit rough today. You could always reschedule for another day."

"I'll let Brent make that call. It's his charter."

Brent entered the marina office to Evan's glib. "He has a question for you." With a toss of his head, Evan disappeared out the door.

"Hello, Rafe. You look as fit as ever. I wish we could've reconnected under different circumstances. But since we're here, what's your question?"

"Me too, Brent. Why did you book this charter? I informed you of the risk you place yourself and Amber in the longer you stay here. This is no game."

"Friendship works both ways, Rafe. We're not leaving right away. We could help you. Have any other questions?"

Brent's firm stance and determined glare reminded Rafe of the old Brent. If only they could recapture those days. Battle lines drawn, Brent gained the upper hand today by default. Paschal and Leah's entry directed the conversation elsewhere.

"As I told Mr. Holcomb earlier, the seas will be a tad

rough as the day progresses. You may want to consider rescheduling for another day." Frustration clouded Rafe's judgment. He knew to cancel the charter. Allowing Brent an option was not an option, yet he succumbed.

"I think we can stand a few turbulent waves. We'll keep it scheduled."

"Your choice. The cost will increase. I hope that's not a problem. Paschal and I will need to accompany you on the trip."

"I'm sure we can manage. No need for that." Brent's jaw flexed.

"Sorry, marina policy. More than six on a boat require a captain and first mate."

Paschal's surprised expression gave way to a deep cough.

"Paschal, is the SJ ready?" Rafe had never been this amped up over a booking, and he knew it confused Paschal.

"All good. Mr. Scott, could you have your party follow me down to the SJ's slip." A swipe of his hand ushered the man out the door."

Leah stood perfectly still, eyeing Rafe. "Mr. Culliver, right?"

"Yes, ma'am. And you're…?"

"Leah Reynolds. The better half of the man you just provoked in that conversation. Care to share why?" Leah's chin lifted.

"You must be mistaken, Ms. Reynolds. I'm only concerned for his safety and that of your other guests. It's my job."

"So, am I to assume you'll be our captain today?"

"That's correct. You might want to hurry; your friends are leaving you behind."

"Oh, I'm not worried. Who better to walk to the slip with than the captain? By the way, how many other charter services are there available on the island?"

"That can handle this large of a group? I'd say three.

Would you like to call another service?"

"No, no, certainly not. It's just now I understand why Brent picked this marina. Lead the way." Her whimsy fueled an already scorching fire.

Rafe griped, anger crawling up his neck while offering a pretentious smile. Brent chose a worthy adversary to spend his life with… that is, if his assumptions were correct.

Rafe heaved his backpack from the rack and closed the door behind him. Concerns over whether Old Man Jenkins would kill him for using the SJ no longer mattered. Odds were against him surviving the day. Jenkins would never have the chance.

~

Amber ran to catch up with Evan, beach bag swinging to and fro, bouncing against her hip. Happy to skirt past the office, she sensed trouble when Evan ignored her calls to wait. He'd seemed indifferent since their cantina visit. She knew he was irritated by the lack of a simple "good night" before retiring. She would've preferred a robust kiss as a substitute for words. She needed to discover why he avoided her, or the blissful kissing days she yearned for were over.

Panic seized her. Brent! Had Brent talked to Evan about Rafe? If he had, Evan may disappear from her life forever.

Amber's trot placed her long legs in perfect step with Evan's. Her bag poked him in the side as she inched closer. A faint giggle caught his attention. Hurt-filled eyes scrutinized her presence.

"If you're going to ignore me all day, maybe I should stay behind." She murmured.

"The trip's for everyone. Your brother wouldn't allow it." He snipped.

"I'm a grown woman. Brent doesn't tell me what to do. Nor does anyone else." Her animosity drove her point home.

"I hope you're right about that." He said and walked away.

The displeasure in Evan's voice gave her an overwhelming feeling of sorrow, giving way to a more important question - had their journey ended after a few short days of bliss? Chips of broken brick lay strewn around her heart. What a colossal mistake she'd made taking down her walls.

She'd played the "passing fancy" role to a "t," much to her dismay. Amber plopped down on the rough pylon, elbow braced on a knee, deep in thought.

What makes him think he can do this to me?

Her chin rose in defiance. No one directed her course. Determination flowed through her veins. No matter what, she'd have a glorious time today. Amber jumped from the prickly seat with a new sense of purpose. A sharp sting told her men weren't the only source of pain in her backside. Her loud "ouch" brought Rhonda rushing forward with Paschal locked about her arm.

"Oh, my dear Amber, what's wrong?" Rhonda's bright smile bragged of her latest conquest.

Her low umhumm never fazed Rhonda. "Just a small splinter, that's all. Hello, Paschal. I never thanked you for the other day." Amber's pearly smile gave rise to Rhonda's obvious annoyance.

Rhonda's fiery eyes grazed over Paschal and released his arm. Tucked underneath Amber's tongue sat a chuckle, longing to escape.

"No worries. There's plenty of sunscreen and water aboard just for you." He grinned.

Rhonda tucked her hand into Paschal's. "Could you help me board, please?"

Paschal's flushed cheeks and enthusiastic nod showed his attraction to Rhonda. Her sly, calculated trip initiated Paschal's welcomed strong embrace around her waist.

Amber moaned. Was there a man alive immune to Rhonda's charms? Probably not. Amber stepped forward, halted by a strong clutch on her left wrist that seared her insides. Both lungs screamed: exhale, breathe. The man whose touch once moved the earth and stars in her world stood inches away. Hazel brown eyes, mysterious as ever, locked onto hers.

"Careful, Ms. Scott." Rafe slid his fingers slowly down her arm, prolonging their connection. "We're in no hurry."

Fireworks pricked her skin. Rafe's seductive scan infused every pore of her being with sensuality. She nervously nibbled her lips, naïve to the effect the action would have on him. His breathy moan drifted to her ears, causing the hairs along her arm to stand on end.

This isn't happening.

Frozen in place, Brent's hand on the small of her back pushed her onto the boat. "Can you let the rest of us aboard, please?"

Assuming Brent saw their heated exchange by the tone of his voice, Amber blinked, issuing a gruff, "Hold on." She'd bet odds that if Brent noticed, he wasn't the only one. Lifting her head, she continued to flinch from Rafe's touch. His flirtatious smile raised her guard.

Oh no, buddy, it's not that easy.

That seductive smile gave way to many a fallen heart in years past. Amber convinced herself that her heart held a failsafe to his charms. And yet, a simple act sent waves of excitement flowing through her, oblivious to her friends' presence.

Charlie's soft tone reeled Amber in. "Do we need to talk?" She whispered. "You might want to wipe the drool from the corner of your mouth and try to hide Mr. Culliver's effect on you. Other people have noticed." She leaned backward, placing Evan in Amber's line of sight.

"That obvious?"

"Afraid so. Leah's suspicious, too. Spend time with Evan before the guys get together, and I'll 'chit chat' with Loverboy. Maybe we can ward off any problems." Charlie winked and joined Rafe by the rail side.

"I think it's too late for that, but I'll try." Amber tucked a fallen strand of hair behind an ear. Her faint smile faltered when she approached Evan. His cold stare chastised her as if she'd committed a mortal sin. Unwilling to relent, Amber met him with an unapologetic welcome.

"Hello, mind if I keep you company for a little while?"

"You sure it's me you want to keep company with? It seems Mr. Culliver desires your undivided attention. You appear to have quite an effect on him, or is it the other way around? Possibly a bit of both." His chiseled features twisted in anger.

"Evan Holcomb, if I didn't think better of you, I'd swear you are wildly jealous."

"Maybe. I'm more concerned about what you're not telling me. A blind man could see you two have chemistry, and you're trying miserably hard to hide it."

Amber's eyelashes fluttered. "I, I .... Have no idea what you're talking about. I came on this trip to be with you, but that's my misjudgment." Her head held high as she stormed off to join the other women.

Evan clasped his head in frustration. "Trouble in Shangri-la, buddy?" Brent asked, pinching the sides of Evan's neck between his fingers.

"I guess." He mumbled. "Your sister has to be the most infuriating female I've ever known."

"You think? I beg to differ. Remember another female named Leah."

Evan paused. "One minute, I want to steal her away from here to be alone, and the next, I want to fling an old-fashioned tongue-lashing on her. She makes me crazy sometimes." His fingers combed through midnight locks.

"You know what they call that, my friend."

"Unfortunately, I do."

"L-o-v-e!" Brent chuckled. "We both have an incurable case."

"It's a two-way street, and I'm unsure if your sister feels the same way, at least not after this morning. Her interactions with our boat captain are very, for lack of a better word, physical. Definitely not something you'd see between two strangers."

"I'm sure it wasn't like that. Amber never meets a stranger. You know her - sweet, kind, friendly."

Evan gave a heavy sigh. "Some of the very reasons I fell in love with her. I hadn't counted on those charms enticing Culliver so quickly.

Brent grimaced. "Remember last night when I said we have serious matters to discuss?"

"Yes?"

"Those matters involve Rafe Culliver."

"I'm not going to like this, am I?"

"Nope." Brent's head hung low.

~

Charlie crossed the SJ decking to join Rafe Culliver. His disappointed expression persisted when he saw Amber standing with the other women. Charlie smiled.

"I don't believe we've met." Hand extended, "Charlie Ashby. Nice to meet you."

"Likewise. Rafe Culliver."

"How is it living life large in this tropical oasis? I'd imagine a man of your caliber would become bored easily." Her nose scrunched. "I mean, even paradise can become mundane at times."

Rafe grinned. "A man of my character welcomes the quiet. Being a lowly boat captain and working at the marina allows me time to fuel my passions."

"And what are those passions? If I may ask."

"If we hadn't just met, Ms. Ashby, I'd swear you're

baiting me. You know, like a reporter on an important story." His spirited stare remained on Charlie. "To answer your question, I'm plotting charts most days, planning my next dive. These reefs host an abundant supply of sea life along with a boat wreck or two."

Charlie masked her amusement. He'd wasted his time if his reporter comment was supposed to fluster her. Confident in her ability to stand "toe-to-toe" with the best interrogators, she continued the game.

"Plotting charts, shipwrecks, and diving sound interesting. Are you searching for a particular wreckage site? I've heard these waters are home to several profitable opportunities."

Rafe tensed. "No particular sites. Taking them one by one. Are you a diver, Ms. Ashby?"

"Call me Charlie, please. As a matter of fact, I am."

"Interesting."

"How so?"

"Never mind. Excuse me. I need to get us moving. Enjoy your day, Charlie."

His lingering speculation indicated her inquiries bothered him. The reporter in her squealed with delight. She felt a strange eeriness around them from their first night on the island. Whether he wanted to admit it, she knew Rafe Culliver's motives for secrecy revolved around more than concealing his past relationship with Amber. Charlie started a mental "tick" sheet. First on the list, she needed to persuade Amber that a frank and truthful conversation regarding Rafe Culliver was a must.

"Thanks. I'm sure I will." She answered, watching him walk away.

~

The "sisters" lounged in the toasty rays of the sun. Legs stretched, feet propped on thick canvas cushions, beverages in hand. Bouts of laughter intermingled with subtle whispers floated among the women.

Rhonda boasted to the other women. "Take lessons, ladies. Flirting 101 has begun. By the end of the day, my sweet Paschal will be eating out of the palm of my hand."

"Paschal will be helping the men all day. The only thing you'll be doing tonight is eating fresh fish." Carol teased.

"Let's say we make a little wager, Carol. I'll bet I make more headway with Paschal than you do with Cooper."

Carol's bright smile faded to a discouraged frown. "I'm not sure what you're talking about. Cooper and I are friends. As I've told you before, no more husbands for me."

"Oh, now. Don't be upset. We all know you're infatuated with Cooper. Your skill set simply needs a little refining. Otherwise, I'd consider your pursuit hopeless." Rhonda smirked, lifting the fluted stem to her red glossed lips.

"There is no pursuit, Rhonda. Only you throw yourself at every man you meet." Carol spouted as she whisked a tear from under her sunglass rim.

"Hey, hey. Enough. I'll not have this. We love each other, for goodness' sake. Rhonda, you pursue whomever you wish and leave Carol alone. She's a grown woman who knows her mind. And we all know being alone is not your strong suit." Amber couldn't help throwing the last jab. Rhonda bullied everyone when it came to men, it was in her nature.

"Well… I never." Rhonda gulped the remainder of her drink and poured another, filling her mouth with an orange slice.

Amber's encouraging wink made Carol gush.

Amused by the banter, Leah, Suzanne, and Kimberly sat side by side with their hands clasped over their mouth. Small giggles escaped from beneath tight-formed fingers. Leah gave a rousing call, "Ding, Ding. Round one goes to Amber."

In on the game, Suzanne and Kimberly shouted, "On to round two."

Amber's hasty throw sent pineapple pieces flying through the air. The three women screamed as yellow chunks struck their midsections. Impressed by her skill, she laughed even harder.

With the mood lighter and "sisterhood" restored, Amber teased, "That'll teach you. Now, can someone point me to the bathroom? Bottomless glasses and this nonsense are placing a heavy strain on my bladder."

"Head up those stairs or down those." Leah pointed. "A boat this size must have more than one."

"Let's try up. I'll be right back."

Amber wrapped the sarong about her waist. She slipped her damp, sticky sandals between her toes and climbed the four small stairs. Unsure of what to expect, a stateroom or galley, her mouth flew open. Confronted with the image before her, she struggled to blink. Her choice of paths led her straight to Rafe standing at the boat's helm. His bare, bronzed chest and ripped abs made her forget her bladder issue. Khaki shorts hung low across his hips, revealing a toned physique undoubtedly enhanced by his endless training hours. She no longer saw the handsome, lanky guy of years gone by; before her stood the perfect male specimen of sexual magnetism.

Unable to look away, she rendered a throat-clearing "hum."

A devious smile covered Rafe's lips. "I wondered how long it would be until you said something."

"Um…Um. I guess I'm a little lost."

"Really? And where are you trying to go? I think you're right where you need to be."

Heat surged through her, settling on her high cheekbones, flushing them. "I was trying to locate a bathroom. Guess I've taken a wrong turn somewhere."

"I'm happy with your choice."

The gleam in his eye rattled her nerves even more. "So… there's one in here?"

"You could say that. Go through the door to your left. Make sure you can find your way back to me. Should be easy for you."

Oh, my goodness! Beads of perspiration framed her upper lip.

Amber hurried to the door, lengthening her steps. Her brain screamed retreat, run, but her heart leaped over Rafe's barely hidden innuendos. The desperate need for a splash of cool water on her face erased as she opened the accordion door. In front of her sat a small black contraption mounted to the floor.

Oh lord. Please don't let this be it.

Nerves, need, and necessity quelled her concerns. She hurried about her business, retied the sarong, and pressed the small foot pedal. Startled by the obnoxious loud suction noises, Amber jumped backward, dislodging the flimsy fabric door, and landed straight into Rafe's arms. His steely biceps wrapped around her waist while his muscular thighs molded to her backside. Their height difference made his catch more sensual than she remembered. Amber stiffened and held her breath. The capability of her lungs to exhale vanished while his hold remained firm.

"Whoa… you good?"

Rafe shifted his hands from her waist, slowly reaching her shoulders, and turned her around. His eyes locked with hers. "You know this is where you should always be – in my arms."

Amber's mouth opened to object, only to discover she couldn't speak. Her clear lack of protest afforded Rafe ample opportunity to reinforce his earlier points. Already weak, her knees buckled when he grazed his lips across hers, lingering to taste the sweetness. Strengthening her stance, his skilled hands glided down to her waist, drawing her upward. She knew her squirming about only amused

Rafe as he maintained his hold, making any attempt to pull away futile. Reluctant at first, Amber released all apprehension, succumbing to his grasp and tender lips. She could no longer fight the past. Her arms instinctively lifted, encircling his neck, her smoldering eyes locked with his. The slight break in their bond granted Amber the seconds she needed to end the encounter. Instead, she pressed into his muscled chest, striving to relive all those blissful moments they'd shared long ago. Yearning to increase the electricity that passed between them, she surrendered to his moist lips. The slight shift of her swimsuit strap exposed a spot on her shoulder for his nip as his firm hand kneaded her collarbone. Amber leaned her head back, engrossed in her memories. Rafe's lips drifted slowly back to her mouth. His fingers toyed with the knot holding the scarf skirt. Agitated by the unyielding tie, Rafe's knee moved to spread the silk covering. Awareness coursed through her body, ringing alarm bells. Amber flinched from the stark truth that surrounded her. Ashamed, embarrassed, and confused, two swift steps away from his arms slowed her heart rate.

"I can't do this," Amber exclaimed.

"Why? Being together feels so right, Amber." He questioned, swallowing hard.

"Right, for whom?"

"Us." Rafe blurted.

"That's laughable. The 'us' you're referring to ended long ago. By your choice, I might add. You left me!"

"Leaving wasn't my decision. I had no other option." Rafe muttered with pleading eyes.

Amber exited the conversation with an irritated huff, no longer willing to hear or be heard.

Sounds of loud clangs mixed with leather slides and an occasional groan alerted the "sisters" of Amber's flustered return.

"I was beginning to think you fell overboard. Did you

get lost?" Leah asked.

"Jumping would be a better idea." Amber retorted. "I wish I had." She plopped down beside Leah, whose unrelenting stare stirred Amber's anxiety.

"Is this boat even going to stop? Any closer to those cliffs, and we'll be here for more than a day. What are we supposed to do way out here while the men fish?"

Charlie's curious once-over sent Amber into a tailspin. Her reckless actions around Rafe betrayed her yet again.

"No need to worry, dear. My sweet Paschal assured me our captain has something exciting planned for us." Rhonda added.

"I'm sure our boat captain has several exciting ideas up his sleeve." Amber's frustrated huff blew the spray of hair from her eye.

"No need to be rude, Amber. You chose to come. Mr. Culliver seems quite capable." Rhonda slid her Ray-Bans down and smiled.

Rafe now stood on the bow and eased his shirt over his head. His presence controlled her will. Angry over Rhonda's ogling, Amber eyed Rafe. Not to her surprise, he ignored her and moved toward Paschal.

Within minutes, he returned to her group, never acknowledging her.

"How do you ladies feel about snorkeling? You can sun on the floating raft for those who prefer something tamer. Who's in?" Rafe's gleaming smile fortified Rhonda's confidence.

"Will you be snorkeling also? I'd try it if a man of your physique accompanied us."

"I'm sorry, I won't. Ms…?"

"Call me Rhonda," standing to strut like a peacock.

"Well, Rhonda, I need to stay on board, but I promise to maintain a watchful eye."

"That's it, sunning for me. Bronzing this body is

always a wise choice."

Rafe's eyes drifted to Amber after Rhonda's comments. She refused to show any sign of jealousy. Saved by Charlie's quick input, "I'm going snorkeling. Amber, do you want to come with me?"

"I'd love to."

His grimace alerted Amber to his disagreement with her choice. "I'll be back in a few minutes after I set things up."

Amber mouthed a silent "thank you" in Charlie's direction, to which she received a response – "We need to talk."

FIFTEEN

High seas hounded the charter boat once they broke open water. Interval swells lapped at the vessel's girth, slowing their arrival. Dropping anchor with the cliffs to their back sheltered the boat from the rougher waters. Behind them, breaks along the cliff line voiced their veracity. Loud crashes slapped against the eroding rocks. Evan's directions to the site had been spot on. Rafe's warnings were also on the mark; however, time left them no option. Brent trusted Evan with his life. If he felt an urgency to revisit the area, Brent saw no need to argue. The women would require constant supervision in the shifting currents. He prayed Rafe remained true to his word to watch over all of them if needed. Not just Amber.

Gathered in a circle, the men eagerly awaited Brent's news. Paschal's job prepping the lines opened a small window of time for frank conversation.

"I'm not going to sugarcoat the facts. We trusted each other in Bridgeport and survived. What I tell you will most likely endanger your lives along with mine. Anyone who prefers to leave now, you should."

"Just tell us." Steve barked.

"Our guide is no ordinary boat captain. I've known Rafe Culliver since high school. He's one of 'The Twelve' - a highly trained team of soldiers. Individuals who possess skills beyond any comprehension. 'The Twelve' handle top-secret covert operations. The Brigadier clip we found belongs to him."

"Dang. I was right all the long." Steve scratched his chin. "Although I've never met one of 'The Twelve,' it all makes sense now."

"Rafe called me while we were in the cantina to warn me that as long as Amber and I remain on this island, we are in extreme danger. He feels our past connections will jeopardize our safety. His orders were to leave, yesterday. Unfortunately, Rafe forgot that I don't take orders well."

"So, your sister has known Rafe for years, also?" Evan questioned.

"Yes."

Evan's pain-filled eyes lifted. "Steve, your inferences seem to be contagious. A lot of things make sense now."

"I believe someone intentionally tampered with the Rover. And it's the same two men Evan encountered here yesterday." Brent continued to brief the men. "Classified mission or not, I can't abandon Rafe. As far as I know, he's alone with no help. Amber and I agree we have to stay. You guys, on the other hand, have a choice. No hard feelings."

"I'm not going anywhere." Evan's bold stare reinforced his pledge.

Steve and Cooper spoke in unison, "Neither are we."

Cooper's eyes glistened and nodded toward the boat's stern, "There's someone else I won't leave unprotected."

"Ditto," Steve replied.

Brent stroked his forehead. "Lord, you guys are hopeless. What has this island done to your independence."

"Probably the same thing that Leah's done to yours," Evan murmured.

"True. No arguing here." He smiled. "Rafe may need all the undercover support we can provide. Steve and Coop, you see what Paschal has to say about the area. Something peaked those thugs' anger at Evan for being here. Evan, you and I will explore the boat while Rafe's preoccupied with the women. We might get lucky. It's worth a shot."

"Question… is Culliver willing to work with us for your and Amber's protection?"

"As much as he's allowed, I hope. Where he fails, you will fill in." Brent slapped Evan's shoulder. "Let's do it."

~

Rafe's frustration creased his brow. Fighting with the oversized raft and babysitting weren't on his agenda when he arrived for work this morning. Air spewed from the spout each time he whisked the air hose away; plugging the safety valve required two people. Anger flushed his skin with reddish hues - Brent's haphazard decision to stay crawled up his spine. Stubbornness and pride had killed many a man. Or woman. Amber's safety hung in the balance, along with Brent's. A few select adjectives fell out of his mouth before he realized she was standing beside him.

"Would you like some help?"

"I think I may need some if you're willing."

"Just tell me what to do." Leah smiled.

"You jab when I pull." Rafe pointed to the plug and air hose.

"Aye, Aye, Captain."

Success! They both exclaimed. He tossed the raft overboard and tied the lines off. His exasperated sigh rang louder than he knew.

"You should've asked someone for help."

"True. But asking for help isn't my strong suit."

"I can tell." Leah grinned.

"Why aren't you with the other ladies? Sunning or snorkeling?"

"I'm fishing with the men. My snorkeling abilities are certainly not up to par for these currents. I'll get enough sun fishing." Leah's captivating smile told Rafe his buddy had succumbed to her charms within minutes.

"Paschal will string a line for you. He's up with the men now. Have fun."

"Hey!" She called, "Wanna tell me who you REALLY are? I'll find out anyway, you know.

Her question stopped Rafe midstride. His rapid about-face highlighted his surprise. An inner voice cried out – steady, maintain. The change in his composure was instantaneous. The curve of his mouth gave way to a midsection chuckle,

"I'm sure you already know."

His contemptuous stare sent her along in a huff, displeased with his answer.

Rafe returned to the snorkeling gear and released another chuckle. His opinion of Leah had changed. Brent deserved someone who pushed him beyond the boundaries of his past. He remained half angry with Brent if he'd told her of his real identity and half amused by her astute promise if he hadn't.

A deep dive into the storage bin produced fins, masks, snorkels, and life vests. Strangely enough, the gear looked brand new, yet Old Man Jenkins never utilized the boat. Rafe couldn't remember the last time he'd taken it out. Maybe the kid cleaned everything after his Bonfire Beach trip. Who cared? At least Amber and Charlie would have safe equipment. Curiosity gnawed at his gut, leading to further speculations, tasking him with one more thing to handle.

Will it ever end?

Lingering on the unknown would only infuriate him more. Handle things as they come - a fresh outlook intended to yield valuable results. Old School. He liked it that way. That is until Amber and Charlie ambushed him from behind.

"Is this for us?" Amber questioned, Charlie close by her side.

Rafe's mischievous smile broadened by her newfound

security blanket. She knew he'd behave with someone else around.

"All yours. Ready for a little adventure?"

"Adventure is my middle name." Charlie teased, grabbed two life vests, and handed one to Amber. "These look brand new. Recently replaced?"

Dang, she noticed everything. But why? He thought for a moment.

Is this woman my backup?

"Rafe, she asked you a question?" Amber thumped his arm.

"Well, Charlie, I'm not sure." He tossed. "But we're using it."

"Whatever," shoulder shrugs greeted him when he turned, arms full of gear. The three moved in silence to the rear ladders. Rafe suppressed his need to touch her. Hold her again.

The uptick in wind sloshed waves against the vessel's sides. Rafe's eyes, shielded by the hat brim, concealed his concern.

"Okay." He breathed. "I've tied a safety line to the SJ. Keep hold of it while you snorkel. Vast amounts of sealife lie beneath and around the boat. There's no need to push our luck by exploring on your own in these currents. Okay, ladies?" He recited his plea to drive home his point to Amber.

"Thanks, Rafe. We'll be fine. I can't wait to see what's here." Charlie bubbled, flippers in hand.

Amber cleared her snorkel with one large blow and began her descent. Rafe's firm clasp on her arm prevented her progress. The safety line on display threaded through his fingers.

"Hold on to that line when you hit the water. Got me." What was supposed to be a request sounded more like an order, as usual. Indignant eyes peered through the glass mask. "Please," he quickly added. Met with a smirk of approval, he watched her until she reached the crisp water and said a prayer.

"When are you ever going to focus on me, handsome?" Red nails flirtatiously twirled a strand of hair as Rhonda turned on her charisma.

Rafe needed a distraction to overcome his worry, but the distraction before him required no introduction. He'd seen it numerous times. His quiet "not interested" intended for her ears only assaulted Rhonda's ego, initiating a rapid "I think I'll skip the raft. I'm staying on board."

"Well, she changed her mind fast. What in the world?"

"I'm not sure, Carol." Rafe retorted. "Guess she realized no one else is interested."

"Not me, that's for sure. I'm perfectly content aboard a steady vessel."

"Can't disagree with you. What about Suzanne and Kimberly? Are they using the sun raft?"

"I don't think so. It's Rhonda's fault you had to blow the monstrosity up. I'm sorry she put you to the trouble of doing it. She can be a bit fickle."

"So, I've noticed. Let me know if you need anything." Her warm "I will" followed him up the stairs into the helm. Rafe smiled. Paschal and Rhonda may be perfect for each other.

Brent's loud rap on the door frame was unexpected. "Hey, man. You busy?"

"Kinda. I planned to watch Amber and Charlie from here. You realize I never want anything to happen to her."

"Your little interlude boarding clued me in. Leave Amber alone if you don't want anything to happen to her, Rafe. Stirring up old memories will end badly for you both. You're like a brother to me. I'd do anything for you except allow you to break my sister's heart again."

"Not my intention." His eyes grew cold as the years of pain welled inside.

"Good." Brent breathed deeply. "I told the other guys about you."

Rafe's voice escalated, "You did what!" Clenched fists reinforced his disbelief.

"Look, not something I intended initially, but we've experienced a couple of bizarre incidents. They needed to know. Between us, there are some pretty influential people in our arena. You may need help."

Rafe hands slid into his pockets, and attempted to calm himself. "Don't think I'm not appreciative. I am. My missions are top secret. Since your group arrived by random design, you have a knack for being in the wrong place at an inopportune time. That spells trouble for both of us."

"Evan was approached by two 'mob' wannabe's on the charter yesterday. Someone cut the battery cables on the Rover. The use of the word trouble is putting it mildly."

Rafe felt a kick in his gut. His shadows were more resourceful than he anticipated. He'd watched the scenario unfold before him through the binocular lens. Rafe fooled himself into believing the encounter left neither him nor Amber in danger.

"I didn't know the Rover had been tampered with."

"Yeah. Someone brazen enough to enter the marina lot in broad daylight concerns me. So, why don't we stop blaming each other for things beyond our control? I couldn't care less about your reason for being here."

"Good, because the less you know, the better." Rafe barked.

"Fine by me. Just know we're around."

"Doesn't look like I have a choice."

"Nope. Time for me to embarrass my buddies with my fishing talents. See you later."

Rafe smiled. He never expected anything less from his old friend, even if staying happened to endanger his life. Chuckling, he peered down through the salt-sprayed window at the women and their security line. Panic coursed throughout his veins. One word burst from his mouth – "Brent."

His foot atop the last step hung midair to the call of Rafe's disturbing tone. "On my way," Brent scaled the stairs in seconds.

Rafe paced about the helm, staring through the binoculars for any sign of Amber and Charlie.

"They're gone…" Rafe's shaky voice greeted Brent upon his return.

SIXTEEN

Amber caught a glimpse of Charlie in her peripheral vision. Charlie grasped the line and started her exploration. Securing her flippers, Amber jumped backward from the ladder's last rung. The undercurrent swept over her, reinforcing Rafe's warnings of treacherous consequences if she disregarded his pleas to hold the line. Although she had been relieved his request wasn't just another command to dictate her actions, she was still semi-frightened. She'd snorkeled many times, and while she had confidence in her abilities, today seemed different. The crystal-clear waters deceived her. It wasn't until she submerged that Rafe's true intention for her safety became apparent.

Distracted by the vivid colorations of a friendly clownfish weaving about her arm, Amber clenched the line tightly and followed the fish's path. Subtle shades of blue led into neon-bright outcroppings of orange coral. Dozens of colorful fish hurried about their business. Amber smiled and wondered how they felt about oversized creatures with flippers entering their domain. What a joy it had to be swimming around all day without a worry in the world. She would love to escape the bewilderment that plagued her. Two vastly different men made her heart sing. One a military hotshot invaluable to the country he served. The other, a man endeared to so many for the livelihood he provided his employees and the nation.

Oh, how did this happen to me?

Rafe shouldn't be an option. He'd wronged her before and left. A quick blow cleared her snorkel and washed away the negativity. She refused to allow anything to ruin the wonderland surrounding her.

With a brisk kick, Amber propelled herself forward and out toward a large underwater ledge. The expanse was so vast that midnight blue enveloped the sea below. Straining the safety line, she noticed small slivers of grey reflected from unknown depths. Her curiosity peaked with wonder. What projected the silver streams from the black abyss? Too frightened to push further, she started her return closer to the SJ, passing Charlie as she glided along, unconcerned, appreciating nature's splendor. Soon, the relentless sea won their match, and she elected to join the other ladies on board, exhausted from the exertion. Amber judged the distance between herself, Charlie, and the SJ to be manageable without rest. She began hand over hand, working her way back up the line, when she saw something strange happening beneath the hull. Air bubbles floated upward as a dark mass emerged, a black tank affixed to the back. Fear clutched at her lungs. Deep inhales only hampered her struggle to breathe. Her mask fogged as the snorkel clogged with splashes of seawater. A diver was under the SJ. Who? Why?

Amber kicked fiercely, franticly moving toward Charlie. The unknown diver swiped at Amber's leg undeterred, missing, and snatched the fin from her left foot. Her screams were rendered useless by the snorkel bit inside her mouth. She clung to the safety line, jostled back and forth, slapping at the water to draw Charlie's attention. Charlie nodded and offered a thumbs up, oblivious to the person in pursuit of Amber. Terror propelled her forward, only feet from Charlie. With one final thrust, hand outstretched, she brushed Charlie's thigh. Her sense of relief was short-lived when she felt a sudden snap—their last hope for rescue, the safety line, floated past the two women, carried by the unforgiving currents.

Charlie realized their peril instantly, screaming, "No!" Their heads bobbed above the water as they were swept away. The SJ became a speck on the horizon.

Spewing water from her mouth, Amber fought to speak before the waves filled it again. "What do we do?"

"What happened?" Charlie breathed in the salt air while she could.

"Someone cut the line. I saw them."

"We're too far away. We'll never make it back to the boat; the current's too strong."

"What if no one knows we're gone?" Panic seized Amber's muscles. Her rigid movements caused more harm than good.

"Calm down. Someone has to know. For now, we need a plan. We can't float around in the ocean until help arrives."

"Rafe will come. He promised to check on us. He'll come." Amber aimlessly attempted to comfort herself and Charlie, praying her words spoke the truth.

"With the movement of the tides, maybe if we kick toward the cliffs instead of away, we could find a ledge to hold onto. Those edges will be razor sharp; try not to get bashed into them."

Amber felt hopelessness consume her. She needed comforting, not Charlie. "That's our only option?"

"Looks like it. You ready?" Charlie grabbed ahold of Amber's hand. "Together."

Amber echoed her sentiment. "Together." If she had to die, at least she wasn't alone.

Amber's one swim fin hampered more than helped her. Aggravated, she slowed Charlie, released the strap, and freed the lone flipper. She'd need to double-time her kicks to Charlie's. The loss of equipment left them more vulnerable to the sea.

"Watch this outcrop," Charlie warned. Crescendos of

water battered them. Amber nodded and thrust her bare feet further apart, fluttering her kicks. Swells tossed over their heads as backlashes from the cliff's sprays roared around them.

Charlie tugged against her friend's arm. "Let's take a short break. 30 seconds, no more."

Amber gripped Charlie's hand tighter, grateful for rest. Cliff walls rose toward the sunlit sky in every direction except the one filled with safety, yet beyond their reach.

"Time's up."

The noise level became deafening. When Charlie's demeanor changed, Amber knew they were in trouble. Her former confident swim turned into cautious threading.

"What's wrong?" She yelled.

Charlie reached to remove her snorkel. "I don't see a spot. We can't stay here. Those cliffs will chew us up."

Amber's head swiveled from side to side with each rise of the waves. She refused to give up. They had made it this far.

"Look!"

Charlie followed the alignment of her shaky finger. Cratered into the walls sat a small opening.

"Will that work?" Amber cried.

"We'll see."

Drained, the two struggled, fighting forward. Losing the battle, Charlie said, "We can't get close enough this way. We have to dive."

"Dive? No…." Amber's head shook from side to side.

"If we go just under the break, we can go faster. It's the only way."

"I'm no fish. I can't hold my breath that long."

"We must. Either dive or die. Eventually, we are going to get hammered into the cliffs. They will cut us to pieces, and then what… bleed to death or have Jaws eat us?" Charlie exclaimed.

Amber's eyes popped wide; the glass mask reflected her fears. "Dive. I'd rather drown than be eaten alive by some sea creature."

"Deep breath in and out. When I pull, we go. Stay just to my side, don't let go. And Amber, do not think about time. It's easier."

Charlie began a series of deep breaths, and Amber followed suit. The yank of Charlie's hand came way before she was ready, but Amber responded as instructed.

Thank God Charlie has diving skills.

In what seemed like seconds, Amber's lungs screamed for relief. Her eyes eased closed, floating beside Charlie. A yank upward returned her to consciousness. She heard gasps and loud coughing. Charlie's hefty slap on Amber's back provoked the same sounds from her.

"Amber, grab the ledge. I can't hold both of us." Her fingertips, pale and weakened, strained Charlie's fragile grip.

Amber's long arm shot forward, cutting her bare knuckles upon the sharp rock ends.

"We made it." Amber cried.

"Can you hoist yourself up?" Charlie asked, throwing her snorkel and mask into the small cavern.

Amber chunked her mask first, cracking the lens, followed by her snorkel. Bearing against the rough surfaces, Amber's arms twitched and shook when she pressed upward. One last "ough," lifted her over the ledge. Instinctively, she reached and hoisted her friend to temporary safety.

The dampness of the tiny recessed cave sent shivers through the two exhausted women.

"Next time you want to go snorkeling, ask anyone else but me." Amber teased.

"Glad to see you still have a sense of humor. You're going to need it."

Amber sighed, drawing her knees to her chin and

squeezing water from her hair. “Give me the bad news first.”

“You asked… we only have hours of sunlight left. Depending on the tides, this whole section could be underwater by that time. If that happens, we’ll float around aimlessly until someone finds us. And it’s an option I prefer not to think about.”

For once, Amber emerged as the confident one, reassuring Charlie. “I promise you, they will find us before that occurs.” Amber hugged her friend and inched closer, each trying to stay warm.

“Your hand’s pretty messed up.” Charlie patted the blood oozing from Amber’s mangled knuckles with the corners of her vest.

“Funny, I haven’t had time to notice.” Amber chuckled, prompting a “giggle-fest.” The release of laughter provided an escape from the fear that gripped them but remained unspoken.

“Charlie… who could’ve cut our line and why?”

Her teeth clicked together, chattering, “If I had to guess, I’d presume it was one of the men you encountered in this area with Evan. They’re too territorial, which reinforces my hunch.”

“Hunch?”

“Men of a certain ‘entrepreneurial spirit’ in these waters have a good reason to keep people away. Most likely a valuable find.”

“Sunken treasures or artifacts?” Amber’s blood warmed. “I saw something just under the boat, starboard side— silvery reflections deep below an underwater ledge.”

“When he finds us, we must tell Brent. We can’t handle this by ourselves. Agreed?”

Charlie smiled. “Agreed. Let’s pray Brent finds us and not our unwanted friend.”

The two women huddled together, staring into the imposing currents, unaware of the danger that lurked beneath them.

SEVENTEEN

"What do you mean they're gone!" Brent's jaws locked, and anger consumed him. "YOU said they'd be safe. YOU were going to watch them from up here."

"We don't have time for the blame game." Rafe spouted. "Tell Paschal to launch the dinghy. NOW."

Brent growled under his breath. "On it." Back down the stairs, intense shouts, "Paschal, Paschal," alerted everyone to signs of trouble.

Evan was the first to reach Brent, "What's wrong?"

"Amber and Charlie are not in sight, anywhere."

"How?" Evan swiped at the tears pooling in his eyes. "This isn't happening."

Rafe met Paschal at the craft. Launched and readied in minutes, Rafe jumped aboard.

Paschal steadied the boat. "I'll stay with the ladies and try to keep them calm. Be safe, dude."

Leah squeezed Brent's hand, "Be careful." With an affectionate wink, Brent followed behind Rafe.

"I'm coming along." Evan prepared to board.

"Sorry, Evan. I need you here." Rafe's sincerity echoed the seriousness of the situation. "Call the Coast Guard and handle things here. Rember the code?"

"908," He snarked. "I've got it."

Paschal shoved the dinghy off and headed toward the ladies. The other three men devised a plan en route to the helm. Evan yelled to his friend, "Brent, find them."

"We will, buddy."

Rafe eased the boat onward, circling all sides of the Savannah Jane, and throttled down into the open seas ahead of them. His sudden stop threw Brent forward. "Rafe, what the…?"

"We're going the wrong way. If the line broke, they wouldn't float into open water—the cliffs. Currents would push them toward the cliffs." Rafe exclaimed.

A quick turnabout had the dinghy roaring back past the SJ.

~

Repetitive distress calls reverberated around the room. "Coast Guard, this is the vessel, Savannah Jane. We require immediate assistance." Each grew more and more direr as the radio remained silent. Unwavering, Evan continued his petitions.

He scoured every inch of the ocean visible from the windows and prayed. His last words to her plagued him. Accusations. He'd accused her of lying and hiding something from him regarding Rafe. Past relationships, sealed by doom, with women interested in his fame, overrode his logic. Evan regretted his statement the minute Amber walked away. *What an idiot*, he thought. Vows to right his wrong the instant she returned lingered.

Radio chatter breached his internal self-reckoning. "Coast Guard, go ahead."

Their requests for coordinates, longitude, and latitude brought Steve to Evan's side. Evan thrust the radio mic into his hand.

"This is the Savannah Jane. We need immediate assistance. Two of our charter boat guests are missing and feared lost in open water."

Responses fueled their hopes with promises of guardsmen en route to their location. Premature sighs of relief washed over the men, only to disappear, with the realization the women were still missing.

"Help's on the way, Evan. Don't worry." Steve patted his friend's shoulder. "Cooper, are you listening?"

Seemingly unphased by Steve's remark, Cooper remained absorbed in another matter. His ill-timed silence brought both men to his side. "Coop, have you heard a word we said?" Evan questioned abruptly.

"Umm, no. Sorry. I was preoccupied with the charts." Cooper kneaded two fingers between scrunched eyes. "Check out this chart. These cliffs have tiny pockets of caverns sprinkled throughout."

"How do you know?" Evan's skepticism prompted a surprised response.

"I'd venture to say the US military would have accurate data, wouldn't you?" Cooper's finger landed on a small watermark – "Classified."

Steve pulled the paper closer and rubbed his thumb over the seal. "He's right. It's legitimate. Where did you find it?"

"I was rummaging through the drawers, and this one sat crammed in the back underneath tide charts and stuff while the others were over there." He directed their gaze to a desk filled with tourist pamphlets. "Those maps only show basic information."

"Steve, you're the expert here. Why have this map?"

"Wait before you answer. Look closely." Cooper handed him a magnifier from the desk. "Scan it. Tell me what you see."

Quiet lingered over the men. Evan could no longer bear the suspense. "Out with it, already. Do you see anything?"

Steve's grim "Yes" started a tirade of questions from Evan. "What? Why here? Does it mean Amber and Charlie are in greater danger? Did Rafe know?"

"Evan, hold on. Small black 'x' marks are scattered throughout the chart. They're very difficult to see without the magnifier. I've never been privy to classified material of this caliber, so I'm unsure of the significance. If I had to guess, I'd say each mark denotes the location of the caverns Cooper referred to earlier. I don't know if Rafe was aware of the information or not. We'll have to ask him when he returns."

"These caverns may be Amber and Charlie's only hope for survival." Cooper beamed. "If by chance they found one, at least they'd have shelter for a few hours."

"How do we get word to Brent and Rafe? They won't know to look for the caves." Worry drove Evan's tone three octaves higher.

"We can't. The guardsmen will be here soon. We can't tell them about the hollows either."

"The heck, I can't," Evan exclaimed. "We need all the help we can get scouring those things for the girls."

Steve breathed deeply, "Evan, this document is top secret. By rights, we shouldn't even know about the alcoves or the map. If we start giving away national secrets, we'll never see the light of day again or the women we care about."

Evan's shoulders slumped. "I hadn't thought about that."

"Cooper, take photos of that map, front and back. Return everything to the exact location where you found it. No one says a word. We're simply guests who followed the instructions of the boat captain to send out distress calls. And Evan, say nothing!"

Evan twisted his neck from side to side, buying time as he contemplated whether to obey Steve's request. Surging sounds of outboard motors upon them gave him no time to choose a different outcome. "Okay."

Shouts from below left them seconds to finish the task.

"Up here." Uniformed saviors entered the helm with questions while other crew members searched the waters.

Steve took the reins and provided any information the

Coast Guard needed. Evan balanced his head between two sweaty palms. His internal cries for the women's safety monopolized all reasoning. Amber would know the depth of his love the instant he laid eyes on her, if he ever saw her again. His sighs abruptly ceased when he heard, "We found something."

~

Rafe pushed the small engine to the breaking point, speeding toward the cliff walls, leaving a wake of foam behind them. Words remained unspoken. Rafe knew his friend blamed him for the disaster that engulfed them. And he was right, even though Brent chose not to verbalize his opinion. Rafe had promised to maintain a watchful eye on the ladies. Doubt rose within him regarding the integrity of the line.

"Rafe, over there." Brent's sighting altered their trajectory.

The dinghy slowed to a crawl. Rafe alerted Brent of the danger ahead, "Be ready. The current will push it past us."

Brent extended his body, leaning out over the translucent water. "Got it." His quick snatch produced a lone swim fin dangling from his grasp.

"Who was wearing these?" Brent screamed.

A small salty droplet of water ran down Rafe's cheek. He whisked away what, unfortunately, wasn't sea spray. "Amber. She had the black fins. Charlie wore blue."

"Those two would never leave one another. Since I don't see blue ones, keep moving."

Rafe, oblivious to everything around him, focused on the single flipper. Consumed with guilt at the potential outcome confronting the men, his grip on the motor remained lifeless.

"Rafe… Rafe." Brent's fury exploded with a sharp right to Rafe's chin. "Man, snap out of it. I know my sister. She'd never give up. She's still out there. Let's go." Brent ordered.

Rafe's melancholy expression transformed into a seething sneer as he stroked his jawline. "Count yourself lucky. I understand your reasoning for doing that."

Brent's impatience sparked, "Go, man."

He chucked the flipper back into the water and revved the engine. In minutes, the small craft glided along the water's edges. Any closer and the boat would succumb to the brash cliff wall's battery. The motor idled, firing in reverse on Rafe's cue, trolling as slowly as possible alongside the rocky abutments.

"See anything?"

Brent's bleak "No, not yet" offered them little hope. Eyes peeled for the smallest sign, the men continued their search.

The sun's setting rays reflected before them with added sparkle. "Wait, what's that?" Brent asked.

A gleam of light bounced from the cliff wall. Just when assurance seized their heart, Rafe stalled the engine. He instinctively peered into the water surrounding them. A swift bump against the dinghy hull prompted Brent's questioning gaze. Rafe angled his finger, covering both lips. Complete quiet stilled the air about them. Small trails of bubbles floated just beneath them. Rafe cautiously eased forward and tugged a large knife from his bag. Mouthing the unspoken words "Someone's down there." He issued Brent a stay-put sign. With one deep intake of air and a jump, Rafe had gained the upper hand on whatever or whoever was under the boat. The sudden jostle sprawled Brent crossways the dinghy's bow, giving him a bird's eye view of the underwater battle below.

Caught off guard, the single diver miscalculated Rafe's detection as he unsuccessfully swiped for the weapon strapped around his ankle. Rafe's taut hold on the man's neck choked off his air supply, ejecting his mouthpiece. Rafe snatched the regulator and refilled his lungs with fresh oxygen. Panicked energy surges to fight Rafe off, further weakening the familiar figure wrestling about. Rafe yanked the long blade across the tank's air hose, shooting a voluminous burst of air toward the surface. One last grab at his ankle gave Rafe's attacker the weapon he required to escape. Exchanging strikes, the metal hit its mark. Rafe inflicted a deep blow, stabbing the man in his side. He dodged the assailant's blade shaft, sending the pointed edge across his bicep. Blood turned the water eerie shades of red. Propelling himself in the opposite direction of Rafe, the lone man swam into the hollows of the cliff banks.

Infuriated, Rafe popped his head up through the water's surface and climbed into the dinghy. He squeezed his upper arm, applying pressure to the wound, and grabbed Brent's hand. Trickles of blood ran down the extremity as Brent scavenged the boat for a makeshift bandage.

"He's much worse off than I am."

"That statement brings back a few memories." Brent laughed and pitched his buddy a pack of gauze.

"I'm afraid to ask, but did you see any sign topside of the women?"

Brent bowed his head.

"Guess we know why Amber and Charlie are in this position."

Eyebrows raised, Brent questioned, "Why?" His eyes narrowed in contempt. "You think that diver had something to do with the rope breaking loose?"

"Don't think, I know. He's the same one I've tussled with several times since my arrival. I'd bet my life he's been following us from a distance most of the day. It's on me. I should have noticed long before we got in this mess."

"You're good at what you do, but there's no way you could have known."

"Wrong! My job requires anticipation of the unexpected. Every time I'm around her, this happens. She consumes me, and my life has no room for love. You know that, Brent. Yet, here I am, going mad with worry, praying to hold her in my arms again."

Brent threw a roll of adhesive tape at Rafe's feet. "If we don't hurry and find them soon, I dare not say the outcome."

The rhythmic sounds of boat motors grew louder as Coast Guard members approached the two men. Grateful for the additional help, Brent updated the newcomers on their efforts.

Rafe interpreted the unspoken meaning behind Brent's statement. Amber must be found safe. Otherwise, Brent would be the one committing murder – HIS.

EIGHTEEN

Water trickled from the weathered cracks embedded in the hard stone. Small crevices shaped the saturated ceiling into lines aged through time. Hurricanes, tropical storms, and unrelenting sea swells helped create the recessed area offering shelter. If only for a short time, the two women could rest. The dark recesses behind them led to a place each was unprepared to explore.

Amber nudged her friend in a futile attempt at humor, "Try to stop your teeth from rattling so loud." She laughed.

"I will if you stop yours." Charlie grinned.

"What should we do? The sun's setting."

A solemn expression shadowed Charlie's features. And a disturbing realization gripped Amber. She'd never seen Charlie worried. Her friend's intuitive skills saved them in Bridgeport, but that was a different scenario. The bleak outlook before them seemed hopeless. Their options were grim. One: return to the rough waters, placing them at the mercy of the sea, and make them more of an open target. Two: remain put, praying the tides won't flood the cavern, and resign themselves to explore the dark expanse behind them for another way out. Or wait for help that may not come?

"Unfortunately, those are our choices. Have a preference?"

"Honestly, I'm not keen on returning to the ocean, but I'm also aware that we have no clue what is back there."

Amber's shriveled, water-logged thumb pitched backward. "Not too appealing, are they?"

"No." Amber jumped to her feet. "There." She pointed. "My gut says we explore."

Charlie rubbed her hands along the chilled bones in her legs. "Stay next to the wall. The only light we have will be the setting sun. As it drops lower, the rays may extend into the cave. Remember, our feet are bare. If the water starts to rise, we'll know it. In that case, we must hustle back, grab our gear, and hit the water, no matter how displeasing it seems."

Amber bobbed her head in agreement and waited for Charlie to take the lead. Charlie slid her palm along the rock wall. Inch by inch, she moved forward with Amber glued to her side. Small beams of sunlight brightened the slippery slope beneath them while lighting a narrow path. Amber hoped their steps weren't leading them to nowhere. Gashes marred their feet as they crept ahead.

"See anything?"

Charlie squinted. "Nothing. The light is dwindling. I'm afraid we'll need to turn around."

"I refuse to accept this. We have to get out of here. Evan is waiting for me."

"And Rafe. Or did you forget about him?" Charlie jested.

"Ugh." Amber moaned. "Let's just push on as long as we can."

"A little further, then we have to go back." The two clenched each other's hand and moved cautiously.

Amber consoled herself with every step, making inward promises she feared she'd never keep. She knew she had to make optimism her guide because the alternative was too dire.

Charlie rubbed her eyes, straining to see. Startled by the soft terrain her bare toes touched, she jerked Amber's hand. "Do you feel that?"

"What is it? Or should I ask?"

"Not the jagged rock we've been on. Stoop down and feel it."

"You feel it!" Amber screeched.

Charlie began her hesitant squat and extended her open palm. Her index finger brushed against the padded surface. Slick from the dew of the cavern, the material felt satiny.

"For heaven's sake, are you going to tell me?"

"I can't. I don't know. The texture is smooth and silky."

"Ewww." Amber cried.

"There's no reasonable explanation for this. We need to go back." Charlie straightened, grabbed Amber's upper arms, and whirled her about-face.

"Go now," Charlie demanded.

"Don't you want to see what's back there?"

"No." Charlie gave Amber a gentle nudge. "I don't think that's our way out. We're better off at the cavern opening."

"I thought you said…."

"We're safe up front. We can try to reflect the sun off our mask lens. Hopefully, someone out there may notice."

Amber retraced their previous steps back to the equipment. Charlie's attitude had flipped on a dime. Although she'd tried to hide her findings, realization resounded in her tone. Charlie was holding back.

A soft landing on her backside had Amber mumbling to herself. Dabbing at the blood oozing from her knuckles and balls of her feet, she asked, "We can't survive if we don't work together."

Charlie's knowing expression returned, reflecting the grimness of their circumstances. "I know. But I'm running on pure speculation." Her outstretched arms wiggled the glass lens, straining to find the perfect angle.

"Hit me with your speculations. What else do we

have to do? Besides, refracting the ideal shift of light to someone out there." She murmured. "Someone who wants to kill us or save us. So, talk."

Charlie continued her quest while Amber listened. "That material under our feet was manufactured, not formed from the earth's elements. The texture reminded me of a parachute. Believe me, I've packed and seen a lot of parachutes. Why there? I can't say."

Horror filled Amber's face. "Someone could be watching us now. They're back there waiting."

"I highly doubt that. No one would've ever let us get that close to whatever's in this place."

"Keep working the lens. The diver beneath the Savannah Jane has something to do with this. I know it."

"You try for a little while." Charlie handed Amber her mask and leaned against the rough wall.

Amber tilted the mask back and forth for what seemed an eternity. "This was a dumb idea. The sun's coming through the lens, not signaling." Overcome with frustration, Amber plopped back down.

"Maybe, but that's all we have to work with." Charlie's dismal response didn't help matters.

"Charlie, do you think we will get out of here?"

"I think the gang's doing everything possible to find us, and we must hold on to hope. I'd be willing to bet you have two gorgeous men out there searching for you." Her brief smile inspired Amber for a moment.

"Well, make that three. I'm sure Brent has threatened to kill all involved if we aren't found safe. He's very protective." She grinned.

"You don't say." Charlie giggled.

The women propped against the cold rock, praying help would arrive soon. Anxiety, worry, and exhaustion gained the upper hand. Sleep prevailed.

The distant cries of her name preyed upon Amber in her slumber. To her right, Evan's calm, reassuring voice beckoned her with his warmth. Her opposing side listened to Rafe's seductive calls to cling to him, if only until his next mission. Amber whimpered, torn in two, split on which man to choose. The voices grew louder and louder with each passing moment until the torment drove her mad. Propelled from the darkness by her screams, Amber struggled to awaken. Light crept into the darkness behind her lids as she fluttered her lashes. A large figure towered over her in that light, filling her with terror. The chokehold on her throat prevented any opportunity for her cries to escape.

NINETEEN

Evan stood aft on the Coast Guard cutter, wind whipping through his thick black hair. Dread overcame him, making his spirit as dark as his locks. Endless hues of blue trailed behind them as the rescue team ended their open-water search and headed for the cliffs. "What ifs" loomed in his subconscious. Was this to be his lot in life – forever miserable over bad decisions? Jealousy had blinded his perception of Amber. In truth, he'd chosen to alienate her earlier. His love for her consumed him, moving from a flicker upon their arrival on the island to a burning flame. Prayers for her safety flowed from his lips. He would find her even if it took every resource at his disposal.

Evan gripped the rails as the cutter slowed, dropping anchor at the outer perimeter of the cliff wall. Guardsmen hurried to secure the vessel. A roaring "there" directed their interest to the water. Floating at the boat's edge, like a sign from the heavens, bobbed a single fin.

The captain looked to Evan. "Have hope. This is good," he said before ushering his swimmers in the waves. Dinghies glided to the water's surface from all sides. Evan marveled at their efficiency. The captain's encouraging words flowed through him once more, reenergizing him.

Left only to pace about the deck, he waited. Boats crisscrossed the sea, searching along the cliff bases. His neck stiffened, and his knuckles cracked under the pressure he applied. Every emotion known to a man overwhelmed his assuredness. Gone were the instincts that propelled him to the top of the entrepreneur lists. Without Amber, he would never return to being that person. He wallowed in self-pity, aware only of his pledge to make her his own.

Radio calls rang out across the craft's speakers, "We've found someone," followed by words that broke him to the core. He fell to his knees.

"They have a severe wound to the abdomen. Call for an airlift."

Evan frantically tugged at the guardsmen's sleeve. Tears streamed down his cheeks.

"Description. What does the person look like? There are two women out there. Which one did he find."

Static now filled the airwaves. Jumbled words Evan couldn't understand crackled sporadically. His death grip on the young seaman's shirt reinforced his need for details. "What's he saying?" He cried.

"Come again. You're breaking up."

"The Bird has departed with a male subject, mid-30s. He said he was exploring the cliffs," rustled through the speakers.

Evan's ears perked. *A male?* His thoughts turned from the women to Brent and Rafe. Had one of them been injured? He massaged his temples. Circumstances were getting worse, not better.

~

Rafe sat still, listening as Brent updated the new arrivals of their failed search efforts. Inquiries regarding his injury and the need for assistance fell upon deaf ears. Rafe's focus lay elsewhere. They were close by. He could feel her presence. It was as though he and Amber's hearts beat as one. He'd stayed in tune with her senses even when they were thousands of miles apart.

With a steadfast plan, each jetty sped in a calculated direction. Rafe and Brent maneuvered between the massive formations.

"You really should've let them bandage your arm better," Brent mumbled.

"I'm good." He muttered and gazed down at the red patch soaking the sterile gauze. "It was very interesting that our 'friend' was rescued before the women. There's no way he could've made it out that quickly. He signaled for help from somewhere."

"True, but how?"

"Not sure. You can bet I'll find out once we know that Amber and Charlie are safe."

An eerie quiet rolled over the boat. Rafe trolled along, barely moving. It was Brent's loud alert that caused his spirit to soar. "Look. Over there," he shouted. His directions guided the men to a tiny section of the cliff wall. Dull, little spots flickered against the opposing rocks. Rafe grinned. Memories of teasing a kitten when the three were younger fueled his hope. The small dot sprang from place to place.

"It's Amber." Rafe headed toward their location.

"My sister's becoming more impressive daily." Brent chuckled.

The boat glided near the cavity inset in the massive stone. Rafe called her name, Brent followed, and their calls were rewarded by two very excited women.

"We're over here," Charlie yelled. She grabbed Amber and cried.

All four shed tears of happiness. Rafe's lantern revealed the severity of the women's experience. Both stood in the mouth of the cavern, bleeding and tired. But alive. When his eyes met with Amber's, the years of life without her no longer mattered. Maybe his time serving everyone but himself should come to an end. Amber would be his priority now if he had his way.

"Thank God you two are safe," Brent said.

His sister's eyes gleamed. "What took you so long!"

Charlie questioned, "What drew you to THIS spot?"

"The person playing cat games." Rafe smiled. "Hold tight while I steady the boat." Rafe tied a small knot and looped it around the jagged tip of rock. "Who's first? That knot won't last long."

Charlie pushed Amber forward.

"You grab her, Brent, if the boat shifts." Amber's extended hand felt shriveled and cold. He squeezed his toasty palm over hers, giving special care to express his excitement with a flirtatious wink.

"Okay. Come here." Brent hugged his sister ever so tightly. "Don't scare me like that again."

"I'll do my best." Her bright smile lifted everyone's mood. "Charlie and I must talk to you ASAP, Brent." She whispered in his ear.

"You mean to us. There's a lot you need to know." Brent replied.

"Do you have anything aboard we could use to mark this spot somehow?" Rafe scrutinized Charlie's question as he reached for her arm to gain her full attention.

"Why?" His forehead tightened. Once more, Charlie's inquisitive nature piqued his interest.

"Take my word for it," she warned.

With both women safely secured on board and the makeshift knot released, Rafe distanced the dinghy from his target. Rafe instructed, "Cover your eyes," before he pulled the emergency flare gun and aimed for the cavern wall. The shot burned a tiny section of the moist edging. He would've remembered the cavern without the torched area. His life had changed forever there.

"Rafe, are you nuts?" Brent shouted.

The fluorescent gun dangled from the end of his finger. "This is all I had to mark a spot."

Brent peered into Rafe's hazel eyes, questioning his answer.

He tilted his head toward Charlie. "Ask her."

No one said a word. Firing off the flare served two

purposes. Charlie's strange request fueled his curiosity. And the Coast Guard jetted over to meet them. One mission accomplished, he sighed. Gratitude overwhelmed him during the trip back to the Savannah Jane. Amber was alive and being treated on the cutter with Charlie. He swore revenge for the trauma she'd experienced. For now, silence provided him with the time he needed to plan his next move. Tonight, Amber would become his again.

~

Orange pops of color exploded against the creamy surfaces.

Not your normal distress signal.

But a positive sign, Evan hoped.

His heart leaped with joy, and his carefully maintained masculine façade crumbled when Amber stepped off the Coast Guard dinghy, Brent and Charlie by her side. Her bare feet shuffled slowly across the deck boarding, bandaged in white dressings to match her hands. Tears flooded cobalt orbs that steeled his handsomeness. Relief, pride, and thankfulness wreaked havoc within him. Amber completed him. Evan realized he must resign himself to the depth of his love. Her sparkling eyes, infectious giggle, and endless compassion transported him to another level - one he planned to remain on forever.

The conversation from below deck sucker-punched him in the gut.

"Who found them?" asked the Coast Guard commander.

"The Savannah Jane captain." Played on repeat, assaulting his ego. Brent insinuated Rafe Culliver and Amber had a past. Based on Culliver's actions, Evan assumed they'd been involved romantically. Clearly, Rafe longed to reignite those flames. One slow breath soothed Evan's emotions. Two bright eyes and a weak smile tugged on his heartstrings.

Culliver would be in a skirmish for the ages, Evan

internally vowed before he barreled down the stairs to hold, console, and love her.

Brent's "hey buddy" went unnoticed, along with everyone and everything surrounding them. His tear-saturated lips moistened hers. Deep and lengthy, their kiss heightened desires he'd pushed aside.

Amber eased backward. "People are watching," she whispered, her cheeks reddening.

"Let them." Evan barked and planted another passionate caress to her sun-scorched lips. Satisfied she comprehended the importance of her safe return, Evan released Amber ever so slightly and snuggled her body against his.

"Thank God you're safe." From the corner of his eye, Charlie's amused smile caught his attention. "You too, Charlie." He smiled.

"Well, thanks, Evan. I know you were concerned for my safety, too." Her teasing induced a chuckle from everyone.

Brent inched between the two love birds, "Think you can release her now? They need checking over."

Brent took his sister's hand and sent her and Charlie on their way, accompanied by the medical crew that had just boarded. A tight squeeze of his friend's shoulder brought forth a wave of relief when Evan's upper torso slumped. "She's going to be fine. A little R & R, and she'll be as good as new." Brent reassured his friends by repeating what the medics had indicated as they boarded the Coast Guard vessel.

"I love Amber with my entire being. If anything happened to her, I'd never survive." Evan pinched his brows and whisked away another tear.

"It won't, I assure you. Amber said there was a diver under the SJ who cut their lifeline. We need to get with Rafe and combine forces to end this. Today could've turned out much worse." Brent bowed his head, relieved for the outcome.

"Anything that will ensure her safety and yours." Evan smiled. "I plan on you being my best man at the wedding."

"Wedding…wait. You asked her to marry you?"

"Not yet. But I will, very soon. My life has no meaning without her, Brent."

"Believe me, I understand. You're preaching to the choir, buddy. And I'm all for the union. It's not me you need to convince."

"Understood. The biggest hurdle is making sure Culliver stays out of my way." Evan grumbled.

"I think that ship sailed a long time ago." Brent grinned at his pun on words.

"Hilarious. We shall see." The "bros" exchanged playful taps.

Interrupted by the Coast Guard commander, the men resumed their masculine personas. "Amber and Charlie have cuts and bruises and appear emotionally and physically drained, but that's the extent. Those two were very lucky. Did they happen to elaborate on the circumstances?" His brow arched beneath his hat brim.

Brent's tone quivered, holding back tears. "I'm sorry, sir, they didn't. We were just so happy to see them, we didn't ask many questions. We squeezed all the air from their lungs with heartfelt hugs."

"Naturally. Should they offer any details, you will let me know. Our tourists' safety is of the utmost importance to us. I'll have someone take you back to the Savannah Jane. Take care, gentlemen." His steady about face returned his focus to his crew and vessel.

Evan's fingers spread over his mouth and smothered a chuckle. "Nice acting job."

Brent beamed, "Let's go." The duo headed to the awaiting boat. Amber and Charlie, already on board, motioned for them to hurry.

Bright, smiling faces lined the railing of the Savannah Jane. Even Rhonda appeared moved beyond words as she ran to hug her two friends. "You gave us such a fright. I'm so sorry if I was harsh. I truly didn't mean to be that way." She cried.

"Brent and Amber Scott. If either of you try something like that again, ever … And you, Charlie, let these two influence you." Leah scolded.

Charlie shrugged her shoulders. "What's a girl to do?" Laughter chimed throughout the boat, a welcome exchange to the edginess and anxiety from earlier in the day.

"You. Come here, please." Brent smiled and united his lips with Leah's.

Paschal even cheered, inching a little closer to Rhonda. The only one excluded from the celebration was Rafe. His taut body leaned against the ship's frame as he observed the spontaneous party. Evan drifted toward him and stood beside the lean man.

"Thank you for what you did today to save her." Their eyes locked on the alluring brunette in the middle of her friends.

"No need. I'd give my life for hers, any day. It's because of me she's in this mess." Rafe's eyes never veered. "She's all I ever wanted."

"Yeah, me too," Evan replied. "Guess we have a problem."

"No doubt. May the best man win." Rafe extended his hand to Evan. The boat captain's firm clasp spoke volumes. Evan had traversed this road before. Brent and Leah, Evan's co-worker, oozed happiness from their pores. The decisions made in Bridgeport had been the right ones. Now, Evan's destiny called him to a different woman. One he intended to spend the remainder of his life pleasing.

Neither man wavered, immovable, bound to their quest.

"Down, boys. We have bigger issues, and they're going to take a small army to resolve. So, play nice." Brent warned.

"I intend to." Evan smiled, throwing a husky wink in Amber's direction.

TWENTY

Amber surveyed her two dilemmas from a purely feminine point of view. The laws of attraction precluded all other rationales. Side by side, they stood at the same height. Rafe's former "hometown jock" notoriety and boyish looks were now gone. Rafe Culliver had matured into a dangerously handsome, beloved military hero. From his mysterious hazel eyes to his sandy brown locks and hunky physique, each one lured you in. She'd experienced the full scope of his "love 'em and leave 'em" attitude. Her world had overflowed with pain, regret, and sorrow for years.

Has he changed?

Rafe's opposite, in every way, towered beside him. Evan's silky black hair and cobalt blue eyes provided the backdrop for chiseled features that melted a girl's heart. Never one to shy away from a challenge, he'd made a name for himself and intended to stay at the top. His life revolved around his company. His word was his bond. Evan would never disappear on her once he committed.

But would he commit to her?

She lowered her head, dizzy with the prospects of a relationship with either man. She longed to lay across her bed at the Vitamin Sea and rest.

"How long will it take us to return to the marina, Paschal?" she called.

"When we get underway, only a little while. You look very tired. Can I get you a cool drink?" His kindness meant the world to her. Perhaps Paschal would teach Rhonda a few lessons, she sighed.

"I'm quite exhausted. Can you ask Rafe to get us on our way?" His smile was all she required.

Paschal's brief exchange with Rafe brought him to her side. "Would you like to join me at the helm? There's a bench where you could lie down." His concern for her welfare was on display. His words dripped like honey from tempting lips. A sensual caress upon her shoulder stirred her so deeply that pops of color enflamed her face.

Amber opened her mouth to speak, unsure of what to say and hesitant to accept his offer based on their earlier escapade. "Umm. I was in there this morning. It's a little small. Thank you, but I'll fare better in the fresh air out here." Eyes slanted from the sun's last rays gave way to a warning each understood.

"Charlie, the same offer is, of course, open to you." Rafe's hand slid off Amber's shoulder and extended to Charlie.

"I think I'll take you up on your invitation. My legs are cramping." She meekly laid her hand on his and off toddled Charlie beside Rafe.

Amber pushed loose strands of hair from her face. Jealousy assaulted her ego over her friend's acceptance. Realizing she'd overreacted, Amber leaned against the leather cushions. Closing her mind to the day's nightmare, visions of warmth and comfort wrapped her in a cocoon. Gentle strokes glided up and down her bare skin. Soft endearments massaged her ears while strong arms snuggled her against a hulky frame. A satisfied smile adorned her lips, allowing a soft moan to escape. Encapsulated in a happy place, she yearned to remain in this dream state forever. Nothing would ever harm her here. Sleep overcame her when exhaustion assumed control.

Jostled awake by an aggressive mooring, Amber lazily lifted her eyelids to find Evan's affectionate gaze.

His tender lips brushed against hers. “Go back to sleep,” he whispered.

“Are we back at the marina?” Long tan legs pushed against the railing, sitting her upright to observe the activities.

“We are. You’re safe.”

“I need to stand. We have quite a walk to the car.” Frail arms eased her from the bench.

“Nope.” Evan declared.

A giggle lodged in her throat when he spun around and extended his full-back to her, ready to hoist.

“Hop on.”

With one short jump, she crossed her arms around his neck, legs spread across, supported by his powerful grip.

“We’re out,” Evan said, stepping onto the bleached planks. “See you back at Vitamin Sea.”

“Wait,” Brent called.

“Can’t. Precious cargo aboard.”

Amber tossed a brief wave and kissed the top of Evan’s head. “Thanks,” she murmured.

During their trek back to the car, Amber toyed with the idea of having a frank conversation with Evan. Deciding she wasn’t in the best frame of mind for seriousness, she splayed his hair to and fro. Twisting dark coils loosely around her bandaged fingertips, she never heard a word of complaint, only deep chuckles.

As the two passed the marina office, their attention diverted to the senior man standing in the doorway. Hands astride his hips, anger curled his upper lip.

“Were you two in the party on the Savannah Jane?” Stern words solicited a direct answer.

Evan gave a squeeze to Amber’s calf. “Yes, we chartered the boat today. Is there a problem?”

“I’d say there’s more than a problem, young man.”

Amber felt Evan’s body tense. He released her legs carefully, sliding her down, stepping between her and the snippy man.

"And… your point?" Evan's tone escalated.

"The Savannah Jane is my private vessel. Rafe and Paschal should never have allowed you to charter in these rough waters. The Coast Guard contacted me about the troubles you experienced."

"They never informed us of your ownership. I'm sorry if we overstepped our bounds. I'm happy to make up any monetary difference you feel is appropriate for our usage."

"No, no, my boy. I'll DEAL with Rafe and Paschal. My concerns were only for the danger you all faced today." The man mellowed once he noticed Amber's bandages. A slight smile emerged. "Miss, is there anything I can do for you?"

Amber poked her head around Evan's broad shoulder. "Thank you, but no. I don't think I will go snorkeling again soon, though."

"No. I don't imagine you will." His eyebrows arched. "Thank goodness you and your friend are safe."

"Is there anything else?" Evan questioned.

"Only if I can make it up to you in any way, let me know. Just don't plan on using the SJ again." He smiled. "By the way, I'm Mr. Jenkins. I own this place."

"Nice to meet you. But I think we've seen our last excursion on the Savannah Jane." Amber said.

"Yes, yes, you have. Have a good night, and stay safe, young lady." The senior adult flicked his cane in the air and returned inside.

Staring after the old man, her curiosity infused, "What do you make of that? I couldn't decide if he was mad or concerned for our safety."

"Don't care. We're going home." Evan paused and stared into the depths of her soul. "Has a nice ring to it."

"What does?"

"WE and HOME." His powerful arms pulled her to

him. A devilish grin preceded a slow, delicate kiss. Brushes of excitement skirted between them when Evan attempted to release her. Amber moved closer, longing for his masculine protection. Bandaged hands stroked his neck, angling for a penetrating kiss meant to last forever. She forced herself to loosen her hold on him after several minutes and smiled.

"Yes, it does."

Words weren't necessary during the journey back to Vitamin Sea. Amber knew Evan's feelings for her had grown. Would Evan consider sharing his future with her? Too drained to ponder the idea further, Amber released her seatbelt as the Rover rolled to a slow stop atop the crunching gravel. Evan leaned his head back against the cool leather seats, staring into the distance.

"Want to tell me?" She asked.

"Nah, it's not important. I have you here beside me, alive and safe; that's all that matters to me." His long arm crossed the padded console, placing her high cheekbone within his reach. Stroking his thumb back and forth, enjoying the feel of her smooth skin, brought him closer.

"Tomorrow, I'd like to discuss something with you if you're feeling better."

Amber blinked, unsure if Evan could read her thoughts or worse, what if she'd talked in her sleep?

"Don't look so frightened." He grinned. "I'm quite sure the conversation will be much easier to handle than anything you experienced today."

Amber's defensive armor made its usual appearance. "I'm not frightened," she sputtered. "Just curious. We can talk now if you like."

Opting to turn on the charm to entice him, she batted her lashes and issued an alluring smile.

Evan's jaws puffed with air, and his lips tightened, suffocating his chuckle. "Oh, we're going to use those tactics, are we?"

Amber grumbled, "What tactics? I have no idea what you're talking about." Her eyes darted to the outside.

Evan pressed the seatbelt release and eased his shirttail from underneath him, giving him wiggle room.

"These," he breathed.

His throaty, sensual tone brought her to full awareness. Bright blue brilliance focused on him, unable to blink. One swift stroke placed her on the small console between them. Pausing to comb the dark whisps from his eye, Evan brushed his knuckles along her jawline. Piercing blue eyes mirrored in the reflection of her own. Agile hands massaged her shoulder blade, leading the path for his damp lips to cover her relaxed muscles. Amber's gasp encouraged further folly, which she welcomed hesitantly. Evan was proving a point, and she enjoyed his methods way too much.

His soft lips found their way down her neck before traveling upward to nibble on her ear. Pleasurable whispers fell from him. Their hearts slowed into a rhythmic beat when he drew her closer to his chest. His guttural moan was silenced by pink lips meeting his. Passion gained control, cuddling them in its breast as their kisses devoured her will. Stirred by the rapping on his window, Evan threw up a hand and waved off their intruder. Amber's eyes never opened, nor did her lips separate from Evan's. Once again, the intensity of their desire fired, only to be doused by harder blows against the door.

Exasperated, Amber jerked from Evan's grasp and issued an irritated "What….?" Her eyes flew wide, prompting Evan's swift turn toward the source of their worry.

Lost in their unspoken words stood the formidable "elephant in the room" – Rafe.

TWENTY-ONE

Rafe docked the SJ and rushed to keep Old Man Jenkins busy until Paschal cleared the boat. He prayed the older man hadn't noticed the absence of his beloved prize. Rafe's trot abruptly stopped when he spotted Jenkins talking to Evan and Amber. Worthy alibies, each with slightly different details, formed in his head. Unable to choose, he'd have to play things by ear to determine which would satisfy the man. Watching Amber astride Evan's back tore his heart in half. Her harrowing experience led a trail back to him. The stakes in the game rose to an unparalleled level today. Resourceful adversaries proved their capability to dispose of any unwanted interference. Rafe knew the day's events sent a clear signal to anyone who crossed their path.

Jenkins' cane wave signaled the end of his conversation with the couple and spurred Rafe to a hasty entrance to the marina office. Almost stepping on the heel of his boss's meticulously polished shoe sparked a flurry of chastisement.

"Young man, explain now. Whatever the reason you deemed it necessary to utilize the Savannah Jane will never be sufficient." Weathered, ruddy cheeks filled with superiority.

"Well, sir, I take full responsibility for the choice. Paschal only complied with my requests." Rafe inhaled. "The charter's cash profit will benefit the marina, and no other vessel could accommodate the party."

"And you feel that is motivation enough to take my prized possession into THESE waters. Not to mention, you placed the whole lot of you in danger."

"Sir, I tried to find an amicable resolution for all parties." Rafe squared his shoulders.

"My boy, you are lucky 'all parties' returned safely. Now, the marina is on the Coast Guard's watch list."

Rafe's back shot straight as a pin.

How did he know?

"Not thinking on your feet will get you killed, young man. Did it not occur to you that they would contact me? I am the owner." Jenkins retorted. "Never mind. What's done is done. But remember, son, you're too valuable to make stupid mistakes."

Jenkins' cryptic scolding made Rafe's jaw drop.

"Don't just stand there with your mouth open, young man. Let Paschal finish here. Get to those two that just left and make sure they aren't going to sue me!" Old Man Jenkins mumbled and picked up the *Island News*.

"Yes, sir," Rafe said and beelined out the door. Thankful the keys dangled in the marina pickup ignition, he fired the engine and sped off. Midway to Vitamin Sea, chuckles rolled deep inside his belly. Lord help, poor Paschal. He had Old Man Jenkins' truck. Hearty laughter filled the crew cab, a welcome change to a miserable day. His mood lightened, and positive thoughts of Amber stirred within him. She would be at the Vitamin Sea by now, and he needed to talk to her, just the two of them. Brent chartered the boat. Holcomb sustained no injuries, not physically, anyway. He saw no need to include him in the conversation.

Rafe eased down the driveway, killing his headlights, hoping to go undetected. If he surprised Amber at the door, he stood a better chance of talking to her without interference. The truck crept to a slow roll behind

Holcomb's Rover.

Outrage crawled over him while warning bells pounded in his ears. The Rover's windows dripped with moisture. A light film of fog covered the front section of the car. Gone were the days when he'd filled a vehicle's windows with that kind of heat. A sharp pain struck him in the gut. Too late to turn around, Rafe opened the door and slammed it closed with purpose. Half tempted to set off the truck's alarm, he plodded forward.

Heartbreak consumed him. He made a last-second decision and tapped on the window. As he predicted, the couple remained unfazed. Anger boiled within him, striking his knuckles in full blows against the glass. Surprised the glass sheet stayed intact, Amber's loud yell stopped his barrage.

Evan shoved the heavy door open and eyed their uninvited guest. "Why are you here?"

Behind him, Rafe watched Amber straighten her hair and slide out the passenger door. She acted shocked and embarrassed as she rounded the vehicle's front. "Did Brent send you?"

"No." He said gruffly. "Mr. Jenkins asked me to ensure your safety and reiterate his willingness to provide any assistance you might need."

"Oh." She whispered.

"By the looks of it, you're fine and 'in good hands,' literally."

Evan's right hand eased Amber back toward the villa. "We're okay. Thank your employer for his concern."

"She's my only concern." Rafe nodded. Both men straightened and prepared for whatever ensued now that the gauntlet had been thrown.

Amber gingerly slid between the two. "Thank you and Mr. Jenkins for checking on me. I'm going to enjoy a hot shower and head to bed. Have a good night, Rafe."

She glided her white fingertips through Evan's and

pulled him along.

"Yeah."

The love of his life strolled into a house with another man, and all he could say was, "Yeah." His life was a debacle.

Hopping back in Jenkins' GMC, Rafe needed an outlet for his fury. The chunky pieces of stone beneath him seemed a good place to start. He stomped on the gas and gripped the wheel. The pristine truck flew down the drive, only slowing to allow an oncoming car sufficient space. Headlights shone brightly on the other driver. Brent brought his vehicle to an abrupt stop when Rafe slammed his brakes.

"Rafe! Are you trying to kill yourself?" Surprised by his appearance, Brent's palm stretched outward from his window. "Slow down, man. How did you end up here?"

"Ask your sister when you see her." His flippant reply left everyone in the van with their mouths gaping when he sped away.

"Well, I never. Rafe's sure different away from the marina." Carol expressed.

Brent shook his head and raised the glass. A weak "hallelujah" rang out when Steve slid open the van door. The weary group trod sluggishly into the welcome warmth of the Vitamin Sea.

Evan's tense body hovered in the foyer. "The chef prepared a light meal for anyone with an appetite."

"Nothing for me. Today has taken years off my life. I need beauty sleep." Rhonda exclaimed, fluffing her blonde tresses.

"Heaven forbid anything interrupts your beauty ritual," Carol bellowed and accompanied Rhonda up the stairs.

Leah clasped Brent's hand, "I'm out too. Walk me upstairs?"

"Right behind you."

Leah released Brent's hand and carefully hugged her friend. "Go rest, you hear me," she warned. Charlie nodded in agreement.

"Gentlemen, bright and early tomorrow, breakfast on the veranda,"

"No more." Leah tugged Brent's arm, dragging him up the steps.

Steve and Cooper followed with Kimberly and Suzanne by their side, leaving Charlie and Evan in the hallway.

"Want to tell me the full story about how you two almost died today?" Evan's stern gaze fixed on Charlie.

"Nope. Not right now. In the morning, we'll talk." Charlie's smirk implied volumes.

"Tomorrow." He demanded. "I'll lock up down here. See you in a few hours."

"Actually. Do you mind if I stay down here for a while?"

"You going to be alright? I can stay with you."

"I just need some time alone, that's all. I can lock up."

"No problem. Wake the staff for anything you might want."

"Thank you. And, Evan, thanks for taking care of Amber today."

"My pleasure. I have a vested interest, you know," Evan smiled proudly and headed to bed.

No more than an hour later, the villa sat wrapped in quiet. Charlie tip-toed through the foyer and snatched car keys from their resting place inside the teakwood bowl. Cautiously, she twisted the handle, slipped through, and closed the door. The loose gravel caused her feet to ache through the thin flip-flops covering her bandaged arches and toes. Grimacing, she hopped in the van and slow-rolled down the long drive. Pleas for success fell from her lips. If all went well, she'd return before anyone noticed her absence.

~

By the time Rafe returned to the marina, blackness had enveloped the boatyard. He yanked the keys from the ignition, upset that he'd let his emotions get the best of him, again. Wrestling with his stupidity, he arrived to find the office door locked, along with a chastising note from Jenkins.

"Under no assumptions that my truck will return in one piece, I had Paschal take me home."

Of course, Jenkins would rub salt in fresh wounds if Rafe's aggressive driving damaged another of his belongings. With darkness hampering a thorough inspection, he shoved the keys in his pocket and started the short walk to his apartment. Strangely enough, his journey was eerily quiet. No shadows lurked about. He presumed one was in the hospital after the Coast Guard chopper's rescue. As for the other, Rafe supposed he wouldn't venture out alone. Tonight, their absence brought a welcome rest.

The crisp air cleared his head, if only for a bit. In desperate need of a hot shower, Rafe reached for the tarnished brass knob prepared to insert his key, but he pulled the wrong set from his frayed pocket. Frustrated, Rafe threw the keys on the ground and drove his fingers deeper for the circular ring. He'd had it with the whole day. As he bent to retrieve the victim of his temper tantrum, a hitch knotted his stomach. In the corner of the rusted doorframe laid his security marker. The tiny section of string had served its purpose. Bloody …. so much for his welcome rest.

Rafe balled his left fist and rotated the door handle with his right hand, LOCKED. Someone knew to relock the door. Maybe his foes were smarter than he gave them credit for.

He crouched by the bright turquoise cement wall,

thankful for the absence of a star-lit sky, and duck-walked into the backyard. Planting his body flat against the cool blocks, he inched toward the sliding glass door and watched for signs of movement. Little by little, he wedged his torso through the tight door gap. The small lamp nestled on the kitchen bar, usually on, shed no light. Prepared for a battle, Rafe lifted a towel off the bed and twined the ends around both palms. Ready for an onslaught, he crept forward, knees bent. Instead, he heard an all too familiar voice, well aware of his entry into the apartment.

"You can put the towel down. I'm unarmed. Although, your 'weapon' wouldn't have helped." She giggled.

"I'm fighting the urge to ask why you're here, but I'm sure I already know."

"Mr. Culliver, look how astute you 'think' you are." Her eyes narrowed.

"You've been conscious of my presence since Day One, haven't you?"

"To be honest, I didn't know it was you, Culliver, until a few days later. Ever heard the saying 'girl's talk'? Fortunately, my friend believes in the concept of trust." She gingerly perched on the loveseat arm and crossed her legs. "A trait you hold most dear."

"Wanna cut the chatter and tell me why you broke into my apartment?"

She puffed her cheeks, indignant to his accusation. "I'm not a criminal. Quite the opposite." A lone key swayed from her forefinger.

"Not technically. But you did enter uninvited," Rafe smirked. He knew asking where or how she obtained a key would be fruitless.

"Wrong again. My invitation just didn't come from you."

Rafe struggled to maintain his temper, remembering he was dealing with a woman. And in his past experiences, women thrived on misdirection. Turning the conversation nasty, he barked, "Not me."

"True enough."

"I thought you would be all nice and comfy, tucked away in bed by now. Considering your condition." Exasperation now molded their interactions.

Eyeing her hands, she replied, "Could be worse."

"What exactly do you want? I'm not in the mood for games."

"Believe me, I too hate them."

"So out with it," Rafe commanded.

"No need to get rude. I'm here for you."

"Me? Why?" First, Rhonda and now her, he assumed the obvious. "Sorry, but I'm not interested."

Incessant laughter pierced his ears. "Oh my, I needed that." She spouted and clutched her belly. "Um. Hold your ego in check. No."

"I stand corrected. My first instinct was right – you're my backup."

"Finally." She flipped her hands up. "You're close, but I'm definitely not your reinforcements, just the messenger. To my surprise, we have mutual friends. Besides Amber." Charlie smiled. "They asked me to play liaison."

"And, in the chain of command, how important are our 'mutual' friends?"

"Quite."

Rafe moved to the sofa and plopped down, dumbfounded by the last ten minutes of word swap.

"Snap out of it, Culliver. Truly, I wish today had gone very differently. Since it didn't, here I am. No one can know that I came here. Understand – no one." She emphasized.

Rafe's eyebrows raised in question, "When you said important, you weren't lying. Am I to assume you have full access to mission details?"

"Oh Lord, no. My message isn't as involved as one might think. Simple and sure."

"I'm waiting," Rafe stated.

"You're being watched from all angles by friends and foes. The message is this – Get your head in the game. Shift your focus back to the matters at hand." Charlie lowered her head. "Sorry. But from my perspective, if it counts, time is running out, and the 'distractions' pulling you away endanger your mission and life."

Rafe threw a few loud grumbles into the air. Bothered by the directive but not surprised, he was well aware of the reason for the warning. Civilian lives intertwined in the mix dramatically changed the operation. "The Twelve" refrained from involving civilians at all costs.

Charlie's compassionate eyes drooped like a wounded puppy's. "She's one of my best friends, and I love her, too."

Rafe rose from the couch, turning his back to brush a droplet off his cheek. "Drink?"

"No thanks. I must return to the villa before someone notices I'm missing. I'll report the message as delivered." Charlie strode to the front door. "Would you mind a little help if I could convince our 'mutual friend' I can be an asset?"

When she hesitated, Rafe questioned, "Enlisted or just skilled?" He stroked his chin.

"Skilled." Charlie laughed. "I've had a lot of off-the-books training, you might say." "What do you know, Charlie?"

"The cavern where you and Brent found us holds more than bits of moss and water. That's all I can say for now." Charlie whirled around and bolted out the door.

Shock over the identity of his intruder subsided. In his gut, Rafe noticed Charlie's aptitude long before today. The "nosy reporter" persona fit her like a glove, perhaps one size too small. Charlie Ashby was a petite force with a powerful punch. Vastly different from Amber, Charlie held her cards close to her chest.

Rafe secured the doors, wandered into the bathroom, and started the shower. Rippled muscles tightened across his midsection as he drew the blood-stained shirt over his head. Recounting the euphoria that seized him when he saw Amber alive, he patted the wound on his bicep and winced in pain. History would repeat itself, this he knew. Amber's forgiveness would flee and turn to anger, and that rage subsided with the love of another.

Hurt, longing, and duty played mind games with him when his head touched the pillow. Gloominess rolled into dreams of loss. Those same dreams had haunted him too many times in the past. He was tired – so very tired.

~

Charlie donned a toothy grin. Her promises to exchange information for permission to remain in the loop had worked. She realized her competency was never an issue – her safety stood at the forefront of his decision. Reluctance turned into acceptance during the course of their conversation. Her promise to provide updates in real time cleared the way. Although this one would never hit the papers, she loved a story!

The van crept to a stop, almost in the exact spot she'd swiped it from. After careful regard to ensure an inconspicuous return, she hustled to open the expansive wooden door as quietly as possible. Pleased with herself, Charlie removed her flops and slinked through the darkness. Edging forward, keys in hand, her reach for the bowl was interrupted by the foyer pendant light's bright beam. Charlie's flabbergasted wail stopped her midstride. "Jeez!"

"Going somewhere? Or should I say – been somewhere?" Amber's brows raised.

"Ummm. I thought I'd go for a short drive, with being unable to sleep and all."

"Seemed to me you were placing the keys back, not taking them out of the bowl."

"No, I was headed out the door. Want to come with me?" Charlie questioned.

"Charlie, remember you said I'm not a good liar? Newsflash, you're not either right now." Amber pulled the ring from Charlie's fingers and laid the keys down.

"So. You almost gave me a heart attack. Can't sleep?" Charlie's diversion worked for two seconds.

"No, sadly. Stop trying to change the subject. Where did you go?"

Charlie rolled her neck in circles. There was no escape. Amber's curiosity persisted. She contemplated whether to discuss her whereabouts with her friend. In reality, the truth endangered Amber more than she ever realized.

"Back to the marina. Regrettably, the office was locked tight, with no other way of entry. So, I came back."

"Why go to the marina at this hour? Of course, no one was there. That was a dangerous move, Charlie. After today, I don't think we should venture too far without one of the guys.

"I left my bag on the boat and wanted to see if Paschal had placed a note on the door or something. The drive's fresh air helped me alleviate some stress and relax. I'm feeling quite tired." Charlie yawned and faked a sleepy stretch.

Amber's suspicious smile never eased. "Whatever you say, Charlie. From here on out, we do everything together with a male. You got me."

Charlie produced a salute. "Yes, ma'am."

"You heading up now?" Amber waited, but there was no response. "Do I need to take those with me?" She said and pointed to the key ring.

"No... I'm grabbing a tiny bite to eat first. As tired as I am, I won't sleep if my stomach's growling."

"We'll talk in a few hours." Amber smiled.

Charlie acknowledged her with a nod and hastily headed toward the kitchen. Great. The list for morning conversation grew from one to two and now three. She second-guessed her earlier request. The necessity of keeping her stories straight could become quite problematic.

Drained and unable to think, Charlie tore a blueberry bagel into small pieces. She popped a bite into her mouth and savored the sweet fruit carb, gazing out over the dark seas. Weary, Charlie downed the tasty snack in minutes. With one last swallow of water to wash down the crumbs, she turned her eyes back toward the ocean. Charlie's palm flew to her forehead, and she slumped over. Not again - lantern lights erratically moved about Bonfire Beach. Only this time, she knew it wasn't Rafe.

TWENTY-TWO

Rafe arose with a sense of dread that no amount of coffee could lighten. He dreaded seeing Old Man Jenkins. Jenkins' wrath, deserving or not, awaited him. The idea of seeing Amber for a final time deflated him. He'd agonized over how to leave her without causing more pain for either of them. Regardless of the methods, the deed had to be done sooner rather than later. Charlie's message reminded him of his duty and the need for vigilance. Confronted with the undeniable voice of reason, Rafe understood Charlie's statement from his commander was an order, not a request. His compliance ensured everyone's safety.

The hard tapping against his front door spurred his quick donning of shorts and a t-shirt. His swift scan of missed text messages decreased his pulse rate. "Yeah, yeah, I'm coming." Paschal's four texts only reinforced the morning's woes. Dragging his feet, Rafe listened for his co-worker's familiar slang, "Hey dude, hurry up." Instead, the rapid cocking sound of a handgun triggered inbred instincts and propelled his flying leap behind the sofa for cover as bullets riddled the mahogany door. Scaling the floor on all fours, he hurried to the end table. Rafe snatched the drawer open, retrieved his weapon, and fired. The door's handle furiously jerked back and forth, followed by hard kicks against the frame. Intent on hitting his mark, Rafe slinked closer and aimed at the target, firing again, prompting the intruder's yell of surprise and hasty retreat. Splinters of light created small white shards scattered about on the vivid tile flooring. Rafe scanned the glass sliding doors at the apartment's rear, unsure of multiple breaches. No activity. He'd averted another assault. Irritated by the brash escalation in aggression, his blood pressure skyrocketed. Whoever these people were, broad daylight no longer served as a deterrent to their attacks.

Rafe rushed into the bedroom and threw whatever he could cram into his old green bag, followed by a speedy sweep of the bathroom for necessities. With a toss of his straw hat upon unkept hair, he slid sandals on his feet and closed the rear glass door behind him. Concerned about a trap, Rafe's legs ached from the flat shoes as he hurdled the neighbors' fences, cutting across their yards instead of taking the normal path to work. The duffle seemed lightweight compared to the first night he'd filled it. Sweat droplets left water stains around the hat's brim. Just a little further lay the sidewalk that led to the marina. Determined footsteps pounded against the concrete, ensuring a safe haven, or so he hoped. Trained eyes scanned every inch of his perimeter. Straight ahead sat Paschal's and Jenkins' trucks side by side, and Rafe was washed with relief the office would be open. Perhaps he'd even be happy to see Old Man Jenkins. Rafe lowered his shoulder, maneuvering the duffle down his arm into ready hands.

His entry clanged the threshold bell. Paschal's horrified face met Rafe's as his swift head movements beckoned for help. Never lowering his newspaper, Jenkins released a crabby, "Good Morning, Culliver. Glad you decided to show up."

"Did you think I wouldn't?"

"I wasn't sure since my truck remained MIA well past closing time. Your actions last night about sent Paschal into cardiac arrest, his having to take me home and such."

"Sir, you did issue me specific instructions. Unfortunately, things took a bit longer than I'd anticipated."

Quizzical eyes peered over the newspaper's top edge. "And were you successful?"

"100 percent." Rafe boasted.

Jenkins neatly folded the *Island News* and rose from his seat, "Glad to know my message made its mark."

Paschal released a deep breath and eased back into his chair as Jenkins' brisk steps moved him toward the door. "Gentlemen, I will leave you to it. See you this afternoon."

As soon as the door shut, Paschal launched a full-scale tirade upon Rafe.

"Dude, how could you do that to me? You know that man gives me bad vibes. Always so rigid and testy."

"All you had to do was take him on a ten-minute drive," Rafe said.

Paschal removed his hat and placed it over his heart. "That drive shaved years off my life. At one point, I wasn't sure Jenkins was even breathing. He never moved, eyes straight ahead, didn't say a word. It was like he was in a trance or something. It was freaky, dude."

Rafe backed against the desk, arms folded, and waited for Paschal to finish.

"And besides that, I had to pick him up this morning. Please don't put me in that position again. Use my truck if you need wheels. You're welcome to it any time." He finished, taking a deep breath.

"Thanks. I may have to take you up on that offer soon." He tossed, plopping the duffle beside him. Rafe pulled the charter clipboard from the bin. "Slow day, huh?"

"Yeah, after yesterday's excitement, I'll take one. A few jet ski rentals, that's all. Mostly locals on the island now. Hey, are you going somewhere, dude? Why the duffle?" Paschal questioned.

"Maybe spending a few nights elsewhere, I'm not sure yet. I thought it would be easier to bring it with me than to head back to the apartment later."

"Hum."

Rafe smiled. "Don't read anything between the lines, buddy."

"Me. Oh, no. The only visual I'm getting is about 5'9" with brown hair and sapphire eyes." Paschal chuckled. "Let me know if you want to visit her. Her friend Rhonda was a gorgeous woman. I wouldn't mind saying hello to her. YOU, I will happily drive."

"Don't tempt me, buddy." Rafe walked toward his co-worker, slapped him on the leg, and pitched the rental list into his lap. "We better get some work done, or else Old Man Jenkins won't be happy."

At the mention of Jenkins' name, Paschal leaped to his feet and hurried out the door. Within minutes, throttle sounds of jet ski motors filled the air. Rafe felt a twinge of shame. He never dreamed Paschal's chauffeuring services would cause him such anxiety. Noting Paschal's apprehensions, he would deal with Jenkins himself from now on and save Paschal the anguish.

Rising, Rafe prepared to assist Paschal with the skis outside until repetitious vibrations from his pocket forced a quick check of his phone - BRENT. He glanced at the number, undecided on his next move. The addition of Charlie as an ally privy to confidential information perpetuated a newfound sense of deliverance. Before yesterday, Brent and Amber remained determined to aid in his safety. The horrific outcomes of the past 24 hours had punched each of them in the gut, offering a stiff dose of reality. Interested in Brent's opinions, Rafe punched redial. A disgruntled "About time" spilled from his cell.

"I've been a little busy this morning." Rafe nonchalantly responded.

"Busy this morning or last night?" Brent asked. "You could've told me you were coming by."

"No time. My boss wanted me to ensure Holcomb or Amber wouldn't place the marina on any court dockets for what happened. And from my observations last night, a lawsuit was the furthest thing from their minds." Rafe jeered.

"Can't say, they were inside when I arrived. Amber's romantic choices are irrelevant now, and you obviously have bigger problems. You and Charlie marked the cavern for a reason. Why?"

"I have no idea. I told you to ask Charlie." Rafe snapped.

"I did. She refuses to tell me unless you're present. Which I find strange."

"Look, Brent. Things got hairy yesterday and worsened this morning, so the further I stay away from you all, the better." His tone resonated with sorrow.

"That's no longer your decision. Charlie won't talk without you. Rafe, you must work with us, or Amber's welfare and Charlie's remain in jeopardy. Both were marked targets while snorkeling. How do we know your adversaries won't go after them again?" His question demanded Rafe's answer.

"Unfortunately, we don't. Brent, helping me is too risky. I survived an attack in broad daylight earlier. I can't say too much for my apartment door, though." Rafe chuckled. "I won't be going back there, that's for sure."

"Will you ever admit that you need help sometimes? You never did when we were younger."

"I appreciate the offer, but I'll handle it. Always have, always will." Rafe's sense of pride took command through his words.

"No way. You're coming to the Vitamin Sea to stay. I'll clear it with Evan."

"Can't do it. Too dangerous." Rafe's conversation was interrupted by Paschal's yells.

"Gotta go. Later, Brent." Rafe frowned and shoved the phone into his shorts pocket. Admitting he needed help meant weakness, a trait he'd never exposed. Rafe knew ample support waited in the wings; however, that individual's identity remained a mystery. First, with Charlie's verbal warning and then Jenkins' cryptic statements, Rafe figured he was on his own until the "powers that be" felt the need to reveal his backup's whereabouts. For all he knew, Paschal could be that person.

Deep chuckles of laughter burst from his lips at the sight outside the marina office. Paschal shuffled about to elude the unmanned jet ski, spinning in circles and shooting sea spray flying. The swirls grew larger as Paschal swam furiously to the dock. *No way Paschal's the man*, Rafe thought, clutching his stomach.

"Should I ask?" Rafe grinned

Saturated from head to toe, water dripped from Paschal's clothing. "The dumb thing wouldn't cut off. The failsafe never killed the engine. The other skis worked fine." He pulled against the hem of his shirt and squeezed. "Strange, dude. Strange. I'm going to change." Water squished from his shoes and trailed behind him down the boardwalk.

Rafe curiously eyed the runaway jet ski. Fluke or planned? He contemplated the disastrous outcome for any inexperienced rider aboard. Thankfully, Paschal's expertise with the machine prevented his injury. Rafe would wait for Paschal's return before he attempted to gain control of the spinning rogue.

He stared into the vast ocean waters, realizing this time might be different. Brent's help could mean the difference between life and death for them all.

A "Hello, sir?" called to him from behind. Prepared to contend with the early arrival of an eager charter, he sighed. One more thing this morning that required his attention. Instead, he saw his young friend.

Shocked by his presence, Rafe began, "Well, you did survive your Bonfire Beach trip. Thank you, by the way, for returning the SJ safely."

“You're welcome. Did you find anything out of order?” The young man questioned.

“No, actually, I should offer my thanks. The SJ glistened like a diamond upon my inspection. You must have worked all night.”

“Pretty much,” he replied. “You allowed me to take the boat out. Cleaning it was the least I could do.” He smiled.

Rafe studied the fellow’s new demeanor. Gone was the cautious college boy who offered to supervise his drunken companions. He exuded confidence from his erect posture to the tilt of his chin.

“Seems we both made a wise choice then.” Rafe smiled. “What brings you here today? Interested in another charter?”

Relaxing, the man casually folded his hands into baggy jean pockets. “Thought I might take the SJ for another run. It’s a beautiful day.”

Raised hairs prickled the back of Rafe’s neck, sending a hesitant awakening through him. “We have a few small crafts that are much newer and sleeker than the SJ. You might want to consider one of those.”

“There are some nice boats here, but I’d like to stick with the Savannah Jane, if that’s okay. I prefer the older ones. They’re built better and speak to you in a different language. The SJ has a backstory all of her own. I bet.” He smiled.

Rafe scanned his new acquaintance with curiosity. “Then we may have a problem. You see, the SJ belongs to the marina owner, and he’s a very protective sort. The charter would need his approval, and he has not arrived yet.”

The young gent rubbed his cheek. “Would it be possible to call him for permission? I wanted to get an early start. I won’t take her out for long, I promise. You know I’m trustworthy.”

Rafe burst into laughter. "Old Man Jenkins isn't the type you can up and call."

"I'd appreciate it if you tried. My name is Wilder James." Amused by his pleas, Rafe reconsidered.

"Well, Wilder, why don't we do that? Let's call." Wilder's continued persistence commanded newfound respect as he extended a hand. "Rafe Culliver. Follow me."

Noting Wilder's firm handshake, Rafe strode up the walkway two steps ahead. The man's relaxed pace perfectly timed in cadence with Rafe's. "You coming?" Rafe questioned.

"Right behind you."

Paschal bumped head-first into Rafe as he entered the office. Bouncing off each other, Rafe tossed, "You may want to sit down, Paschal. It's going to be a bit."

Stunned, Paschal stepped back, ogling the young man following Rafe. He drifted back toward his favorite spot, an old recliner, and stood still in anticipation.

"Hey, Wilder James." He said with a head toss.

"Nice to meet you. Are you chartering a boat?" Paschal asked.

"Trying to. The Savannah Jane. Rafe's calling the owner to get his permission."

When Paschal heard Savannah Jane and the words "calling the owner," he grabbed the recliner's arm and fell backward. Anxious hands massaged the worn leather.

Rafe knew Jenkins' contact information was off-limits. Jenkins had instructed that he never be contacted unless there was a true emergency. Rafe pressed on and dialed the number. Curiosity guided his actions now.

Propped against a chair without a care in the world, Wilder surveyed the office, checking out the charts and books.

A moody "Who is it, "three rings in, echoed from Rafe's phone. "Sorry to bother you, sir. This is Rafe." Before Rafe could continue, Jenkins blasted him with questions.

"Why are you calling me? What's wrong? Couldn't whatever this is have waited until my morning visit?"

Rafe waited for Jenkins to pause and interjected, "Sir, a minute, please."

"Oh, go ahead." Jenkins retorted.

"Someone here wants to charter the Savannah Jane. I've offered other vessels, but he's insistent on using the SJ. After yesterday, I was under the impression the SJ was permanently unavailable. Is that correct?"

"Darn right, it is. I won't allow another fiasco. Common sense should have told you my answer, Culliver."

"Understood. Sorry to bother you, sir. I will relay your response to Mr. James."

"Response to whom?" Jenkins coughed.

"A young man named Wilder James.

"He's at the marina now?" The older man's voice escalated.

"Yes, sir."

"Ahh, let him take her out. Give him strict instructions from me that the SJ is to be back at the dock in no more than four hours. You straight on that, Culliver."

"But…"

"But nothing. We could use a bit of capital in the bank, just in case the Scott fellow decides he wants his money returned. After all, the trip maimed his sister and her friend." Jenkins scolded.

"Understood." Rafe's reply never reached Jenkins' ears. The phone fell silent. Obviously, Jenkins had changed his mind. He owned the SJ, and the decision was his alone, no matter how strange.

Wilder James watched Rafe smiling, whistling a low tune, poised for the owner's reply. Rafe sensed Wilder James somehow knew before he revealed Jenkins' answer.

"Marina owner said you have four hours. Not a minute more. The Savannah Jane is to be docked and secured precisely at that time."

Paschal's choked coughs prompted hasty gulps of water. With the bottle drained, he whispered, "Swallowed my gum."

Rafe shook his head in amusement at Paschal's ridiculous attempts to hide his surprise.

Wilder James displayed a broad grin. "Fantastic. Tell him thanks for me. I'll have her back as ordered."

Rafe passed the SJ keys to eager hands. "I appreciate it." Wilder James was halfway out the door when he turned to Rafe. "Your protection means a lot… to the owner, I'm sure. See you later."

No sooner than the door struck James in the rear, Paschal launched to his feet. "That young dude is questionable. Cool but strange. He…." Paschal stopped mid-sentence when James popped his head back through the door, grinning like a Cheshire cat.

"You all know there's a jet ski running in circles in the harbor, right?"

Rafe moaned and leaned his head back. "Yeah, we know. Hadn't you better get started? Your time is ticking away."

"True. Later." And James was off.

"Like I was saying, he's too quiet for me, kind of like Jenkins, dude. Another question: why would Jenkins allow him to take out the SJ? He raked us over the coals yesterday. Jenkins swore she'd never leave the dock again. I don't get it."

Paschal's points were valid ones. Rafe, too, questioned Jenkins' rationale while acutely aware his opinion of the decision mattered not to the boat's owner.

Rafe looked at Paschal. "For his sake, James better have the Savannah Jane back on time." He refused to vouch for the young man if he failed. "We should try to rein in the ski before Jenkins sees it. We don't need any more trouble with him. "

Paschal groaned, pushed his slumped body to its feet, and shook his head. "Today keeps getting weirder and weirder."

Rafe stood on the marina boardwalk in awe of the strange occurrences preceding the Savannah Jane's full throttle into the harbor. Where was the young man headed, and why the SJ? With his apartment out of the equation, Rafe succumbed to the surreal decision that he had little choice but to accept Brent's offer. He'd stay at the Vitamin Sea tonight, with or without Holcomb's approval.

~

Evan tugged at his coal-black hair, ready to snatch out a patch or two. For the first time in a long while, his hand itched and ached to strike something or someone.

"Evan, it's to our advantage to have him stay here," Brent said cautiously from several feet away.

"Advantage for whom? From my perspective, Culliver's the one who'll reap the rewards." Irritation coursed through his reply.

"We need him more than he needs us. Remember, somebody tried to kill my sister yesterday? Like it or not, Amber and Charlie are dead in the mix of whatever's happening."

"Not a good play on words, Brent." Evan huffed.

"Rafe can handle himself. He'll do what he can to protect them. His mission must and will always come first. He could disappear at any moment. When or if that happens, WE have to be ready."

Brent's enunciation of "we" drove the demons that lurked within his emotions to the surface. Evan realized his insecurities mattered only to him. Amber's safety was the important thing in this whole scenario. Culliver's expertise was invaluable, and they had to toss the dice.

"Go pick him up." Evan raked cool fingers across the back of his neck. "I still say we're inviting trouble straight to our front door."

"Maybe, but it's a chance we have to take, you know that."

Leah's entrance brought the room to a hush. "This is not happening." She said, drawing a triangle in the air between the three. "I'm growing tired of the shifty looks, hushed conversations, and the sudden appearance of a mysterious boat captain by the name of Rafe Culliver. Who, by the way, appears very familiar with you, Brent Scott, and your sister."

Brent's neck rolled back and forth, increasing Leah's annoyance, evident by her whispered slow count to ten.

Evan, unwilling to deal with her fury, declared, "Brent will tell you."

"Me." He piped. "Oh, come on," Brent reached for Leah's hand, "We have to pick someone up. I'll fill you in during the ride. Women." Brent mumbled.

Leah grinned and hurried out the door, led by Brent's firm grip.

Evan's head, clouded with indecision, fear, and uncertainty, drove him to the crystal decanter for a stout snip. The thick glass weighted his hand as it rose and lowered. Half determined to throw it through the window, he gently returned the glass to the cart. Gloom gnawed at his gut. Vitamin Sea had been his sanctuary in bad times, lifting his spirits after his parent's deaths. Now, his tropical oasis surrounded its guests in the unknown.

The high tide's thundering roar drew him to the expansive picturesque view. Waves tumbled over, sweeping in and rolling out, dragging loose objects into the shallows. The irony of the images racked his once-confident muscular build. Bending, he bore his palms down for support against the mahogany window casing. His heart somersaulted every time Amber approached. Indecision had dragged him to the lowest depths of despair mere hours earlier. Culliver's past relationship with Amber no longer mattered. Amber and only Amber possessed the key to his heart, his whole heart. Not bits and pieces drudged up by ebbing tides of ever-changing circumstances. Whispered vows and prayers flowed from his lips. For the first time since his parents' deaths, he unshakably loved someone – mind, body, and soul.

Self-absorbed in his plans for a path forward, he didn't notice Amber's gentle stroke on his shoulder. Her slim finger poking into his muscled bicep brought a smile to his face.

"Would you prefer to be alone?"

Evan rotated and eased down, sitting on the wooden encasement. His eyes left one paradise to view another. Her long brown tresses coiled into a messy bun that sprouted loose "getaways" of strands framing her face. Her brilliant blue, uncertain stare and tilted head made his heart soar.

"Never." A loving pull of her body accompanied his husky reply. Inches apart, their eyes locked, giving total acceptance to the other. Snuggling into his hulky frame, she laid her head on his shoulder. Warmth and comfort encased the two in a cocoon, sheltered from the outside world. Minutes, possibly hours, seemed to pass before he felt the subtle rise of Amber's head.

"The sound of your heartbeat relaxes me so. I'm afraid I've kept you in quite an uncomfortable position. Are your legs asleep?" She giggled, backing out of his embrace

Evan smiled. "Let's see." His attempt to stand was thwarted, as she thought, by tingling limbs and a slight misstep.

"Oh, my goodness." She encircled his waist with her arm, balancing his heavy form.

"Can you hobble to the chair?" Evan nodded and clung to her tighter.

Within a step or two, Amber's body tumbled onto his sprawled frame, their topple cushioned by the mammoth leather chaise behind them. Deep chuckles accompanied the rise and fall of his belly beneath her. Amber's laughter abruptly stopped when she realized Evan had duped her.

"Evan Holcomb, you faker," she yelled before planting a pillow against his forehead.

Evan's hand flew to his throat, pretending he couldn't breathe, prompting a gasp and Amber's hasty lift of the cushion.

"Are you teasing? Can you breathe now?" Concern etched across her brow.

"No, but it's not the pillow, my dear. I've laughed too hard." The rascally gleam in his eye forced a loud "Ughh" as she wiggled to remove herself from his grasp.

Unwilling to relent, Evan squeezed her tighter, entangling her limbs, and rained kisses on her cheekbone. Amber relaxed into his comforting embrace. Her chin lifted to entice him with dewy lips. The sensuality of her gift encouraged his throaty growl as he tasted the ripe fullness of her lips. Drawing her ever closer beside him, he glided his fingers up and down her back, massaging her weary muscles with broad strokes. Evan's fingertips shifted, sending deeper caresses along her spine, initiating her raspy whimper. Amber's back quickly arched, followed by her soft "Ouch" as her mouth raised from his.

"Sorry." He apologized, wearing a thin smile. "I thought a massage might alleviate some of the soreness." He closed his eyes and exhaled.

"No worries." Her fingertips feathered along his lip line with tender touches. Evan lazily lifted his eyelids, unwilling to move. He saw hesitant eyes that spoke to his soul.

"Evan, we should talk about this." She tapped her nails across his chest and back to hers. "Us."

He rushed to place his finger over her lips. "We should." His back straightened, pulling her with him into a sitting position on the chaise.

"Amber, I should apologize for my behavior. I let jealousy control me when you were around Rafe Culliver on the Savannah Jane. I've been ashamed and bothered by my unfounded accusations following your interactions."

"Wait," she cried. "Remember when you first asked me about Rafe before our boat trip? Everything is my fault. You gave me the opportunity to tell you, and I hesitated. Well, no more hesitation. You deserve to know the truth. And when you do, I'm the one who should be embarrassed." Her eyes welled with tears.

"Don't cry, please." He brushed a tear from her lash.

"I'm not." She said, steeling her frame and rubbing the tip of her nose.

"You see, Rafe and I have known each other most of our lives. He was like a big brother to me. Then, in high school, out of the blue, our feelings changed, and we became a couple. A hot and heavy couple, much to Brent's dismay, I might add." Her cheeks flushed.

With a deep inhale, she continued. "We both knew Rafe would be leaving soon to join the armed forces. Oh, we declared undying love for one another and promised our sole devotion. Vowing nothing would separate us, we agreed to get married when he finished his four-year tour. During Rafe's first two years, I pursued my career, training as a flight attendant, before returning to my base in Charlotte. Life seemed grand until one weekend, he came home on leave, ecstatic over a new opportunity his commanders had presented to him. During that visit, we stole away as much as possible to be alone and talk about our lives. I never noticed any change in his demeanor. As far as I was concerned, our relationship was perfect. He packed up, kissed me goodbye, and promised to see me soon." A small sniffle halted her words, followed by a shaky breath.

"I never talked to or saw him again after that day. He stopped all communication. Brent's efforts to find Rafe led him down a rabbit hole. After a while, he became a stranger to me, a remnant of a former life I preferred to forget. It took years for me to mend. That's why his sudden appearance at the marina shocked me so." She lowered her head. Remembrance spread across her beautiful features, twisting them from the pain.

Evan placed a gentle kiss on the tip of her nose. "You have nothing to be embarrassed about. You were young, impressionable, and believed his promises."

"What if it is me? Something about me? My personality, my looks, or a heart that makes me undesirable. Or am I just a temporary distraction? Perhaps I'm not relationship material in men's eyes." Her doe eyes blinked, fighting back the tears again.

"I'd say Culliver was the idiot. It's not you, my dear."

"You think?" Amber's eyes opened wide, questioning his statement.

Evan tilted her head, gazing into blue sapphires filled with uncertainty. "Amber, never doubt your self-worth. No matter what a man tells you, know you are an angel God has placed on this earth. There's not enough time to list all of your wonderful qualities."

"Really?" Her lashes batted up and down above cherry cheeks.

"Your beauty, kindness, and generosity captivated me from the moment I met you. You fill my soul with goodness. A couple of days ago, you told me that if Leah had chosen me, you wouldn't be in turmoil over lowering your barriers. I have thanked God every day that she selected Brent because that choice sent me to you."

Amber's brows arched in disbelief. Her mouthed reply was quieted by the mission-filled pulsation of his hungry lips on hers. Her innocent realization prompted a declaration of his love, desire, and need to become her only option for companionship. Hesitation no longer existed for either of them. He absorbed every part of her love that she was willing to give. Pink swollen lips fused to his warm mouth. Husky moans and feminine sighs transported them into a dreamland.

Evan slowly eased back and gingerly pulled on the clasp, securing Amber's bun. Sun-drenched strands fell about her shoulders, enhancing a natural beauty created only for his angel. Masculine hands dove deep into the long locks, providing a path for his exploration. Soft lips grazed her cheekbone before his breathy murmur. "I love you."

Amber's startled jump interrupted the pleasures beneath Evan's exploring lips. Seemingly unhappy with her pause, he whispered, "Come here," tugging on Amber, only to be met with unbridled resistance.

"Wait…" Two firm palms pressed against his shoulders.

"We're wasting time." He chuckled. "Is there a problem?"

Her face paled, "Oh, there's no problem. You're inherently aware of how you make me feel. Did you…?"

Evan wondered if his confession had gone unnoticed in the heat of the moment.

Guess not!

"Yes, I did." His eyes flickered with devilish intent. "Amber Scott, I love you with every fiber of my being. You consume me. My life would be nothing without you."

Amber threw her arms around his neck and squeezed, smiling. Evan coughed and coughed again. His firm grasp dragged her arms from him and pushed her backward. Questioning eyes, saturated with rejection, stared back at him before she lowered her head.

His vocal cords inflected with raspiness, "You were choking me." He smiled and stroked her hair. "I didn't want to die from strangulation since you might feel inclined to reciprocate my feelings." He said impishly.

"Oh, shut up!" Amber lunged forward, grabbing his cheeks and lavished kisses upon his willing lips, only to hear Rhonda's disgruntled, "Um. Uhhh," which they both ignored.

Her second request, "If I could...." was met with Amber's resounding, "No, and close the door on your way out."

Rhonda's furious stomps banged on the ceramic tile floor, followed by the deafening slam of the door.

To which Evan touted, "And that, Ms. Scott, is one of the reasons why I love you."

TWENTY-THREE

Leah puckered her lips and sat quietly. Brent's endless stall tactics had placed him in a precarious position. He now had a long story to tell in a minimal amount of time. From the corner of his eye, he saw a flurry of scoldings brewing that would soon pierce his ears.

Brent reached for Leah's hand, "I need you to remain level-headed, okay? I didn't want to alarm you until I had facts."

"Well, would you like to elaborate, or should I tell you what I already know?" Her shoulders squared as she squeezed his hand in determination.

"I guess tell me." Brent sighed.

"For one, it's blatantly obvious Amber and our boat captain had a romantic connection at one time or another. Secondly, you are more than just THE brother. And thirdly, the odds are Mr. Culliver sent the mysterious signal a few days ago. Am I warm?"

Brent bowed his head in defeat. "No, you're hot." Attempting to lighten the mood, he spouted, "in more ways than one," and grinned.

"I love you, but that won't work this time." Leah folded her arms, ready to battle.

Time was up. Brent rushed his explanation, hoping to stave off any interruptions. "Rafe Culliver and I are old friends. I haven't seen him in years…." Brent finished his story's condensed version within a mile of the marina.

"Are you angry with me?" He meekly asked.

Leah's warm smile rolled over him, to which he released a short exhale. "I'm not angry. Hurt a little. We agreed, after Bridgeport, to be honest, no secrets, although I understand your rationale. More importantly, though, how are we going to handle the situation?"

Brent's reply accompanied the Rover's rolling stop in the parking lot. "One moment at a time." He smiled with confidence.

"Then, let's go get your friend." She replied, placing a peck on his cheek as she popped open the door.

Brent looked to the heavens and counted his blessings. Leah Reynolds never ceased to amaze him. He'd die to protect the ones he loved. Gone were the days of just himself and his sister. That list had surged to nine over the past year. Brent exhaled at the daunting task and exited the Rover. Hand in hand, the couple moved toward the marina door, lost in the thickening plot set before them.

Armed for a verbal fight with Rafe, Brent stopped mid-stride. Handwritten bold red letters stretched across the stark white paper. "BACK IN TWO HOURS." Brent fought to restrain his annoyance. Rafe Culliver wouldn't readily accept help. He never had.

"Quite the phantom, isn't he?" Leah spouted.

"You have no idea. Let's go." Brent marched back to the car, his shoes pushed into the crushed rock, leaving fragments stuck between the sole's wide tread.

"Where?" Leah questioned.

"Back to the Vitamin Sea for reinforcements. Culliver is on his own tonight. Tomorrow, we implement a new plan."

~

Rafe peered over the boat's console, dropping the engine back to slow its pace. Paschal perched on the starboard side, legs stretched, one hand atop his favorite straw hat. The wind swept over them once they reached the open seas. Free of the jet ski fiasco, both men agreed Wilder James carried a mysterious aura about him. Even more strange were the circumstances surrounding his sudden appearance. Limited by a two-hour window of opportunity, Rafe decided to try to locate the SJ, if possible. Without hesitation, his instincts propelled the boat and his new cohort straight to the cliffs. Only this time, their arrival placed them much further away than he preferred. The long-range binoculars delivered vivid images of the coastline encompassing his target.

"You think he's here, dude?" Paschal slowly shifted his position to the bow for a better view.

"I'd bet my life on it. We just need to determine where."

"Wonder what he's doing here? You think he found some long-lost pirate's booty?" Excitement rolled from Paschal, his deep brown eyes alight. "Oh, dude, if I'd found some billion-dollar stash, I'd act sketchy too."

"If we're lucky, we'll find out." Rafe scanned the cliffs for the area he and Charlie marked with the flare. No activity.

Rafe motored the sleek boat to a new vantage point and killed the engine, electing to float freely in the vast waters. An hour later, the SJ came into view. The vessel lay nestled in the outer cliff walls near where Rafe anchored a day earlier. A diver's flag swayed from atop a makeshift mast. Hindered by the limitations of the binoculars, Rafe slammed them against the steering column.

Paschal's daily nap, interrupted by the loud bang, propelled him to his feet. "Where are they? I'll get them." His fists balled, ready for a fight.

Rafe's laughter over Paschal's miscue lightened his mood. "Sorry, I was venting my frustration."

"Dude, we've been gone over an hour. Shouldn't we be heading back?" He asked between a gaping yawn and oversized stretch.

"Oh, crap." A quick key twist and the engine fired, followed by Rafe's full throttle. Salty mists of sea spray flew over the sides of the speeding boat. The craft slammed against the waves, launching the bow several feet into the air, a testament to the high speed at which they traveled. Rafe glanced beside him. Paschal hunkered down, hat in hand, gripping the bright silver railing. Rafe pushed the craft to its limit, keenly aware of the problems that awaited them if the two-hour benchmark expired.

The men worked on autopilot, instinctively, securing the boat and handling necessary tasks in record time to maintain their air of secrecy. The SJ coasted in and docked precisely at four hours. Rafe watched young Wilder James with curious eyes from a parallel slip, hosing and whisking the wood planking. James was no amateur boater; the precision with which James battened down the SJ and meticulously cleaned the deck spoke volumes. Caught off guard by James' friendly wave, Rafe stroked his brow, realizing he was losing his touch.

So much for being inconspicuous!

Rafe waved in return and called, "How was your outing?"

James smiled. "Great! Perfect way to relax before moving on to the unpleasant duties of the day." His toothy grin was wide and genuine. "Hang on. I'll be over in a second. I need to check below real quick. He scaled the stairs and was out of sight.

Rafe fiddled around the slip and pretended to do his job. Oddly enough, he was doing exactly that, his job. The irony produced a low chuckle, interrupted by a friendly "Thanks, man." Small flicks of hair rose on the back of Rafe's neck for some unknown reason.

"No problem. Glad to see you're prompt. Any later, Jenkins would have our heads."

"Couldn't let that happen." Wilder drew his palm through cropped locks uneasily.

"What did you find out there to do for four hours? Pay another visit to Bonfire Beach?" Rafe laughed.

"How'd you know? I love that place. I could sit there forever and listen to the waves roll. No one there made for a perfect day."

"Really? By yourself on Bonfire Beach isn't the norm."

"Yup, I've learned to enjoy the solitude of being alone." James quipped in total awareness of Rafe's implication."

"Yeah, sometimes women can be more trouble than not." Rafe spouted, thinking of his woes concerning Amber.

"Agreed. Thanks again. I'll be seeing you." Wilder James spun around and disappeared as mysteriously as he had arrived.

Paschal's speedy pace carried him to Rafe's side no sooner than James passed the marina door. "What'd he say? What'd he say?" Paschal repeated anxiously.

Rafe had grown fond of Paschal and once again wrestled with how much of the truth he should share. Too much could get him killed, not enough, and he'd drive Rafe's patience level to the brink. Rafe chose to feed his curiosity with small tidbits to quench his thirst and no more.

"He was at Bonfire Beach – alone." Rafe jested.

"Oh, dude, we know that's not true. No one goes to Bonfire Beach alone." Paschal winked, slyly making his point clear. "He's found golden doubloons or something out there and is covering his tracks."

"I'd say he's located something. But for now, our best bet is to sit quietly. We can't stir up the locals by giving away our secret."

"For real. Good idea. Too many noisy islanders. No one will suspect me since I'm one of them. I'll keep my eye out for anything unusual." Paschal stood tall and straightened his hat, eagerly accepting his latest role.

Rafe slapped Paschal on the back. "Perfect plan. I'm hungry, you?"

"Always, dude." Paschal rubbed his protruded belly.

"My turn," Rafe called from the marina's drive. "Back in a few."

Rafe's walk to their usual restaurant gave him time to organize his thoughts. Mystery shrouded Wilder James; however, several things now fell into place. The existence of the new snorkeling gear aboard the SJ for one. Along with the pristine state of the Savannah Jane, although she remained continuously docked due to the lean rental requests. James seemed to possess a unique familiarity with the vessel.

Perhaps he's been sneaking the craft out at night.

Rafe wanted to rap his knuckles atop his head, indicative of an old V-8 commercial. The night Rafe interacted with the partygoers, Wilder James had stepped from the group to captain, holding the swinging key between his fingers. His instincts, rattled from the fist-a-cuff with his assailants, prevented him from realizing the importance of that fact before now.

My focus always deteriorates around her.

Rafe mumbled all the way to the restaurant, launching a self-induced lecture on what must happen. Cheerfully greeted on his arrival, the spunky jack-of-all-trades local ushered him to the bar.

"Your turn for lunch, yeh?" She grinned. "The usual?"

"Please." Rafe's down-turned mouth, burdened by his duties, alerted the woman.

"Troubles, mon? Is that why we haven't seen ya here in a few nights?" A bar mop cloth dangled from her hand.

"You might say that," he moaned.

"Hope your friend's injury hasn't worsened?" She asked.

Rafe's brows raised. "What friend?"

"Two were here, asking if you'd been in lately. The tall guy said he'd been injured on a dive and didn't move around too well. They said they wanted to chat; hadn't seen ya in a while."

Shivers coursed down his spine. As expected, the visit to his apartment was by design. His stalkers' inability to locate him forced them to take drastic measures.

"Ah, nah, I think he's doing well. Could you do me a favor? If they come back in, will you text or call me?" Rafe held the sticky pen between his fingers and scribbled his number on a cocktail napkin.

"Sure! Been wanting your number anyway." The fiery islander winked and headed through the swinging kitchen door.

Back before he could blink, the server placed a brown, oily paper sack in his hand. The air was saturated with the aroma of hot fries and burgers.

Rafe dug into worn khaki shorts, "How much do I owe?"

"On the house." She smiled. "Ya number's worth way more than a bag of fries."

He offered her his thanks and laughed. His problem had never been getting women; it was finding a way to keep them longer than a week. The sun warming his body, and the scent of food lightened his mood. Whistling a rhythmic tune as he beat a path back to the docks, Rafe abruptly froze, his feet heavy as concrete. Parked at the rear of the marina sat Jenkins' truck. Inside were the silhouettes of an unlikely pair. The sight of Jenkins and James sent him scurrying behind an enormous Sego palm. Both men's bodies sunken down, barely visible from his vantage point. Rafe's mouth curled into a small grin at the notion that Old Man Jenkins could even twist his body into that position.

By all appearances, the men were having a cordial chat. *About what?* Unable to venture closer, Rafe struggled to read their lips, to no avail. The once-tasty lunch turned into a bag of cold grease in Rafe's tight grasp. Roughly five minutes later, James jumped from the truck and hurried into a thick grove of palms. Jenkins started the white GMC and maneuvered into his designated parking place in front of the office door. His tall outline strode up the sidewalk to the click of his cane. Rafe pushed the palm fronds aside and followed, enlightened by his witness of Jenkins' encounter.

"You'll need to use the microwave," Rafe pitched the tattered oily bag to Paschal upon his return.

"Dude, what the heck? The cook didn't show up again, did he?" Fussing all the way over to the ancient silver box, Paschal threw the brown paper sack in and pressed 00:60.

Old Man Jenkins focused on the *Island News* stretched between each hand, never acknowledging Rafe's arrival.

"Afternoon, sir."

"Afternoon, Culliver. I assume you ensured the Savannah Jane was back on time."

Rafe smiled. He'd play the game. "Yes, sir. Back safe and sound as requested."

Paschal reappeared, two plates in hand, and shoved one toward Rafe. His complaint, stifled by a mouth overflowing with food, "Dude, this bread's hard as a rock. Wait until I see them tonight. I'm going to complain."

Jenkins piped, "Serves you right for eating junk," and returned to his newspaper.

Rafe pushed the boundaries, probing for answers, "Sir, Wilder James seemed VERY comfortable behind the SJ wheel. Has he chartered the SJ before?"

Shifty slants eyeballed Rafe over the top of his paper. "Can't say that he has. I'd have to check the logs. You're in charge of those things, Culliver, not me."

"I don't recall him ever chartering; however, it could be my error. Perhaps he's just an adept boatman." Rafe continued the ruse, shrugged his shoulders, and reached for the cold plate of food.

Jenkins slapped the thin, crumpled newspaper's pages together and shot up from his chair. "Culliver, the Savannah Jane is as much your responsibility to protect as mine. Take heed in who you let near her." Stern words meant to reinforce the importance of his beloved possession flowed from the senior's protruded lips.

With a snatch of his cane, Jenkins perfectly angled the captain's hat atop his brows and announced, "Gentlemen, my day has come to an end. I'll be heading home now. Lock up tight." The salt-worn corroded bell above the door clanged, signaling his departure.

"Dang, that dude rattles me more every day." Paschal clutched his chest. "Between him and that excuse for a burger I ate, I could die tonight." Rumblings and small belches bubbled from his mouth. "Can we shut down early, dude?"

"Appears we may need to," Rafe smiled, referring to the greenish tinge flooding Paschal's cheeks. "Feel like giving me a lift somewhere?"

Paschal's hands rubbed in circular motions, round and round his bulging stomach. "Sure, no problem. Where?"

"The Vitamin Sea."

Paschal froze. "For real? You sure?"

"100 percent."

TWENTY-FOUR

Slim clutched his side, winced in agony, and climbed into the passenger's seat of the four-door. The blade's deep puncture of flesh immobilized him, hampering his ability to fulfill his boss's orders. Surgical bandages, staples, and pain medications impeded his progress, forcing him to down the faithful drugs like candy.

"They are coming out now," Slim announced.

The brawny driver started the sleek sedan and gripped the wheel. They waited and watched as the aged, faded red truck rolled to a stop and took an unexpected turn left. Hesitation allowed their prey to garner a lead on them.

"Hurry, make a U-turn, you idiot." Slim barked.

His burly friend snarled back, revved the engine, and whipped the steering wheel in the opposite direction. Black tread marks covered the grey asphalt as the luxurious sedan's squealing tires peeled out in pursuit.

"That hunk of junk can't be too far ahead. Faster." Slim dug into his shirt pocket, popped the white cap off the golden bottle, and swallowed two thick pink capsules. The sedan, forced to make another abrupt stop, screeched to a halt, allowing a handful of tourists access to traverse the small crosswalk. Slim seethed with fury as he screamed at the group, unfazed by his obscenities.

"Go…Go."

Slim's driver accelerated, quickly gaining speed. The four-door vehicle weaved across the two-lane road, dodging oncoming traffic.

"Look." Slim's crooked finger pointed. "On the left."

A dented red tailgate rounded the corner onto a gravel drive.

"Slow down."

Tired of being bossed around, the ogre driving barked, "Make up your mind," gripping the wheel tighter. Easing his pace, the sedan crept down the drive, hidden by the dry, dusty shield ahead of them. Rolling cautiously down the lengthy road, the two men assumed they were on a private estate due to the lush, manicured landscaping. Unwilling to disclose their presence, necessity dictated the urgency to locate a hiding spot for the car. Slim motioned toward a dirt-laden, overgrown utility path. Low-hanging tropical branches scraped and scratched the car's shiny black finish as it rolled deeper into the unforgiving foliage.

Slim slipped out the door and eased it closed. Electing to shuffle through the greenery, Slim and his partner crept closer to the Vitamin Sea. The sprawling villa riffed with laughter and conversation. Out front sat their source of contention, Paschal's red truck.

"What next?" questioned Slim's muscular friend.

"We wait for dark. Get comfortable." Slim groaned, propping his chin on his palm.

They can't stay inside forever.

~

Rhonda's irritated huff, hands firmly planted on her hips, met Leah and Brent at the villa's entry door. "Don't go in there unless you want Amber to bite your head off." Her flustered motion directed their line of vision to the study door.

Leah turned to Brent and grinned, "Didn't we go through this the other day?"

"Must be something special about that room. Want to explore for ourselves later tonight?" He teased.

"You have yourself a date," Leah said, planting a

preview of her intentions square on Brent's curved lips.

"Not y'all, too." Rhonda huffed. "Everywhere I go, even Carol. She's snuggled up to Cooper, Kimberly's practically falling over Steve, so that leaves Suzanne and me as the lone wolves out there." She pitched her thumb over her shoulder and pounded up the stairs.

Laughter, music, and the odor of the fiery grill drifted through the open veranda doors. Curtains billowed back and forth, flowing with the wind and ushering the tasty smells inside the villa.

Leah rolled her eyes and tossed a nod toward the study. "Do we dare interrupt? Evan should know we were unsuccessful."

"Nah, they'll come up for air at some point. Besides, our failure will be welcome news to Evan's ears. Let them enjoy their solitude. Come on. I'm hungry." Brent hooked his arm through Leah's and led her out to the party.

~

Amber rummaged underneath the leather chaise, patting her hand here and there on the jute rug in search of her missing diamond stud. The pair, a gift from her mother years ago, were her favorites. And while she would never complain about the manner in which it was jostled free, her heart might break if she couldn't locate the prized possession.

A broad smile pinched her cheeks into round, bright red circles. Blissfully content, her eyes closed, remembering Evan's words, "I love you." Stunned by his frank admission, she chose to withhold her feelings, determining that was the best option for the time being. Amber eased her lids slowly open to drink in Evan's hunky physique. The tropical sun's kisses enhanced his chiseled jawline and raven-colored locks. Freshly tanned skin, rugged and masculine, screamed to her feminine sensibilities. Her yearning for his devotion grew deeper every day. Amber's lashes fluttered over sparkling blue orbs, blinking in disbelief at her good fortune.

There before her lay Charlotte's most eligible bachelor, snoring. Amber's slim fingers hovered over her mouth, trapping a giggle.

Even heartthrobs have their faults.

She fought the urge to wake him and willed her attention back to the matter at hand: the cherished diamond stud. Balanced on all fours, Amber launched her bottom in the air, arched her back, and shimmied further under the lounger for a closer look. A short puff of exasperation blew loose coils from her face as her "pat down" continued. Hoping for a tiny feel of the earring's post, she extended her reach. No luck. Withdrawing slowly, reluctant to end her search, she ducked her head, slid backward, and sighed. *I have to find it…*

Amber casually raised her head, perplexed at the whereabouts of her earring, only to find herself eye-to-eye with Evan. Still on her hands and knees, she remained motionless and peered through fly-away hair strands. Blue devilish eyes returned her stare as he balanced his chin on the chair's edge.

"Should I ask what you're doing?" He snickered.

A quick exhale and blow sent brunette wisps flying over her head. "It seems I've lost an earring. Would you like to help me?" she asked, maneuvering her limbs to a different section of the rug.

"I'm quite comfortable with the view from here." His gaze washed over her body.

"Oh, you." Amber propped on her knees, shoved her hair to the side, and wiggled her earlobe. "You're looking for one of these."

"Perhaps I need a closer look," he proposed, sliding off the lounger and cozying up beside her. Evan's rascally grin grew broader as his fingers glided up behind her neck, drawing her into his waiting lips. Playful pecks preceded his moist kisses that flowed from hungry lips, quelling

Amber's earring worries for a moment. Evan Holcomb certainly knew how to push her buttons, igniting a firestorm. She released a soft moan of pleasure, sidetracked once again by his effect on her.

She leaned her head back, exposing her bare earlobe to his lips' continued quest. "You know… this is exactly how I lost the first one?"

"Doesn't seem like a bad way to lose it to me." He growled in a breathy tone.

Raspy whispers, describing all the reasons why they were her favorites, never reached his ears. Evan silenced her explanations with passionate tenderness as he caressed her lips once more. He gently rolled onto his back and stared at the ceiling with a content smile, drawing her closer to his side. Eager to comply, Amber wiggled closer and laid her head on his chest, feeling the rise and fall of relaxed breaths until a loud "oww" interrupted her peacefulness.

Evan shot straight up. "I think I found your missing earring," he said, rubbing his lower back.

"Where, where?" She cried.

Evan skimmed his hand along the braided jute and edged the stud from its hiding place. Amber plucked the prize from his upright palm and grinned. Her happiness restored, grateful arms encircled his neck in a tight grasp, "Oh, I love you."

The realization of her statement prompted her to quickly release her grip. Shuffling backward, she stuttered, "I…"

"You what?" Evan questioned, his eyes gleaming. "You appreciate my finding your mother's gift?"

"Yes, yes, I do." Amber lifted her chin and looked away.

"Is that all?" Evan asked, attempting to coax more from her with a soft nudge.

Gone were the days when Amber felt she needed to

keep her heart locked away. She placed her fingertip beneath Evan's chin and guided his mouth closer as her moistened lips converged on his. The deeper she dove, the more he gave.

Intending to make her true feelings known, she withdrew from her oasis of splendor and stammered. "I have a confession to make." Her eyes darted from the floor to the ceiling, landing anywhere but his face. Evan's tranquil gaze and playful squeeze of her knee encouraged her to continue.

"When I met you in Baton Rouge, I was jealous of your affections toward Leah. Every night, I'd give myself a stern lecture about how you shouldn't stab your best friend in the back over a man. I felt quite guilty about my 'semi-obsessive' behavior. I've never told Leah about those feelings." Her face brightened, "But since she chose my wonderful brother, I see no need for that."

Evan's plea for honesty continued, his hands motioning for her to proceed with her confession.

"Anyway, never mind that. Oh… you already know," Amber exclaimed as she threw her hands in the air. "Evan Holcomb, I love you! I have from the time we had dinner at that dumb Cajun restaurant with terrible food that made me sick."

"Amber Scott, you talk too much."

His impassioned capture of her lips muffled her reply. Evan's taut embrace entangled her long locks about his fingers as he deepened his kiss. Unwilling to move, Amber lingered in the joy his presence brought her. Sure he was aware of the depth of her love for him, Amber slowly lifted her lips. The twinkle in his eyes played upon hers, fortifying the promise of more mischief from him, causing her cheeks to flush. Amber realized it would be in her best interest to get some fresh air, fast. She reinserted her earring and nudged Evan's arm. "Are you hungry?"

"I'll always hunger for you." He gleamed, giving her

a roguish wink.

Her face flushed from the implication of his statement. "For food, silly. I am."

"Me too." He quickly grabbed her by the hand and tugged, moving the couple into the foyer toward the grill's beckoning fragrance. Carol whirled past them in a dream-like state. "Hey, Carol." Amber voiced.

"I'm fine. I'm just fine.... heading to fetch my wrap. Cooper and I are going for a stroll on the beach." Carol's lively reply raised the couple's eyebrows.

Thunderous knocking behind Amber drowned out her response. Questioning, she eyed the door, then Evan. "Expecting someone?" she asked.

"Unfortunately." He grumbled and eased open the door.

Amber stood there stunned and watched Evan usher in Rafe and Paschal, who wore a broad grin.

"Hey. Hey." Paschal tipped his hat.

Ghostly white, Amber's ogle moved from Evan to Rafe and back to Evan. Not now. She pleaded from within. Go away, go away. Amber squinched and reopened her eyes, but Rafe's image remained in the doorway. Her hope that she was dreaming shattered when Evan spoke.

"Where's Brent and Leah?"

Rafe's disgruntled response fueled Evan's mire. "How should I know? I haven't seen them."

"Then why are you here?" Evan questioned, clasping the door handle tighter.

"Brent called and offered me a place to stay for a little while." Rafe's stance widened in the challenge of his competition. "I had a little mishap at my apartment this morning. I don't like unwanted guests at my door." Rafe declared through clenched teeth.

"Neither do I, Culliver. And now you've probably brought them here. Did you ever consider that?" Evan's face reddened with anger.

Amber retreated to the foyer's side chair, away from the tension escalating between the two loves of her life - one long forgotten and one she'd never forget.

"Um, I didn't mean to cause any trouble," Paschal stammered, somewhat embarrassed by the unwanted guest comment. "I know you weren't expecting me. I'm only acting as Rafe's chauffeur, that's all. I'll head out." He lowered his head and scuffed the tip of his shoe against the concrete.

"Paschal, you're welcome to stay if you like. I'm afraid my statements require clarification that I cannot give you. Culliver, however, knows the full scope of their meaning."

Amber felt a burdening sense of guilt. Paschal was an innocent bystander in another sick game played by devious individuals, along with Charlie and possibly everyone else in the villa. Waves of nausea washed over her. Amber jumped from her seat, unable to hold her stomach or her tears. "I'm not feeling well. Excuse me." She exclaimed and bolted up the stairs.

"She's had a hard time since the first time she visited the marina." Paschal professed in sorrow. "I feel for her, dude. Would it be alright if I go check on her?" He looked to Evan for approval.

"Yes." Simultaneous replies of concern erupted from both men.

"Up the stairs and take a right," Evan said. "Thank you, Paschal."

Paschal removed his hat and started up the steps, only to be met by Carol's lively tone. "Goodness, what are you doing here, Paschal? I'll have to send Rhonda in. She'll be very happy to see you." Carol beamed, secured her wrap around her torso, and headed into the hallway. "Oh my, you're here too!" Her gaping mouth marked her surprise. "Well, hello and goodbye, Rafe. Evan, Cooper, and I are heading for a nice stroll along the surf. We won't be gone long." She grinned.

"Have a pleasant time, Carol," Evan replied, then confronted Rafe.

"It's just you and me, man to man. Culliver, care to come clean because I'm afraid I cannot be responsible for my actions if further harm comes to Amber." Evan's fists tightened while he moved a step closer to Rafe.

Ready for the fight, Rafe dropped his bag to the floor and chuckled, "You really want to do this?"

Before Evan could respond, Brent and Charlie's head-on sprint placed them between the two men. It was Charlie who spoke first in her matter-of-fact tone. "Gentlemen, I think we should talk. Follow me." Her frank statement left no room for questions, only compliance.

Brent jockeyed for position among his two friends as the three followed Charlie into the study.

~

Slim sat concealed in the damp foliage with a wet butt and a brewing migraine. His cohort leaned back against a tree that provided the perfect environment for a nap. Slim's continual use of pain medication fueled his inability to sleep. His lack of rest hampered the healing process for the worrisome abdominal wound. Grimacing, he clutched his midsection and side. He was in a "catch-22". His life revolved around one dilemma after another. Slim had gravely underestimated Rafe Culliver's abilities. Each had years of military training, but he knew Culliver was a different breed of warrior. Slim mumbled "what ifs" under his breath, irritated by his employer's deficiency in due diligence. He would never have accepted this job if he'd known the full scope of his duties. The sizeable payoff could set him up for life, but he needed to survive the gauntlet to enjoy the enormous sum. Rounds of orders that trickled down somehow never reached his ears until it was too late. He remained cognizant that his life meant little to them since they'd never bothered to disclose the contents of the cargo lying in the ocean. Slim vowed his brawny partner would be doing all the diving from now on when another excruciating pain shot through his wound.

Movements and voices crept up on him from the beachfront. Slim's swift kick woke his pal, who let out a roar. "Shut up, they'll hear you," Slim scolded.

He quickly shuffled through the landscaping and down a slight hill to the beach side of the villa. There, canoodling in the moonlight, stood a man and woman. He grumbled to himself, upset that the two strangers were not the targets he'd hoped to see.

"Ain't love grand?" His muscular cohort chimed and snorted a laugh.

"We're moving in some. I need to hear what they are saying. And be quiet." Slim ordered.

Met with a mean growl, the two drifted closer to the couple hidden by the lush plants. Slim tapped the side of his ear, signaling his partner to stay silent and listen.

A female's voice floated on the wind, "I simply don't understand why there's so much trouble afoot when Rafe Culliver is around. And why is he here at the Vitamin Sea? I tell you, strange things are going on between those three men."

Slim's sidekick shrugged and whispered, "What three?"

"That's what I'd like to know," Slim asked, leaning in as he strained to hear specifics.

The woman's lover boy patted her shoulder, "Brent and Evan have a vivid imagination. Those two let their curiosity get the best of them at times." He laughed. "Don't worry."

Slim sported a sly smile and nodded to his partner. Slim knew it wouldn't be hard to identify their last names. The odds were favorable that one belonged to the charter captain they'd encountered a few days ago.

His burly friend, overcome with satisfaction, reached

over to nudge Slim's shoulder only to discover his footing on the hillside was unstable. Frantic grasps for Slim's hand proved useless. Slim writhed in pain from the strenuous tugs, rapidly withdrawing, leaving the big man plummeting from their perch right into the couple's beachfront rendezvous.

Slim watched his incompetent partner's futile attempts to run, sinking deeper in the cool sand and falling again. The woman's terrified screams pierced the once-peaceful serenity. Her companion jumped atop their intruder, wrestling with Slim's cohort, exchanging blows. Finally, Slim's sidekick gained traction and some leverage over his opponent, but not before Slim yelled, "Car, now, hurry," and shuffled back through the greenery to the black sedan. His buffoon of a partner was on his own. Slim would be generous and give his accomplice five minutes to show up, then he would be gone. Slim complained inwardly, fussing that the man had caused problems from day one, but he kept moving. A brisk retreat had worked in his favor as he scurried along undetected. Back at the car, he jumped in the driver's seat and started the ignition. Slim threw the sedan in reverse and marked his watch – 5:00.

Revving the engine, Slim slid the transmission into drive when his countdown reached 0:01. Ready to bail, his vexed comrade's strong bang on the passenger's door paused Slim's getaway. The sand-covered man leaped in and slammed the door. A simultaneous crash on the car's trunk moved Slim into overdrive, sending the vehicle speeding down the gravel to safety.

"You're lucky." Slim chided. "We need a new plan." He mumbled before pressing the gas pedal to the floorboard.

~

Charlie sprang from the wingback chair, her features distorted with terror. "What was that?" Her impromptu meeting with Evan, Rafe, and Brent was interrupted before it started. The woman's spine-tingling shrieks continued, bringing the three men to their feet.

"That's Carol," Charlie exclaimed. "I'm certain of it. Sounds like it's coming from the beach."

Evan bolted for the study door. "She was going for a walk on the beach with Cooper."

Amber and Paschal ran down the stairs. Rhonda, Leah, and the remaining party rushed toward Evan's voice.

"What's happening? That sounds like Carol!" Amber yelled.

"Brent, hurry," Leah shouted.

"Everyone else stays here," Evan shouted as he flew past the gathering onto the veranda and down to the water.

Brent and Rafe, hot on Evan's trail, made a beeline toward the screams. Charlie stopped to grab a sizeable iron paperweight from the desk and hurried behind them. If she ever doubted the necessity to update her friends on their precarious circumstances, her uncertainty no longer existed.

Evan's heels dug into the moist sand, marking a path for Brent and Rafe to follow. Carol's screeches led him straight to the couple. Sitting upright in the surf, rubbing his jaw, Cooper twisted his neck back and forth, clearly dazed from the skirmish. Brent ran to help with Cooper while Rafe rushed to Carol's side. Carol clung to Rafe's arm, crying, "Who was that?"

Charlie's intuitive grab for a weapon delayed her arrival just enough to see a hulky silhouette bounding through the trees. Without hesitation, she changed directions in pursuit of the intruder. Her petite frame weaved, undeterred by the greenery's growth, to within yards of the injured man as he lunged for the sedan's door handle. Unable to see the vehicle's tag, she angrily hurled the paperweight toward the car's rear end. A loud thump brought a smile to her face. At least she'd marked the speeding vehicle.

Alert to the absence of further screaming, Charlie

hustled down to the beach. Carol stood frozen in place, whimpering, Rafe's arm draped over her shoulders. Charlie's foreboding stare met Rafe's as she took his place by Carol's side.

"He just came rolling down the hill and landed practically at our feet," Carol managed between tearful sniffles. "Poor Cooper didn't even have time to react. That ape of a man just walloped him in the jaw."

"Did he say anything to you?" Charlie probed for information.

"No, never a word that I heard." Carol was now crying again. "He ruined our evening. What was he doing here?" Alarm seized her expression. "Cooper could've been killed. Ohhh……" Her distraught cries grew louder.

Eyeing the men with bewilderment, Charlie spoke. "Gentlemen, we have a serious problem. I'll see you inside." She cradled Carol's elbow, leading her back to the villa. "Come on, Carol, let's get you back to safety."

Evan and Brent grabbed ahold of Cooper's arms, veering him down the path behind Charlie and Carol. Rafe followed quietly.

Charlie nudged Carol through the veranda doors into the tender care of her other "sisters." The women encircled their friend with hugs and ushered her up the stairs. Only Charlie remained downstairs.

"You coming?" Amber questioned with pleading eyes.

"I'll be there in a moment. I want to make sure Cooper's okay. I haven't had a chance to talk with him."

Amber's fake smile warned Charlie of impending trouble. The rash of "unexplained accidents" involving her friends had not gone unnoticed. Tonight's adventure verified her earlier fears. Rafe's adversaries possessed minimal worthy skills. However, their connections provided financial backing from another entity, presenting bigger problems than physical danger alone. She dared not withhold this latest update, or else her highly-ranked source would sever their connection. Charlie clutched her cell, held her breath, and slipped into the garage. No matter how unpleasant, the deed must be done. She sighed and pressed the star key on her phone.

~

Rafe watched Evan and Brent haul their buddy's limp body into the kitchen, easing him down into the ladder-back chair. Cooper's head and forearms had multiple cuts and abrasions. His swollen jawline flamed red from the sucker punch he suffered. From the looks of it, Cooper's attacker had the upper hand in both size and strength. Without a doubt, Rafe knew the identity of Cooper's assailant. Carol's description, "the ape of a man," reinforced his conclusion. Only one question remained – where was his "slim" partner? The restaurant's petite bartender had informed him that the man's injuries weren't healing as expected. Maybe the burly man decided to continue the job with his injured partner. Nonetheless, Rafe never considered the idea that the thug would follow him to the Vitamin Sea. He'd led them straight to Amber and the people he was trying to protect.

Cooper twisted around, staring blankly at Rafe, "When did you get here?"

"Right before your moonlight stroll took a turn for the worse." Rafe tossed.

"Where's Carol? How is she?" Cooper attempted to stand, bending his legs to give a push upward, only to be shoved back in his seat by Steve.

"She's with the other women. They'll take care of her." Steve reassured his friend.

Bright red splotches formed across Cooper's face and down his neck. Ravaged with anger, he bellowed, "If that idiot touched her, I'll find him. He'll pay. Mark my words."

"Down, boy," Brent teased. "He never made it near her. You seemed to keep him quite occupied."

Evan grabbed a frozen sack of peas and rotated his hand against Cooper's jaw. "Have you ever seen the man before?"

Cooper flinched from the touch of the cold bag. "Nope. He was a big one, though. I still can't believe that happened, and it was the craziest thing. Guy just came rolling across the sand."

Evan leered at Brent. "Don't say I didn't warn you. Right to the front door." His gaze moved from Brent to Rafe.

Rafe's concerned, half-angry glare bore directly on Evan. "I don't know the breadth of your conversation, but I assure you, I would never have come if I thought those idiots were smart enough to follow me here."

Paschal stood silent, palms tucked in his back pockets, watching. Rafe had forgotten he was there until, without notice, Paschal cleared his throat, looked at Rafe, and announced, "Dude, the three of you seem to have an awful lot in common to have just met a few days ago."

Rafe tossed his hands up, annoyed with the turn of events, and spilled his backstory. "Brent is an old friend. I had no clue who Evan was until he chartered the boat and brought the long-lost love of my life aboard."

Paschal grinned. "Dang, dude, that explains things. I don't know the entire story, but count on ole Paschal to be in on the action. I made a promise to you the other day, and Paschal never breaks his promises." He strolled over to Rafe and slapped him on the back, maintaining his proud grin.

"Thanks, Paschal." Rafe never doubted his co-worker's loyalty since he hadn't allowed Paschal to get that close to the activity.

Steve stepped forward, prompting Rafe to moan over the probability of an impending lecture. Motionless Rafe awaited Steve's solemn address. "I don't know you or the scope of your authority; however, I'd venture to say anyone who carries the *Brigadier* medal is highly regarded and will always have my full support and admiration."

Cooper piped in, "Mine too. Even though, at first, I thought it was a fake trinket."

Roars of laughter rumbled throughout the kitchen as the men covered their mouths, attempting to mask their amusement over Cooper's honesty.

"Laugh all you want. Ask me who found the secret map?" He beamed.

Cooper's comment stunned the gathering, their earlier chuckles giving way to silence. Three men's faces reddened, and three stood clueless. Brent's face twisted into a mask of disbelief.

"Secret map? You guys didn't think that might have been important to tell me?" Brent barked.

Evan cast his eyes downward, looking at the floor. "That's my fault," he confessed. "I was so upset over Amber's trauma that I completely forgot about it."

Steve mumbled, "Evan, you can't take all the blame. Cooper found the map before the Coast Guard arrived. We should have mentioned it to you sooner. I apologize, Brent. Some rather mysterious events keep interrupting our plan."

Cooper quickly pointed to the frozen vegetables pressed upon his jaw, then at Steve, and nodded in agreement.

"Rafe, did you know anything about a map?" Brent questioned.

Rafe scrubbed his thumb across his chin, amazed by the group of sleuths' abilities. "Can't say that I did. No doubt that map is the root of all our troubles."

Brent positioned himself beside Rafe. "You guys are like my brothers, but we've run out of time. As I see it, here are our options: we confide in each other and help Rafe," Brent held up one finger. "Or we let our insecurities and jealousy rule our decisions," he said as he held up a second finger before continuing, "and someone could die."

Rafe stared at Brent in wonder. Not only was his old friend willing to risk his life, but Brent implored the assistance of men who were complete strangers to Rafe.

Evan stepped up first, "You're well aware of my feelings. And while I have nothing personal against you, Rafe, I won't allow you to hurt Amber again. When the time comes, I'll be by your side to help in any way I can out of respect for your service and for Brent."

Steve seconded, "Me too."

Cooper gave Rafe a thumbs up, followed by Paschal's hat tip and a nod.

Evan inhaled deeply. "How about we get down to business."

The men sat around the expansive table sharing, confiding, and promising. In the end, a pact of total secrecy birthed newfound plans that each prayed would work.

Unbeknownst to them, a larger problem loomed on the other side of the wall—seven women filled with an undeniable spirit of self-determination, led by a pro … Charlie Ashby.

TWENTY-FIVE

The sisters huddled outside the kitchen doorway, quiet as mice, absorbing every morsel of information they could to prepare their own plan. Fear of being discovered sent the group tip-toeing back upstairs and into Amber's room. The expansive bedroom offered their weary bodies refuge with its plush furnishings. Opting to sit on the floor, Amber slowly squatted until her legs gave way, dropping her frame atop the thick, cushioned floral rug. Her sisters followed suit, forming a circle, as they sat in the Lotus position. They looked more like a yoga class than a group of headstrong amateur detectives. Lost in the sea of details they'd acquired only moments ago, silence and confusion encompassed them.

Enraged by the attack on Carol, Charlie took the reins. "If anyone is in doubt what we heard is true, you can stow your doubt. It's true." Stunned expressions from everyone except Leah and Amber stared back at her.

"Cooper's attack wasn't the first." Shocked eyes locked on Charlie as she continued. "A diver under the boat cut our safety line, leaving us at the mercy of the open seas. Amber and Evan also had a dicey encounter with two less-than-desirable henchmen on their charter. One of which, I'd be willing to bet, was the same man I followed through the trees to a hidden vehicle tonight." Charlie's stern words sent a chill through the room, accomplishing her intended objective.

Rhonda, Kimberly, and Suzanne exchanged horrified stares while Carol's sobs started once more. Leah squeezed the "mother hen's" hand and placed a light blanket from the foot of Amber's bed around Carol's shaking body.

Charlie's frame stiffened, "Carol, I know your experience was unpleasant; however, now is not the time to fall apart. It's time to mount a unified front."

Rhonda's uncharacteristically humbled tone resonated with the women. "I'll gladly accept whatever role you assign me, Charlie. I must admit I'm sometimes difficult to deal with. I'm sorry about that."

Carol wiped her tears and threw a wadded ball of damp tissue at Rhonda's head. "Sometimes?" She asked, a watery smile lighting up her face. "Tell us what you want us to do, Charlie."

Charlie's heart warmed at the profound confidence her "sisters" placed in her. "Here's my plan."

Spirited whisperings continued well into the night. It wasn't until the group heard a light rapping on Amber's door that the women realized the time.

Amber shot to her feet. "Just one moment," she called.

The seven females scurried about the room, dragging bed linens to the floor and lining pillows in a row. Leah tossed Amber a thumbs up and nuzzled the covers under her chin.

"Coming." Amber eased open the door and faked a giant yawn, unprepared for the surprise on the other side.

Glancing down at his watch and then back at Amber, Rafe's cheeks flushed. "I guess I didn't realize the time. Go back to sleep."

"Wait, do you need something?" Amber sheepishly questioned.

"Only a few moments alone with you." His eyes flickered with desire until he heard a resounding "Ohhhh."

Charlie stuck her head through the crack, releasing a

knowing, "Hey, Rafe," and opened the door to reveal the floor covered with sisters.

Shades of red crawled from his neck into his face and down his muscular arms. Stammering, he uttered, "Um, I can see now's not the time. Good night, ladies."

A booming, unified "Good night, Rafe," followed him down the hallway as he made his hasty retreat.

Charlie looked at Amber sympathetically and whispered, "You know you're going to have to choose soon?"

Her question sent Amber fleeing back to the makeshift beds and the security of her friends.

~

Amber rubbed her eyes with one hand and her back with the other. Maybe the spontaneous sleepover wasn't such a good idea. Her attempt to sit up produced loud cracking noises and her body ached from little to no sleep. Rafe's image floated in and out of her short dreams, filling her head with his delusions of grandeur. Amber gnawed at her bottom lip. Anxiety seized her, rendering her unable to breathe. She'd listened to the men's conversation. There was never a doubt that Rafe was in danger. Until last night, she remained foolishly unaware of the full extent of his vulnerability.

In her younger days, she would have jumped from the tallest pine if Rafe had told her to. She loved him unconditionally during their budding romance, believing his happiness was all that mattered, and she sacrificed her own to maintain his. Long gone were those times. Amber understood the true meaning of love now through Evan's eyes. Evan showered her with the kind of affection she once bestowed on Rafe, but with one difference: Rafe never truly reciprocated the purity of real love. Rafe's commitment to his job and country would always be his first choice. Surprisingly enough, the thought no longer upset her. Amber finally looked upon Rafe as she should have since childhood - another brother. And she'd fight for his safety just as she would Brent's.

Relief flooded her soul. For a girl with little to no rest, the epiphany fueled her need to see Evan pronto. Amber threw the covers back and jumped to her feet, startling her other bed buddies.

"Ugh, go back to sleep," Rhonda moaned.

Amber tugged the white linens and removed the blanket covering, "Time to get up. Lots to do today." Her count of the complainers lying around her fell short by one – Charlie. Amber knew her friend. Charlie's absence signaled a plan she'd contrived all on her own.

Amber gently nudged Leah in the ribs, whispering, "Get up, Charlie's not here."

Leah's eyes flew open, "How long has she been gone?"

"No clue."

Leah sprang to her feet and smoothed her brown locks down. "Get dressed and meet me downstairs as soon as you can."

"I will. Leah, there's someone I need to talk to before we leave." Amber smiled broadly.

Leah tossed her a knowing wink and hurried to the door. "I said as soon as you can." She teased.

Rhonda bolted straight up. Strands of blonde hair shot up in the air, charged with electricity from the plush rug. "Would you two please go back to sleep? Make that you three!" she muttered, falling backward and dragging the blanket over her staticky locks.

Amber never saw the other women move. They remained oblivious to Rhonda's complaints. Deciding they were better left alone, Amber scooted to take a hot shower, throw on clothes, and see her man. The words "her man" had a nice ring to it, brightening her face with a radiant glow.

Amber's slim fingers curled and tapped on Evan's

door thirty minutes later. His raspy "Who is it?" stirred her core, making her stomach flip like a ride on an amusement park roller coaster.

"It's me," Amber answered softly.

Determined footsteps pounded the wooden flooring, "I said, who is it?" Evan yelled, jerking the door open.

Amber's mouth opened, yet nothing flowed from her lips. The image before her took her breath. Wrapped in a towel, face half-shaven, stood a man nothing short of perfection. Piercing blue eyes sparkled back at her. The white cream smeared across one cheek created a mesmerizing contrast with his pitch-black locks. Evan's toned physique was relaxed. A curved smile greeted her.

Evan's tanned, hunky frame remained inches from her, rendering her speechless, as Amber's gaze floated between muscled biceps and chiseled abs, eventually shifting back to his broad chest.

Evan's chuckle drew her obvious admiration to his wicked, twinkling eyes. "Get in here," he laughed. He yanked her into his room and kicked the door close. Amber's lungs tightened as he led her to a chair and eased her down. The aromatic elixir of body wash or cologne filled the room with an irresistible fragrance that spiked her desires. The need to quell her emotions erupted, sending her into dangerous territory.

Evan's devilish grin moved into a deep laugh. "I'll be right back." He drew the ends of the towel tighter, leaned down, and kissed Amber's cheek.

"Impish rogue," she huffed.

Amber scanned the room during his absence for a speedy escape route, none of which existed since Evan's room was on the third floor, and his door was tightly closed. The overwhelming combination of visuals and fragrances blended with the warm caress of his touch concocted a deadly mixture of desire and sensuality. Amber bowed her head, willing her emotions to remain in check.

Weary of the struggle, Amber leaned back and tried her deep breathing skills. Her body began to relax, and her heart rate slowed. Proud her technique worked, she opened her eyes, instilled with a new sense of confidence. Evan sat opposite Amber's wingback chair, his arms crossed. Sporting a wicked grin, Evan tossed her a wink, amused by her zen moment. "Feel better?" He asked.

Amber straightened her back, insistent Evan's sexy charms would not sidetrack her purpose for being there. Oddly enough, those charms were why she'd visited his room. Her chin lifted, "Evan Holcomb, you are the most exasperating man on earth at times, and your incessant teasing pushes my buttons, but I can't imagine my life any other way. I realized last night that Rafe was a part of my past and always will be. My only feelings for Rafe are those of a brotherly nature."

Her eyes glistened with innocence. "I really should thank you for helping me destroy the defensive barriers I erected from my pain and heartache. And for teaching me that I, Amber Scott, am enough." Pride echoed in her statement while tiny droplets spilled down her cheeks.

Overcome with joy, she sprang from the chair and flew into his arms. Strong and protective, they encircled her as Evan shed his own tears.

"When my parents died, I locked my personal life away in a box, obsessed with my work and the care of my siblings. Leah is a wonderful woman, and I'm happy for Brent, but God's plan is always the best. We were meant to be. I wouldn't trade you for anything in this world." Evan collapsed against her. His confession was as pure as hers.

Amber marveled how perfectly timed their hearts beat as one. Content to stay right where she was for the remainder of the day, Leah's bothersome yells disturbed Amber's tranquility.

"Can't you just tell her to go away for now?" Evan smiled.

"I wish I could. We are going out for a little while. You know, shopping and such." Amber teased. "I'll be back soon," trailing a finger from his cheek toward waiting lips. Her teasing nips about his upper lip prepared the way for the bold, passionate promise her moist kiss left until her return. His frustrated moans grew louder when she slowly wiggled from his grasp and backed away in response to the endless calls of her name.

"Leah, I'm coming," Amber half whispered.

"When, next week?" Leah complained.

Amber's slow approach to the door reinforced her reluctance to leave. She stifled a laugh at the sight of his tall frame stretched half on and half off the wingback chair, balanced by his long legs. "Evan, I love you," she smiled and rushed out, leaving him with a satisfied grin.

Hurried steps propelled her down the staircase. Not so pleased with her delay, Leah paced back and forth, hands on her hips. "As soon as you can doesn't mean two hours!" Leah ranted.

"Has it been two hours?" Amber asked, her face aglow.

"No, but it seems like it."

Amber reached for Leah's hand and tugged. "Then come on. We have to find Charlie."

"Any clue as to where we should look first?" Leah questioned, snagging the Rover keys from their resting place.

"My instincts tell me the marina. Charlie told me some stupid story about leaving her bag there when I caught her sneaking back in the other night. She totally lied."

"The question is, why?" Leah asked.

"No idea, but Mr. Jenkins seemed a little too quirky for my taste the other day. I say we head there first."

Leah shuffled into the driver's seat and asked, "Did you tell Evan what we were doing?"

Amber pulled the passenger door closed as quietly as possible. "Shopping, of course. Brent?" Amber's eyebrows rose in wonder.

"Not a word. Brent will be ready to kill me. Again." Leah chuckled.

"What number are we on now?" Amber jested. Both women knew they would get a severe scolding should Evan and Brent learn the truth.

"So, to the marina?" Leah asked.

Amber nodded in agreement.

With a quick buckle of their seat belts, Leah steered the Rover down an all too familiar path – straight into trouble.

TWENTY-SIX

Rafe sluggishly gravitated toward the aroma of fresh ground beans. Sunshine spilled onto the coffee bar countertop, inviting early risers to its warmth and piping hot brew. Carafes percolated steam funnels from the white spouts for any taste – decaffeinated, caffeinated, coconut, rum-infused. Rafe groaned and reached for the strongest available. Disappointment had prevented him from drifting to sleep. His decision to visit Amber's room haunted him this morning. Every female in the villa overheard his request, providing an outlet for each lady's imagination to run amuck.

How could I have known they'd all be there?

His inner voice caused turmoil and beat him ruthlessly each time he closed his eyes for not following his commander's directions. Thankful that Holcomb's room was on the third floor, Rafe shook his head, both amused and annoyed at his stupidity for the stunt. Evan Holcomb appeared capable of handling himself in just about any situation. Brent's friends' sincerity touched Rafe in ways he hadn't felt since boot camp. Being a "ghost" to everything others hold dear was tiring.

Rafe and his cup of caffeinated motivation moved to the veranda for solitude, a short-lived idea interrupted by the scraping sound of chair legs upon concrete. Brent slid into the seat beside him. "Mind if I sit down?"

"Would it matter if I did?" Rafe grumbled.

"Not, really. I'm not leaving." Brent grinned. "We need to get moving as soon as the other guys come down. Could Paschal search the SJ this morning when he arrives at the marina? We have to consider someone may have found the map by now. Steve's forethought of taking photos will be useful if that's the case."

"Brent, you and your friends have no idea what you're up against, not to mention my superiors highly discourage civilian assistance."

Brent smiled, "Yeah, I thought about that. Technically, Steve, Cooper, and I are not just civilians. We are veterans. We served in separate branches but are still brothers and love our country. Could you stop trying to push us away? You need help right now, and we can provide that help."

"Okay." Rafe agreed reluctantly. "There is one thing you should know." Rafe paused. "Charlie's in on the action, too."

"Charlie? How?" Brent's expression shifted from momentary satisfaction to shock.

"Believe me, I was as shocked as you are. All I know is that Charlie has ties to people with a rank much higher than mine."

"Have you seen her this morning?" Brent anxiously questioned.

"No, you're the only one. Everyone else must still be asleep."

Brent whirled around, flinging the chair away from the table, and rushed back into the villa.

Rafe jumped to his feet in pursuit, "Brent, what's going on? Is there a problem?"

His mouth tightened, yielding a terse reply. "You don't want to know. We have bigger issues than you can imagine. And if my instincts are correct, Leah and Amber are directly in the middle of it." He groaned through clenched teeth.

Brent whisked through the villa's rooms, stopped at the bottom of the staircase, looked upward, and shouted, "Leah!"

The "sisters" spilled from Amber's room to Brent's deafening yells. Rhonda looking whimsical in a bathrobe, silk pajamas that clung to her legs, hair strands on end, and hands clutched to her ears, questioned, "Why is everyone yelling this morning? First Amber, and now you guys? How's a girl supposed to get rest?"

Rafe's pulse quickened, visible in stretched neck tendons, *Amber*. "Why was Amber yelling?"

Rhonda ranted, "Oh, for goodness' sake. I don't know. The rest of us were trying to sleep."

"Who's the rest of us?" Brent demanded.

"Um, I didn't take a count, Brent. I think Kimberly, Carol, Suzanne, and maybe Leah. I'm heading to shower. Since no one can sleep this morning." Rhonda huffed.

"Leah…." Brent climbed the stairs, shouting again and awakening the rest of the entire villa.

"Brent, calm down," Evan announced, strolling onto the upper balcony.

"Leah's missing. You calm down." Brent shouted.

Evan's chuckle clashed with Brent's disdain. "She's with Amber. I saw Amber earlier this morning. Amber said she and Leah were going shopping. I think they are fine."

Rafe's painful awareness of Evan's proclamation tested his fortitude. Everything within his core wanted to punch Evan square in the jaw. He'd tried to talk with Amber "earlier this morning" only to be turned away. A stark revelation swirled through his mind while chaos ensued around him.

"Evan, take my word for it, they are not fine. Those two are up to something. In all probability, Charlie's in the thick of the mess, too. Did it ever occur to you that it's only 7 a.m.? Tell me a shop that's open at 7 a.m." Brent lectured, combing his fingers through his hair.

Rafe mumbled, "The marina." Horror contorted his and Brent's features simultaneously.

Evan peered over the railing and watched Kimberly, Suzanne, and Carol scurry back into Amber's room without a word. The air fell silent except for the swift click of the door's lock.

Evan's loud grumble spoke volumes. "I'll get Steve and Cooper."

"Better make it fast," Brent spouted as he reached for the nonexistent van and Range Rover keys.

~

Charlie's stealthy maneuvers placed her outside and in the van before dawn. Marveling at how soundly her friends slept, she capitalized on the perfect environment to achieve her hasty departure. The "sisters" were up well into the night, devising a fictional plan Charlie had no intention of implementing. Each eventually succumbed to unwanted exhaustion. Only Rhonda flinched when Charlie eased the gauzy coverlet back, mumbling Paschal's name. Makeshift pillows supported their heads, which would give rise to some very sore necks, causing her to smile. A quick snag of her shoes and she was on her way. Even Leah and Amber remained motionless.

Last night's telephone conversation with her contact placed her in a precarious position. While her "sisters" pledged their assistance in any manner needed, Charlie knew the women were unprepared to handle the degree of danger surrounding them. However, due to the escalation of Cooper's attack, her confidant warned her of the increased urgency to expedite a resolution that ensured the original mission's success. Of course, she had no one to blame but herself. As usual, her "nose for news" had landed her smack dab in the middle of a perilous situation few could control. Her role as messenger had quickly changed to active participant.

She drove slowly to the marina while on guard for

any signs of a tail. Thankfully, the dented black sedan remained out of sight. Her initial drive-by of the parking lot yielded nothing but darkness and a lone truck. Charlie circled the block and pulled into the narrow entrance. After locating the perfect space, she eased the van backward into the shadowy spot and shut off the ignition. Flashlight in hand, Charlie jumped from the vehicle and ran down the old wood planking straight to the Savannah Jane. One leg over the railing, she halted her approach. The sounds of paper crumpling and heavy footsteps rang from the helm. Cabinet doors creaked and closed.

Charlie readied her petite frame and stepped onto the SJ with a resounding sense of purpose. A quick flip of her light produced a thick, weighted baton angled to create maximum pain. She moved one foot quietly in front of the other, creeping toward the helm. Fortunately, the burglar remained engrossed in his search, unaware of her arrival. Charlie knew without a doubt that only one of them would leave the SJ successful and vowed it would be her.

She shifted closer to the entryway. Her grip tightened on the black wand. Leaping into the dark room, Charlie leveled her weapon and lunged at her opponent's kneecap. The blow placed him sprawled out on the floor, yelping, his lantern rolling about around his head.

Charlie drew back, poised to strike again, until the tumbling light illuminated a familiar face.

"You?" she cried.

"Charlie? Stop, it's me. You about killed me." Paschal pleaded. Riddled with pain, he coiled into the fetal position.

"Paschal, why are you here?" Charlie asked curiously.

"After Cooper's attack, we devised a plan. I'm supposed to find a map. Why are you here? Did Rafe send you?" Confused and hurt, Paschal massaged his knee.

Paschal had just provided her with the perfect alibi. Charlie replied, "Yes, Rafe thought you might need help."

Paschal's hand waved back and forth, and stammered, "If Rafe sent you, why did you try to kill me with that thing?"

"It's pitch black in here. I couldn't tell if that was you, and I certainly wasn't going to take a chance on someone else leaving here with that map." Charlie bent down to heave Paschal up. "Grab my arm."

"OWWWW. I think you broke my kneecap." Paschal moaned as he hopped to a bench.

"Sorry, sorry. I'll cover your medical expenses. Right now, I need to know if you were successful?"

"No sign of it. Cooper told me to look in that cabinet." Paschal pointed to a row of old storage cabinets. "Except nothing's in there but tide charts and crap. Someone had to move it."

"Who could have moved it, I wonder." Charlie's suspicions returned to Rafe. Had he sent all of them on a wild goose chase as a ruse? If that were true, she would be ready to whack him with her baton.

Paschal tried to smile, then winced, "Odds are it was that sketchy young dude. James something…Wilder James, that's him. He took the SJ out yesterday morning. Rafe had to call Old Man Jenkins for approval. That little dude is sly. We followed him out to the cliffs. The SJ was flying a diver's flag. I told Rafe he's found treasure."

Charlie's stomach churned. The name Wilder James sounded all too familiar, but she didn't know why.

"Let me rummage through the cabinet to see if you missed something, and then we'll get you to a doctor. Sit still."

Paschal cried, "Don't worry," clutching his knee.

Unsuccessful as predicted, Charlie slid her arm around Paschal's waist, bearing the brunt of his weight as they limped down the walkway. Her quick boost landed him in the van's front seat just before dawn broke over the horizon.

Charlie knew she wouldn't find what she was looking for. Paschal, for all intents and purposes, was correct. The tropical waters sported all types of treasures. Wilder James assuredly stole the map, yet an important question loomed over her: was James friend or foe? Until she remembered the connection, it was in the best interest of them all to assume foe.

~

"Look." Amber leaned in closer to the dashboard, squinting. "There she goes." The two women watched as the Vitamin Sea's white utility van eased from the marina parking lot and traveled leisurely to the town's trendy east side. A mecca of restaurants, shops, and old museums comprised the square. They loved the area and had spent much of their time exploring its diverse attractions since their arrival on the island.

"Why is she coming here?" Leah asked.

The vehicle methodically took a sharp right and whizzed by the businesses, moving on inland.

"Guess she's not." Amber giggled.

"Oh, stop it. Where could Charlie be going?" Concern flowed through Leah.

Charlie drove the vehicle around a median and hung another right, only this time Amber spotted a silhouette in the passenger seat. "Someone's with her. Keep going."

"Who would be with her?" Leah chewed her bottom lip. "This early?"

Leaving enough space between the Rover and Charlie, Leah gripped the wheel and carried on. Within a few minutes, the Vitamin Sea's van slow-rolled under a canopy attached to the island's small hospital. Amber, unconcerned whether Charlie knew they were tailing her, feared the worst. She shouted at Leah, "Go. Go."

Amber popped the latch on the glove compartment and searched for some semblance of a weapon, just in case. Swinging a flashlight from her left hand, she gave directions. "You get to Charlie. I'll get the passenger."

Their plan intact, Leah skidded the Range Rover to a stop just inches from the van's bumper. Before Charlie could crack her door, Leah was by her side. Amber yanked open the opposite door, ready to strike, only to be met by Paschal's yelp. "Not you, too! Wait."

Amber's surprise sent the light crashing onto the curb. Charlie emerged from the rear of the van with Leah in tow. "You two are some of the worst drivers I've ever seen. I've known you were behind me a block after we left the marina." Charlie's endless bursts of laughter trailed around her. Amber watched in amazement as Charlie nonchalantly maneuvered between her and the car door and grabbed Paschal's arm.

Paschal slid from the seat, favoring his left leg. "What is it with you women and flashlights?" He shook his head. "Making you three angry is not in a man's best interest."

Charlie tossed a determined "Follow me." Leah and Amber dared not balk at the command and followed her into the hospital in silence. The tiny ten-bed facility displayed minimal equipment or supplies and even less staff to administer care. The handwritten cardboard sign "Ring in an emergency" propped beside a rusty bell evoked little to no confidence from the three females. Amber tapped the bell four times, rendering a faint "clang."

Paschal joked, "Now you know why we airlift significant injuries out of here." Hopping to a chair, he sat down and extended his leg. "I should be okay with a few pain pills and a brace unless… she broke my kneecap." He spouted and pointed to Charlie.

Charlie unveiled an apologetic smile, "I said I was sorry."

Paschal grinned, "I know. I'm teasing ya."

"Can one of you enlighten us on what either of you are talking about and why we're in a hospital at 7:30 in the morning?" Leah's frustration was evident by the escalation of her tone.

“I think what Leah is trying to say is… we were very concerned about you,” Amber added and patted Leah’s arm, conveying patience.

Charlie’s eyes glistened. “Paschal and I were on a sort of mission.” Her further explanation was interrupted by the appearance of a scraggly, yawning orderly.

“One of you need something?” He scratched his head, struggling to open his eyes.

Paschal piped up, “Yeah, dude, you see my knee.” He exclaimed and pointed to the swollen, purple flesh on his leg.

“Wow. That looks painful, man. I’m the only one here this early. I can take an x-ray before I call the doc in. Want a wheelchair?” The sleepy man questioned and leaned on the counter.

“What do you think, dude?” Paschal hurled.

“Okay, okay.” The man shuffled gingerly down the hall in no hurry, his worn Crocs squeaking on the linoleum flooring. Amber focused on Charlie. Her rigid body stood motionless, her attention span sparse and preoccupied. Charlie’s pitiful cover story meant nothing. Amber wasn’t buying it, nor would Leah.

The orderly returned pushing a battered black wheelchair with one hand, the other filled with a tattered clipboard securing paperwork. “Your ride, man.” He grinned while Paschal limped into the chair. “One of you will need to fill these out.”

Amber’s response was cut short by Charlie’s reach for the papers and a meek, “I’ll do it.”

“Thanks,” Paschal called. “If I’m not back in an hour, come save me, ladies.”

“We will,” Amber yelled.

Charlie sifted through the pages. Amber watched her friend, filling in the bare minimum since none of the women knew much about Paschal, finishing the stack with her personal insurance and payment information.

With Leah's annoyance quelled, Amber softly asked, "Charlie, want to tell us how we got here?"

"You two heard the men last night referencing a confidential chart. We need it. I figured I could beat the guys to it."

"That wasn't in the gameplan we made as a group, Charlie," Leah interjected, a hint of anger lingering in her tone.

"Plan or not, the map wasn't there. But before you bash me for my actions, Leah, consider this. Rafe instructed Paschal to retrieve the thing early, before dawn, which means he strayed from the men's proposed plot. So, what does that tell you?" Charlie murmured. "That's why we are here. I nailed Paschal with a club on the Savannah Jane this morning. I didn't know it was him." Regret brimmed from within her.

Leah rushed to embrace her friend, "I didn't mean to sound angry. Your disappearance scared us. You told us never to deviate from a plan; if you do, disaster strikes."

"Good advice." Charlie moaned, eyeing their present location.

Amber clutched her friends in a bear hug. "We'll survive this too." Her reassurance brought the women to tears.

Met with Paschal's gleeful, "Ladies, don't cry for ole Paschal. I'll be up and about in no time. No breaks!" The women squeezed him from all sides and cried. "Ohhh, Paschal."

A broad grin formed on his lips, "I have to wait for the doctor. Go. I'll have a friend come pick me up. Charlie, find that map."

"You can count on it," Charlie said as they ran toward the exit doors.

The scrawny hospital attendant tapped Paschal's shoulder, "Man, if I were you, I'd considered busting up my other leg for those three." He grinned.

Paschal flicked his curled fingers across proud shoulders and smiled.

~

Vitamin Sea's luxurious offerings provided everything a guest could want, excluding a vast array of vehicles from which to choose. Brent charged into the garage, disappointed by the stark emptiness of the three-car bay. Covered in the last spot sat what appeared to be a sports car. Brent yanked the cover back, confirming his earlier conclusion – a black Porsche Carrera. A true gem by all standards, except under present conditions. Another model better suited to Brent's needs would have been nice.

Grumbling, Brent marched back into the villa, meeting the other men coming out. "Evan, tell me you have another SUV stashed somewhere."

"Amber and Leah took the Rover, but we can use the van. Not the most luxurious mode of transportation, however…"

"Wrong." Brent's aggravation added an ire to his reply. "Van's MIA. Charlie probably has it. Before you ask…don't."

"They've done it again, haven't they?" Evan's face glowed red with anger.

"Yep. That fancy little Carrera won't work. Any ideas?" Brent paced back and forth, deep in thought, his hands jammed into his pockets.

Evan walked to the empty mahogany bowl, picked it up, and then slammed it back down. "Next time I visit the Vitamin Sea, this estate will have ample transportation and hidden keys."

Steve, Cooper, and Rafe stood in the doorway, waiting patiently. Cooper's fanciful admiration floated past Steve as he reared his shoulders and grinned. Steve followed his gaze to the bottom of the staircase. Carol halted her entry into the makeshift meeting and smiled.

"Oh my, morning, gentlemen. Have I missed something?" Her probing stare landed on Brent.

"Carol, where are Leah, Amber, and Charlie?" Brent's annoyed groan brought Cooper to Carol's defense.

"Brent, hold on now, how would she know?"

"Believe me, she knows," Evan added.

Carol's smiling eyes met Cooper's. "Actually, I do. Although I'm not sure what all the fuss is about. They're right outside on the veranda. Everyone is waiting on me for breakfast."

"No way," Rafe muttered, crossing through the group straight onto the porch.

"You fellows might want to head back to bed or pour yourselves a stout cup of caffeine." Carol chided, gliding through the testosterone-infused air.

"She's telling the truth. The three are having coffee, chit-chatting with Suzanne and Kimberly." Rafe's report had each of them scratching their head. "And look what I found on the kitchen counter." He declared, opening his palm. Inside lay the Rover and van keys.

Brent shot to the window and gazed across the front lawn. Parked in the garage sat the two vehicles in question. Filled with disbelief, he exclaimed, "You have to be kidding me."

Cooper spoke first, "See, and you all were trying to blame Carol for something."

Evan noted, "They are good. Scary good. And she was in the thick of it, believe me."

"Looks like we need to have a frank discussion with those three." Brent's annoyance was on full display. His swift turn toward the veranda cleared a path for the other men in line behind him as they marched into the sunlight.

"Leah….," Irritation pricked like needles on Brent's neck.

"Morning, babe. You guys are late risers this morning." She cheerfully tossed. "We've been up for hours."

Amber fidgeted with the napkin on her lap, "Geez, you all look so serious. Want me to pour you some coffee?" She offered, rising from the wrought iron chair.

Evan blared, "Thought you were going shopping?"

Amber returned to her seat and reached for her cup, "Evan, where in the world would we go shopping this early, silly? That's what we're doing later."

Charlie grinned. "Goodness." Her stare fixed on Rafe. "Why all the suspicious questioning? You accosted poor Carol and upset her all over again."

Suzanne and Kimberly covered their mouth and stifled giggles over Carol's pretense of dabbing tears from her eyes.

Rafe reciprocated Charlie's glare. "Brent and I checked earlier. The Range Rover and van were not in the garage. Any explanation for that?"

"Did you look in the drive? Maybe the staff moved them." Amber asked.

"Okay, enough, we all know the story you're feeding us is crap. You forget I'm your brother, Amber. And you, I love dearly, but I know when you're lying," Brent bellowed, pointing to Leah.

Charlie straightened her back and confessed. "We've been trying to protect him; however, you men can't let anything go. It seems there's no way to hide it anymore. We went to help Paschal."

Rafe's wild-eyed glare shot straight to Charlie. "Help Paschal?"

Charlie's words weaved a web of concern among her male friends, "Poor Paschal had an accident earlier this morning and needed a ride to the hospital. In excruciating pain, he called me since I was the last person he spoke with. I guess it was a reflex sort of thing." Charlie shrugged her shoulders.

"What kind of accident? Was he hurt bad?" Rafe's

scrutinized the details of her story. "Where was he?"

"He was at the marina getting an early start on the day and fell on the wet planking. Of course, I hurried to his aide, never considering I may not be able to lift him by myself. So, I contacted Leah and Amber. There was no need to wake and worry everyone in the house. The three of us handled things. His knee did look pretty terrible. Didn't it, ladies?" Charlie paused.

"Paschal was fine when we left him. The x-ray showed no breaks. He thanked us for helping him, and we returned here." Leah added. "Although I must admit, the medical facilities on the island appear quite archaic." She professed, batting her eyes at Brent.

"Paschal has been so kind to me. I wouldn't want Mr. Jenkins to reprimand him or worse for an unavoidable incident." Amber interjected.

Charlie coughed and focused on Rafe. "Contrary to your conclusion, Amber. The accident was avoidable. His decision to follow directions landed him where he is now. Unfortunate from all angles."

"Do you three know how infuriating you can be at times?" Brent announced. His cheeks reddened with frustration. As good as their story sounded, Brent knew there was only one way to confirm the tale, and Paschal was the only person who could do that.

"Come on, Culliver," Brent called. "Evan, mind if we use the Range Rover?"

"I'll come with you. No. Someone needs to watch Leah, Amber, and Charlie." Brent tossed a thumb over his shoulder in Cooper and Steve's direction, pointing out their infatuation with their breakfast companions, Carol and Kimberly. "I'm afraid Cooper and Steve will be an easy target since the 'island love bug' has also sunk its teeth into them. You, however, can't be entirely swayed by my sister's charms, right?" Brent's eyebrows rose in question.

"Yeah, sure, he can't. He's the one who thought they

were going shopping at 7:00 a.m." Rafe interjected, jealousy dripping from his words.

Evan's chest broadened, fury flickered in his usually tranquil blue eyes, "At least I know her worth and won't leave her," he whispered to Rafe, fists clenched.

Brent grabbed Rafe's shirt sleeve and pulled Rafe through the door. "Not now." He warned. "We'll be back in a little while. And Leah, don't go anywhere."

"Why would I? We have hours before we visit the boutiques. Love you." She yelled.

~

Leah pushed the warm iron chair from the table, "I'm heading in for a refill."

"Me too," Amber said. Charlie's "sounds good" soon followed.

Evan's inquisitive eye watched the three culprits prance to the coffee bar. Giggles and whispers echoed from inside the villa.

Where could they go? Steve and Cooper are inside.

He basked in the sun's warmth, casting his anger with Amber to the wind. He kept his eyes closed and listened. Female voices coursed through the air. Unable to decipher the words, he found comfort in the conversation. If he could hear them, they undoubtedly were nearby. Evan remained intently still, attempting to lure the women into a false sense of security. Bits and pieces of their discussion floated on the wind, but not enough to discover any discernable plan.

Leah peered around the corner at Evan's relaxed posturing, "Amber, you're going to have to keep him occupied while Charlie and I sneak out. I am confident that won't be a miserable challenge for you." Her low-pitched statement rolled into a laugh.

"Leah, you heard Brent. He will be ready to kill you, us, that is."

"Charlie needs my help. Besides, we covered our

tracks earlier and can do it again."

"Where are you going? You can't take the van, and the Range Rover is gone." Amber's head swiveled back around, staring from Evan to Leah. "And Evan may see through my ruse."

Charlie giggled. "He could, but I doubt he'll complain. Nor will you, for that matter."

Amber succumbed to her friend's pressure. "Okay. On one condition. Tell me where you are going?"

"Two times now, in the dead of night, I've seen a light roving about that peninsula, and I want to know why." Charlie's smile widened.

"One small problem: how are we going to get there?" Leah asked.

"Those two beach cruisers in the garage." Charlie grinned. "Hope you remember how to ride a bike." She giggled, dragging Leah upstairs, leaving Amber to do her job.

Evan's body tensed from the sudden pause in the ladies' discussion. It was too quiet. He popped open his eyes to see Amber's silhouette surrounded by the sun's rays, creating a halo around her. He had to be dreaming, which accounted for the sparse conversation. Her beautiful aura enriched his soul. Kindness and love oozed from her like a flowing river. The nudge of his knee aroused him from his utopia.

"Hey, your juice was cold when I brought it out." She smiled. "Must have been some dream you were having. Want to fill me in?"

Evan removed the two glasses from her hands, clanging the glass against the wrought iron when he sat them down.

"Oops." She giggled.

Her pearly grin encouraged his playful tug, placing her on his lap. Amber curled her legs up and laid her head on his chest. Her long sun-spritzed hair smelled of fresh lavender, and her soft skin teased his nose with a tranquil effusion of eucalyptus. Evan looked to the heavens, thankful for the private dose of tropical splendor and joy that filled his heart. He squeezed her tightly and whispered, "You are my whole world. Never doubt how much I love you and always will."

"I won't." She replied, snuggling closer.

"You covered your tracks this morning like a pro." He chuckled.

Amber lifted her head. "You knew? And didn't say anything?"

"Of course, I knew. You did come to my room quite early." His eyes twinkled in remembrance.

"But… you didn't give us away… why?"

Amber's perplexed expression made Evan laugh. "Because you don't betray the ones you love. What good would it have done? All three of you were back here safe and sound before the rest of us could even make it into the kitchen. Now, had you not returned in a reasonable time, that's a different story."

Her soft "thank you" sent his heart leaping.

"Brent and Rafe wanted to kill us." She laughed.

"Brent, I support in most cases. Rafe's opinion didn't matter to me." Evan inhaled and pushed his animosity for Rafe out of the picture.

"By the way, was your tale true? Is Paschal injured?" Curious eyes stared into Amber's, praying for the truth but ready for a tale that protected her friends.

Her gaze fell away from his for a second, then returned. "Yes, Paschal's knee is hurt – not broken. If it's okay, I'd prefer not to divulge exactly how it happened." Wide eyes blinked back at him.

"The simple fact that you asked my preference is all that matters." Evan bent down and kissed her lips, twinged with the tartness from the orange juice. "How fond are you of OJ?"

Amber scrunched her forehead, "Not too."

"Good, your lips are much sweeter than I just tasted." He teased, pinching her in the side.

Her giggles and squirming drew him closer to her goodness and joy. He smothered her full lips with his in search of that joy, stopping her laughter and starting his sweet deliverance. A magical spell spread over his body when her arms encircled his neck. The world's worries disappeared as the nectar of her kisses emboldened him to new heights. She returned his kiss with a passion and fire that never subsided but instead grew stronger each time he basked in her loving arms. Evan's low moan of satisfaction floated in the air between them.

Amber's frame relaxed against Evan, tipping the tabletop just enough to one side to send the juice glasses crashing onto the tiles. Neither of them moved. Evan willed away the problems beneath their feet and continued his search for happiness, sliding caresses down the side of her neck. With one eye open, Evan lifted his head and whispered, "Don't step down. We have a mess, and you're barefoot."

Amber pressed dewy lips against his cheek and murmured, "No sir, my heels just now healed."

Evan's housekeeper's swats with the coarse broom hairs forced Evan to break their embrace. Dust pan in hand, her warnings to shoo away the couple from the slivers of glass prompted him to tenderly lift her body into his arms as he rose from the chair.

Chastising him for his delay, the housekeeper popped him on the butt with the dustpan. "I'm going. I'm going." Evan cried while Amber stifled her giggles by burying her head into his muscular chest.

Steve ran onto the veranda, "Well, did you ever mess up." Steve quipped, "Romeo, where were you when they slipped past us again.?"

"Who?" Evan knew the answer before he asked.

"Leah and Charlie, of course." Steve fussed. "You were our last line of defense."

Evan sat Amber gently down on the outdoor lounger and stared deep into her eyes, "What do you know about this?"

Amber's sorrowful cry told him everything he needed to know.

"Amber, where were they going?" He asked calmly, tucking a strand of hair behind her ear, clearing a path for his questioning look.

A tear trickled down her cheek. "You don't betray the ones you love," she cried. "I'm sorry, Evan. They were only going over to the peninsula to explore. They took the beach cruisers. How dangerous could that be?"

His patience echoed in his words." Amber, you have no concept of how far away that is by car, much less bicycle."

Evan stood slowly and steeled his gaze on Steve. "God help us when I tell Brent. You and Cooper get the van."

"I'm going too. I helped start this mess. Charlie and Leah weren't the only ones. I'm just as guilty in a sense." Amber nervously looked at Evan. "I understand if you're mad with me."

"That's good because that means you grasp the severity of the unnecessary risk those two have placed themselves in. Your brother will have our heads. Let's go."

Evan marched across the lavish green lawn to the garage servant's door with Amber on his heels. When he yanked it open, he found Steve on his knees by the van. "What now?" He asked, throwing his hands in the air.

Steve scrubbed his chin in disbelief. "The tire's flat." He smiled and shook his head. "Can't say those two aren't resourceful."

Amber expelled a disgruntled, "Ugh, I can't believe them."

"And why are you mad?" Evan's eyebrows raised, questioning.

"They flattened the tire as a backup because they didn't trust me to hold my tongue and not tell you what was happening. The gall of those two." Amber exclaimed, stomping her foot in irritation.

Evan burst into a fit of laughter. "Steve, do we have a spare?"

"Yup, but it's going to take a bit of time to change. I'll get started." Steve reached for the lug wrench and went to work.

Amber strolled to the concrete stoop, planted her bottom on the step, and huffed.

"Now you know how I feel." Evan chuckled and tossed a frisky wink before leaving Amber to stew over the antics of her friends. Who were, by his guess, regretting their choice of transportation.

TWENTY-SEVEN

The white Range Rover sped down the estate's drive as if on autopilot to the marina's parking lot. Rafe stared straight ahead in awe. How could the events that now consumed his life involve his long-lost friend? Riding alongside Brent produced vivid flashbacks of their younger years - some great and some not-so-great. Brent never questioned his judgment in those days, standing by him through thick and thin. Who knew ten years later, this is where the men would end up – guarding each other's back again.

Rafe watched the island's scenic beauty whiz past him through the passenger window, much like his life. Everything had turned upside down when he made the difficult selection between his career and Amber. His ill-considered decision haunted him daily, never ceasing to remind him of the devasting choice. Their reconnection stoked a fire within him, left smoldering for way too long. All his thoughts lingered on her lips' taste, her skin's smell, and the flirtatious giggles. His senses struggled to weather the assault. Unsuccessful, Rafe dug into his neck muscles with anxious fingers.

"Rafe, you have to forget her." Brent's frank statement hurt.

"Believe me, I've tried. My decision forever torments me. I've wrestled my demons hundreds of miles away from her and lost the battle. You have no clue what she does to me, Brent. And now, seeing Amber all wrapped up in Evan Holcomb is driving me insane. I want her to choose me." Unsettling emotions seized control, his shaky tone riddled with regrets.

"Buddy, no good will come from the two of you rekindling a decade-old romance. You can't go back. It's too late, and that reunion will cause you more pain than happiness. Rafe, you'll forever be on some covert operation in who knows where. Worry, fear, and doubt would eat her alive."

Brent wheeled the Rover into the marina lot, rolling to a stop beside Paschal's red truck. "She's my sister, Rafe, and you're like a brother. I only want what's best for you and Amber, and 'together' is not the answer."

"I hear you, Brent. Still, a man can hope, can't he? Let's go. Paschal is probably going nuts alone in there with Jenkins." Rafe rounded the hood, slapped Brent on the shoulder, and muttered, "Thanks for always having my back."

Brent smiled, "Any time, man."

Rafe hustled to the office in search of his friend. "Paschal," he called.

Jenkins shifted the *Island News* from one page to the next, engrossed in the daily gossip. "Stop yelling. He's not here. I was hoping you could tell me why." Jenkins' curt reply left his lips a bit too soon.

"That's concerning since his truck's parked beside ours." Brent's presence and snarky comment startled Old Man Jenkins. Flustered, his hasty discard of the *Island News* sent his prized cap clambering onto the floor.

"Well… my boy, I didn't know you were here. How's your lovely sister and her nice friend?" Jenkins eyed Brent coolly.

"Doing better, thank you. We appreciate all of your concern."

"Of course, of course. Our clients and their safety are

of the utmost importance to us. How much longer will you be visiting our little paradise?"

Rafe noted Jenkins' prying questions. He sensed Old Man Jenkins would never be happy until Brent and Evan's entire party left his island.

"Soon. We still have a few more places to explore. Right now, I'm more concerned about Paschal than whether we extend our vacation. Any idea where he could be?" It was Brent's turn to prod Jenkins for answers.

Jenkins' disapproving stare locked with Brent's. Old Man Jenkins disliked anyone who challenged him, and Rafe knew he saw Brent as a challenge.

"How should I know?" Jenkins grumbled, returning to his paper. "Culliver, that's your job."

Rafe rummaged through the old file. "I've got it. We can call him on the way." He shoved the address in his pocket and addressed Jenkins in his preferred manner. "I'll do my best to return within the hour, sir. Okay?" His attempt to soothe the older man's ruffled temper seemed to work.

"Do what you must, young man. I'll be here a while longer." Jenkins raised his hand and shooed Rafe on his way.

Brent hopped back in the Rover and scrubbed his chin. "He's a testy one, isn't he?"

"You get used to him." Rafe laughed and dialed Paschal's number, anticipating his usual upbeat vibe. Instead, the voice of his sassy, petite island bartender greeted him. "Hello." Confused, Rafe stared at the display. It was Paschal's.

Griping "hello's" echoed from the receiver. "Look, ya gotta talk to me, or I'm hangin' up." The woman spouted, smacking her gum.

"Don't hang up. It's Rafe Culliver. Is Paschal close by?"

"Oh…. Heyyy…I didn't recognize ya number." Joy

radiated from her now-friendly tone. "He's wit' me." She tossed nonchalantly.

"With you? Can I speak to him?" Rafe shook his head. Another conquest added to Paschal's long list.

"Sure, hold on. Hey, ya wanna meet me later?" Her feisty island slang dripped with endless promise.

"Um, can't tonight. Thanks, though." Rafe muted his phone when he noticed Brent's insinuating smile, "Don't even." He growled.

"Rafe, what up, dude. I guess Charlie told you about our eventful morning." He laughed.

"Yes and no. Charlie gave me her side, which isn't important right now. Are you good?"

"Yeah, dude, no breaks. I should be up and moving around with a brace in a day. May not be fast." Paschal's cheery attitude never faltered.

"Good to hear, buddy. Were you successful?"

Rafe knew the hitch in Paschal's breathing spelled trouble. "Um, Charlie didn't tell you?"

"Tell me what?"

"Nothing, dude. These pain pills are doing a number on me. Nope, it wasn't there. I searched everywhere. Sorry."

"No worries," Rafe murmured in dismay. "Rest today. I'll cover with Jenkins. Mind if I borrow your truck?"

"No problem. Keys are inside, under the driver's seat. Be good to her." Paschal laughed.

"Definitely. Don't worry about work. Talk to you tomorrow."

Paschal's hasty "Thanks, dude," drove Rafe to distraction. Charlie, as usual, knew more than she'd let on, along with Paschal. Irritated, he tucked the phone beneath his leg and groaned.

"Rafe, where does he live? I can't keep driving in circles." Brent asked, rounding the street corner for the third time.

"We're not going to see him. Paschal is predisposed. Head back to the marina. Jenkins will want an explanation, and I'm going to grab Paschal's truck."

"Truck? Then what?" Brent questioned.

"Back to the Vitamin Sea. The women did a number on us this morning. The story they concocted was BS. If my instincts are correct, Charlie's gone off on some rogue mission, and we may need another vehicle." Rafe buried his head in sweaty palms. His life was spinning out of control.

Brent cracked his neck, releasing his pent-up stress with a loud pop. "Dang, I knew Leah wasn't being honest. That woman can make my blood boil." Brent jerked his phone from the console. "Looks like I should make some calls, and someone better answer."

Brent's face flushed redder with each unanswered call, sending Rafe into a full-blown rant over his sister's actions.

"Amber has never listened to us. She'll never learn. She makes me crazy." Rafe raked his fingers across the top of his head.

"And your point is?" Brent ranted. "You're not telling me anything I don't already know."

Brent pressed the Range Rover's "AC" button, placing it on the lowest setting. Both men fumed over the women's trickery. Their blood pressures surged to explosive levels during their return to the marina office. Rafe exited the Rover and promised to meet Brent in an hour. He sighed. More dubious behavior was on the rise from the entire group.

This mission's going to kill me.

Stabbing pains rolled through his head. Anger and worry preoccupied his thoughts. The unknown overrode his usual precise, rationalized approach to success. Rafe remained convinced the map held the key to his mission.

His troubled footsteps creaked on the old planking, carrying him back to another source of concern, Jenkins.

Rafe returned to the office to discover Jenkins bent over the *Island News*, pen in hand, engrossed in the small six-page daily periodical. His unexpected arrival threw the elder into a tizzy, slapping the papers closed and secured with a quick fold.

"Back so soon?" Jenkins' icy stare didn't fool Rafe this time.

"Unfortunately, Paschal's not well, and he won't be able to make it in today," Rafe reported.

"I'm not surprised. Paschal eats crap. Can't keep a body lean and trim, ingesting junk." The man proclaimed, rapping his palm against his stomach. "As usual, you're in charge, Culliver. Make me proud." He smiled, retrieved his cap and cane, and headed for the door.

"Mr. Jenkins," Rafe called.

Paused in mid-stride, his boss spun about, "What?" He snarled.

"Mind if I close a little early?"

"Why, have some impending obligations to fulfill with that new crew of yours?" Jenkins croaked in a superior tone.

"Possibly." Rafe mimicked Jenkins - a man of few words.

"Wise choices always prevail over impulsive ones, my boy. Therefore, I assume you have a good reason. Close whenever." Jenkins replied, and he was gone.

Rafe's opinion of Jenkins never swayed. The man's broken heart over the loss of his love had made him stern, straightforward, and disciplined, much like himself after his loss of Amber. Perhaps that explained why Rafe felt comfortable around the man. They suffered from a similar plight, only years apart.

As Rafe reached for the office key, his hand brushed the neatly folded *Island News* nestled on the desk's corner.

Jenkins never left his paper behind. Rafe picked up the paper. His intention to return the item to Jenkins before his departure was doused with disaster. Due to a hasty grab, the flimsy pages fell disheveled all over the floor. Shuffling the printed mess into a pile, he noticed a series of odd handwritten doodles.

Once in order, the thin newspaper Jenkins submersed himself in each morning displayed the normal mundane island articles: weather, events, local happenings. However, Rafe's attention veered to the paper's random offset printing. Jenkins had encircled single alphabetic characters exposed by the black ink rings. The letters intermittently linked to scribbles and notes at the bottom of the page. Intrigued, Rafe settled on the stool and jotted the letters down, forming his version of an anagram. A jumbled hodgepodge jumped to life before him in a message that chilled Rafe to the bone.

Twelve's time running short – storm coming – make the move.

TWENTY-EIGHT

Charlie and Leah guided their bicycles from the gravel drive onto the winding road. The white beach cruisers modeled the iconic style of Miss Gulch from The Wizard of Oz. Pedaling faster or slower made no difference. The build of their transportation screamed "tourist," and it went at only one speed. Charlie took the lead; their preplanned route piped through her phone to ear pods. She tried to hide her displeasure in front of Leah. The peninsula by road versus water was much further than she'd anticipated, especially on the touring relics they rode. Left with no option, they'd need to make the best of it.

Her beckoning hand wave encouraged Leah to move closer. Leah was lagging too far behind, adding concern to Charlie's already restricted time constraints. Charlie extended her arm and pointed to the small sandy clearing on their right. She eased her cruiser to a stop and cringed as Leah stopped her bicycle inches from Charlie's calf.

"Having trouble?" Charlie asked.

"This seat hurts my butt, the whole frame wobbles, and the brakes are crap. Any other questions?" Leah complained. "I don't know why I let you talk me into this."

"You have to stay closer. We don't have a lot of time, Leah."

"Then we should have taken the van." She hissed.

"You know that wasn't an option. Cooper and Steve would've noticed immediately. Just try to keep up with me." Charlie planted her foot in the sand and pushed off.

"Ugh, okay…." Leah moaned, shoving the ancient hunk of junk back onto the asphalt.

Charlie breathed a sigh of relief. Leah's bike hugged the white line and her fender as the two pedaled onward. Traffic was sparse, allowing the women to venture further out in the lane. She was ever so grateful that there were no hills on their route. Aided by the smooth surface, they could make up a bit of time.

Charlie glanced over her shoulder and tossed a thumbs-up of encouragement to Leah, receiving a toothy grin in response. Charlie giggled. She knew Leah was complaining under her breath, but her friend carried on in support of Charlie's mission.

Unable to resist the temptation, Charlie turned and stuck out her tongue, egging Leah on in jest. Rattled by the vehicle speeding up behind them, her cruiser's front tire strayed onto the loose gravel, shaking the frame. Her knuckles washed white in her tight grip on the handlebars.

Charlie wrestled the bicycle back to the flat ground and yelled, "Leah, don't stop. Keep pedaling as fast as you can."

"Won't do any good. These things have one speed." Leah's oblivious reaction was a good sign. She followed Charlie's earlier directions and stayed safely on her tail. If Leah panicked, they were both going down quickly, making themselves prime targets.

Leah shouted, "Think we should let this black car go by us? There's a dirt road ahead."

"NO!" Charlie screamed. "The peninsula is just past that road."

Charlie's internal "red alert" flashed franticly. Even though Charlie couldn't see the back half of the sedan, she recognized the sizeable frame in the passenger's seat. With no plan other than to pedal - and run when necessary - she and Leah steered straight by the little dirt path to the narrow trail leading them onto the peninsula and Bonfire Beach.

Leah's front tire scraped against Charlie's fender. "He's going to hit me." She cried, pushed closer and closer to Charlie's bike by the speeding car.

"Hang on," Charlie yelled. Her bicycle darted across the path into the tree line. "We're almost there."

Charlie maneuvered the cruiser through the tropical forest. The black sedan followed in hot pursuit, paralleling their movements along the makeshift road.

"Get ready to jump off and run, Leah." The old bike's wheels, entangled with green vines, slowed on the overgrown path as it narrowed. Forced to ditch the bikes, Charlie shouted, "Now," shoving her bike to the ground, and cried, "Leah, hurry." Charlie eyed her pursuer's vehicle, their quest stalled by the dead-end road.

Leah threw her bike down and grabbed Charlie's shirttail. "Who are they?"

"Not sure, but I don't think they're interested in being friends. Run!"

In a sprint, the women raced toward the sounds of crashing waves. Close by, loud commands, "Get them," spurred their steps. Charlie's outstretched palms pushed overgrown bushes from her eyes. Cracks of open sky filtered the sun's rays ahead of her as encroaching footsteps hustled behind. Caught in between, Charlie scrambled, pressing forward, Leah in tow.

Just a couple more steps…

Stopped mid-dash by a tight grip on her forearm, Charlie lurched backward, sending Leah into a panic, terror-stricken by the man's sudden appearance. Leah released a blood-curdling scream.

Charlie's shocked expression disappeared as she struggled for release. His firm grasp embedded indentations on her arm, ensuring her compliance. Unable to move, she paused.

"I'm here to help you," He whispered.

"Who?" Her mysterious helper placed a finger to his lips, silencing her questions.

"You two were about to go off that embankment head first."

Doubting his claim, Charlie peered past the tree fronds. One step further would've sent them tumbling down a massive drop-off onto the beach. Leah stood horrified, her open mouth clamped shut by Charlie's flat palm.

"Go that way." He pointed to their new route. "The drop is shorter. Jump and head straight for the dock. I'll send these two on a different path. Hurry." The man smiled and headed back into the foliage.

Charlie issued a swift "thanks" and pulled Leah along. Their feet flew as if carried on angel's wings, bringing them to the short slope. Skidding down the hill on their bottoms, Charlie and Leah spotted the tip of the dock protruding into the clear waters. Leah's sandals filled with sand, slowing her pace as Charlie dropped back and yanked her friend's hand. The two hurried around the curve to safety. In just a few yards, they were home free. Their joy was short-lived as the two out-of-breath women eyed the dock, then stopped motionless on the beach, bent over.

Home free, indeed. Nothing could be further from the truth.

Poised, ready for a battle, stood three very angry men only yards away: Brent, Rafe, and Evan.

TWENTY-NINE

Displeased with his partner's botched shenanigans, Slim sat behind the steering wheel this time. Pleased he had followed his gut, Slim watched and waited. Parked catty-cornered to the vast estate's driveway gave him an expansive view of its tenants' comings and goings. His futile efforts to catch Culliver in a vulnerable position had miserably failed countless times. So, Slim contrived a plot to glean information from a different source. It made no matter to him whether the provider was male or female. His mark just needed to be an easy target, ripe for the taking.

Their short wait afforded the henchmen a golden opportunity. Like a brightly-wrapped gift, the two women strolled to the end of the drive. Their mode of transportation elated Slim. The old wide-tire bicycles they mounted offered no challenge to his mission. It would be a breeze to overtake them, force the women off the side, and choose one.

Slim's sly grin encouraged his hulky friend. "We've got them now," he bragged.

He watched the two glide down the road, headed away from town. It was an unexpected but welcome choice, with less traffic and even fewer witnesses. Angry that he hadn't considered this plan earlier, Slim fussed over the time lost while he edged onto the blacktop two-lane.

"Go get 'em." His passenger ordered.

"Not yet. Let's see where they're going." Slim's

speed kept him well behind the bicycles during their journey.

"Those two stupid bikes are worthless. They could never outrun us. Can't we take care of this?" Two oversized fists pounded on the dash in frustration.

For once, Slim's brawny partner made sense. He was growing tired of the endless trips to nowhere. All the signs directed him to a dead end ahead. Slim's firm press of the gas pedal propelled him to within a foot of the second bicycle's back tire. The frightened woman peered at him over her shoulder. His partner's sneaky grin greeted her, prompting hasty increased pedaling. The women's feet slipped off the wide foot pedals in their fight to place a gap between them and the sedan.

"Look." His friend chuckled at their pointless efforts.

Slim released a small chuckle of his own. Being the bad guy was starting to feel too good to him. Amused by the fact his prey actually believed they could get away.

The bicycles' sharp turn onto a narrow path forced Slim to steer the car down an adjacent dirt road. He glared at the two from his window and watched them jump off. The women dropped the old two-wheelers to the ground and ran. Unable to advance the car further, Slim threw the vehicle into park, left the motor running, and ordered his partner's pursuit of the fleeing females.

Slim pounded on the steering wheel in frustration over his injury. In his current condition, he would never be able to traverse the dense brush fast enough to overtake them. He could hear his mammoth friend crashing through the overgrowth, expelling an angry "ouch" periodically.

His cohort returned minutes later, livid and cut up. "It's too overgrown, and I swear I heard a man's voice. I told you to snag them on the road." He exclaimed, pulling ripped vine leaves from his hair and clothes.

Enough is enough, he mumbled to himself. While grand in stature and intimidating in looks, his partner lacked the mobility and brains required to succeed with any plan. He needed another able-bodied individual to help since his injury hadn't healed. His boss would have to cough up the cash if he wanted the cargo that bad. Slim flipped the car's blue tooth off and placed the call.

Happy with the outcome, Slim smiled. Someone was already in place on the island.

~

Brent's panicked tone jarred Rafe from the chilling decoded message laid before him. He stood still, dumbfounded that Old Man Jenkins was involved. That thought boggled his mind.

"Give me ten." He blurted.

"Wait, Evan and I are on our way to you. We could use your help."

"What now?" Rafe questioned.

"We're going to need a boat, quick. Leah and Charlie decided that they would explore the peninsula alone."

"We can be there in no time by water. I'll meet you on the docks."

"Be there in five." Brent voiced.

Rafe closed the cryptic newspaper and stuffed it inside his shirt. What role did Jenkins play in this never-ending saga? He had stumbled upon the message out of sheer luck. Jenkins made it a habit of tucking the paper under his arm before donning his favored cap. Until today. Had Brent's "noncompliance" rattled the man so much that he left without it? Or was his "error" a calculated move? Either way, Rafe would closely monitor Jenkins' activities in the coming days.

With a slam of the office door, Rafe sprinted toward the Contender. The vessel sat fueled and readied within minutes. Brent, Evan, and Amber rushed aboard the boat, silent and expressionless.

Why is she here?

Amber's blatant avoidance of interaction with him

spoke volumes. His stomach lurched. Deep down, the truth gnawed at his insides. Rafe wrestled with his bruised feelings as he listened to Brent's backstory on why they were speeding to the peninsula. Brent's words passed through one ear and out the other. Rafe couldn't process anything except the pain of knowing it was his fault he'd lost Amber.

The sleek craft crossed the distance at top speeds. Once tethered to the battered, rusted cleats, the group leaped onto the rickety, splintered dock.

"Listen," Amber lowered her head and strained. "You hear that?"

Her comment brought the three men into formation in front of her, forming a human shield.

Rafe, in tune with the rustling through the foliage, struggled to see the cause. Green outgrowths swayed to and fro.

Is it just the wind or the women…

"I'm heading up to the tree line. I'll sweep left to right." Brent barreled to the dock's end with Rafe and Evan close behind. Evan pointed to his right before the men's feet could hit the sand. Running full speed around the curved inlet were Leah and Charlie.

Brent's clenched jaw riffled in anger. "That look means trouble. Did either of you see anything?"

"Not yet," Evan said, his body tensed.

"Nope." Rafe signaled, eyeing their perimeter.

No one budged, including the ladies on the beach. The rustling continued briefly, and then the air fell silent. Leah and Charlie slowly, sheepishly, moved toward the three men. Rafe marveled at Brent's composure with Leah. He would have spewed a spirit-filled tongue-lashing regarding her actions; however, Brent's gentle grasp of her hand professed concern, not anger.

One day, I'll experience that joy.

"Leah, do I need to ask what you were thinking?"

Brent coolly stroked her palm with his thumb.

Charlie spoke up in her friend's defense. "I'm afraid this is all my doing. The investigator side of me felt compelled to come here. There's something strange about this peninsula. And as usual, my instincts were on target. The same henchman that attacked Cooper last night tried to abduct us."

Rafe scrutinized her story, "How could you know that?"

Charlie's brown eyes glowed when she announced. "Because I followed him on the grounds back to his partner and getaway car. There's no mistaking this man. He fits Carol's description to the letter. He's quite brawny."

"Why didn't you tell us this last night?" Brent groaned.

Charlie spouted back, "Remember, the four of us were supposed to share our ideas. That is, before Carol's fright, when you gentlemen conceived your own plan." Her knowing glare ended any further argument from the men.

Leah encircled Brent's waist and cuddled him close. "And the Hulk would have succeeded in his pursuit if our guardian angel hadn't shown up."

Amber's blue eyes popped open. "What guardian angel?"

"Out of nowhere, the man said he was there to help us. Without him, we would have plunged into certain disaster. He pointed us to the beach and led our attackers away. He was a Godsend." Leah's face washed with relief.

Brent's brows drew together. "Really…and what did this guardian look like?"

"You don't believe me?" Leah puffed.

"I didn't say that, now did I?" Brent's tone mellowed.

"Well, for your information," she huffed. "The young man was about your height, athletic build, very clean cut."

Rafe's quick inhale resulted in two words. "Wilder James."

Charlie froze. “Who?”

“Someone I met at the marina,” Rafe muttered.

“Rafe, should we assume there’s a connection between you and Wilder James?” Brent asked.

“No assumptions needed. Wilder’s appearance here aligns with my earlier conclusions, validating one important factor. He’s on our side.” Rafe’s face washed with relief. “Where did he go, Charlie?”

Charlie’s wise smile locked on Rafe. “He led the Hulk away long enough for us to escape, and we never saw him again. My guess would be back to his safe zone, which I’m betting is somewhere on this peninsula.” She beamed.

“If you two could stop challenging each other,” Evan directed his statements to Charlie and Rafe with the whisk of his finger. “And share what you know, we’d all be better off.”

“Holcomb, are you implying…?” Rafe’s temperament sharply rose.

Evan dropped his head and rubbed tight neck muscles. “Good Lord, you two don’t even see it.”

Brent nudged Evan in the side. “They will,” he said.

Evan placed his arm around Amber’s shoulders and escorted her back to the boat. Brent followed suit, easing Leah and Amber in their seat, leaving them sporting blank stares into each other's eyes.

Now alone with Rafe on the dock, Charlie lifted her head, staring up at Rafe’s tall frame.

“We don’t have much time,” Rafe professed. “Old Man Jenkins is involved somehow, and now Wilder. The attacks are escalating. Don’t you think it would be easier if we worked together instead of trying to one-up each other?”

“Why, Mr. Culliver, you took the words right out of my mouth.” Charlie nodded toward the boat. “They’ll have to know too.”

“I know.” He moaned. “My career’s probably over

after this anyway. I've screwed this thing up in every way possible."

"I'd beg to differ. I think you're doing just fine, considering." Charlie grinned.

Rafe sensed watchful eyes on them as he and Charlie drifted back to the Contender. One final check of the foliage provided no insight into who watched from beyond the beach.

Charlie shrugged her shoulders and tossed Evan a smile. "Guess you'll have to buy new cruisers for the Vitamin Sea."

Leah grumbled, wiggling around on the cushion. "Oh Lord, don't mention those bikes. Ditching those was one of the best things that could have happened. My bum will be sore for weeks."

"Nice cool pool water will loosen your muscles, my dear. I'm ready to relax." Brent's teasing grin rolled over Leah.

"I'll need it." Leah sobbed, her stiff arms lifting her bottom from the seat each time the boat bounced on a wave. Spontaneous laughter rolled across the craft. Rafe's participation was a cover to lure his friends' focus away from the impending troubles. He had little choice. Rafe angled the Contender back into the slip, burdened by the day's events. His head ached from trying to force the puzzle pieces together, and time was slipping away. Chattering all the way down the boardwalk, the group started for their cars, issuing promises to see Rafe in an hour.

Rafe bent down, checking the tied rope cleats one final time when he heard a soft "Hey." Towering over him stood Amber, hands on her hips. "Think we could talk for a minute?" She smiled.

Rising slowly, he couldn't help but think his bad day was about to get worse. "Sure," Rafe grunted.

Amber headed to a weathered bench outside the

marina office, barely large enough to seat them. Rafe watched her scoot to the far edge of the splintering wood before squeezing in beside her, drinking in all of her beauty in the tropical sun. Bright blue eyes stared into his. His body tensed in remembrance. Their moonlit nights, sensual kisses, and shared promises created a smoldering flame within him through her eyes. From her perspective, Rafe saw only pain, not joy, and that pierced his heart like a sharp knife.

Her intense gaze displayed a newfound strength Rafe had never seen. Her lips parted as she whispered, “Rafe, I’m so thankful your family chose the house across from mine all those years ago. We had so many good times then, but those days are over. Our plan just went awry somewhere, changed by life’s circumstances. I don’t blame you for leaving. Truly. We will never be the couple our younger selves pretended we could. Our lives are too different. I know your career means the world to you, and I’d never ask you to change that now. I prefer you look at me as a sister rather than an annoying nuisance holding you back.” Amber playfully nudged his shoulder. “And honestly, it makes me breathe a little easier at night knowing you’re out there protecting people from the world's evils.”

Her pause gave Rafe one final moment to linger in her angelic eyes. “While my heart is breaking, if I said I was surprised, it would be a lie. I made my mistake years ago when I decided the excitement of the adventure outweighed the idea of married life in a small town. My unwillingness to settle for the white picket fence has caused me many sleepless nights. If a sister is all I can have, then a sister is what I’ll take. Besides, Holcomb doesn’t seem all that bad.” Rafe tossed her a playful wink.

Amber placed a quick kiss on his cheek and patted his knee. “Come on. We start fresh tomorrow. Time for some fun.”

"I'll be there soon. Go ahead." He struggled to keep up the façade and hide his pain. Her wide grin filled one of the small holes in his heart as she walked away. The rest would take time. Day by day, his heart would mend, he hoped.

THIRTY

A renewed sense of confidence flooded Amber's soul. Her straight frame and effortless stride caught Evan's attention, causing his swift turn for a second glance. Amber immediately noticed his pearly white smile, to which she tossed a sexy wink. Heavy-laden years of anxiety, despair, and "what ifs" released their bonds the moment her honest conversation with Rafe ended. She smiled inwardly. This Amber Scott was a new woman, hopelessly in love with the gorgeous male specimen sitting across the room.

Sunshine, the infinity pool's glistening water, and her cheerful mood emboldened her decision. Sauntering up to the group of men, she leaned down and placed a breathy whisper in Evan's ear. With a confident toss of her sarong, Amber headed into the pool with a grin. Red-faced and exuberant, Evan hastily shoved his chair from the table. His abrupt "Excuse me, gentlemen" left his friend's mouths gaping.

Amber purposefully swam to the far ledge, propped her elbows on the seamless wall, and balanced her floating lower torso, fluttering kicks underneath the water. Her attention centered on the one man in this world who loved her for her and all her glorious imperfections, Evan Holcomb. With smooth, effortless strokes, he glided up beside her, sporting a brilliant smile.

"I'm not sure what has come over you, but if my opinion matters, I like it." He grinned.

Amber whisked her toes along his calf, urging him closer with a nod. The cool pool relaxed her tired muscles and offered a final release of stress. The two turned toward the open seas, absorbing the panoramic setting sun's radiance.

"Evan," she said softly. "You know I stayed behind today to talk to Rafe."

The corners of his mouth curved downward. "I do."

"We had a long overdue heart-to-heart."

"And…?" His cobalt eyes never left the falling sunset.

"I clarified my feelings for him. He's a friend and a second brother, no more. Rafe understands now that we could never be a 'couple.' And I must admit a heavy weight lifted from my chest as the words left my lips. I can truly breathe for the first time in quite a while." Amber stammered, "Truth be told, I think there's only one person who will now and forever more hold my heart."

Evan focused his slanted gaze in Amber's direction. "Really, now. Do I know him?"

"Forever, teasing," she exclaimed, slapping her palm on the water, sending a soaking splash in his face.

Releasing a low chuckle, Evan wiped the salty spray from his eyes. "You," he bellowed, showering her with a drenching twice as large. She ducked under the water and surfaced behind him.

Evan quickly spun around to face her head on. Hands cupped, waiting for more. Unconcerned about her friends mingling at the pool, Amber paddled closer and hooked her arms through Evan's, their bodies floating in the cool, refreshing water. She searched his eyes, gazing into his soul. What she saw warmed her heart beyond measure. Beside her was a man filled with compassion, hope, yearning, and, most importantly, love. His brilliant blue, serene gaze brought forth an inner peace that calmed her like never before. Overcome with happiness, Amber brushed her wet, salty lips across his as she absorbed the strength and positivity that flowed from him and filled her. She knew trouble lurked on their doorstep, and more lay ahead, but for tonight, she would enjoy being in Evan's arms surrounded by their friends. Her heart finally felt free and alive.

Shouts of happiness flooded the veranda and pool when Paschal arrived. He struck a pose in his new protective boot, not a cast. The petite female beside him shook her head in jest over his antics.

"See, I said you could count on old Paschal no matter what, even though I may not be able to run. I won't need to if you guys rough 'em up before they get to me." He laughed. "Hey, everyone, this is Jaden. She was kind enough to chauffeur me around all day.

"Thank you, Jaden," Charlie gratefully shouted. "Join us."

"If ya sure, don't want to impose." She smiled.

"We don't want to disrupt your evening if you have other plans. I'd be happy to care for Paschal for the rest of the evening." Rhonda's sassy comment proclaimed her plans for Paschal.

"Really now? I know Paschal pretty good, ya see, and he can be a lot to handle." Jaden's feisty island temper flared. "I'd love to stay wit' ya and enjoy some grilled splendor." She pointed toward the smoking outdoor barbeque before glaring at Rhonda.

"Awe, ladies, I'll take all the help I can get from you two beautiful women." Paschal smiled at Rhonda and hobbled over to the rattan lounger.

"Great." Rhonda huffed, beating a path to the beverage bar.

Amber and Evan dangled their bodies from the pool wall and watched the sparks fly. Evan noted Rhonda's fiery red cheeks and turned to Amber, "Think she'll ever change?"

"Unfortunately, not when it comes to men." Amber giggled. "Want to go join them?"

The familiar athletic frame's appearance under the veranda canopy prompted Evan's hasty response, "Nope, no, I do not. I'm happy right here." He smiled and hugged Amber tight. His husky laughter was the last thing she heard when he pushed her beneath the water as if attempting to conceal her presence. A pinch of Evan's leg brought her to the surface, expelling giggles.

"Let's sit," Amber said, leading Evan to the shallow end. Perched on the submerged bar stool, Evan by her side, Amber watched Rafe. She tossed a wave of reassurance in his direction. Rafe's faint smile and return wave meant he was okay. Or so Amber hoped. She eyed his confident stride. If he weren't, she nor anyone else would ever know.

~

Rafe's penetrating observance of the playful couple found its way to the pool long before anybody noticed his arrival. Amber and Evan suited one another, much to his dismay. Unwilling to rehash Amber's decision, he scanned the impromptu party for Brent. Floored by the 5'2" frame sitting beside Paschal, balled fists rubbed his astonished eyes for a clearer view. Confounded by the vision, Rafe paused. What was she doing here?

The petite woman's spirited smile greeted Rafe's gaze. Jaden motioned him over and touched the chair next to her. Sandwiched in between Rhonda and Jaden sat an elated Paschal. His magnetism must render him irresistible with the ladies. Rafe's amused look stilled on Paschal, who responded with a shoulder shrug.

"Surprise," chuckled the island beauty.

"Like my chauffeur, dude? Jaden's been carting me around all day."

"At least I know ya told me the truth about being busy tonight."

"Honesty is one of my more admirable qualities."

Rafe jested.

"Most of the time." Charlie's exclamation from behind Rafe wasn't a shock, considering the bubbling camaraderie brewing between the two. And he kind of liked it.

"Of course, you would say that." He mumbled.

"Sorry, it's a personal opinion. Not shared by those two, obviously." Charlie's twinkling eyes landed on Jaden and Paschal.

Keenly aware of Charlie's antics, Rafe quickly steered the conversation elsewhere, "Seen Brent?"

"Huddled up at the table with Leah and the others. Why don't we join them." She tucked her arm under his and whisked Rafe away from Jaden. "We need to get rid of her." Charlie's tense demand returned Rafe's thoughts to the cryptic newspaper warning.

"I know that. Have any suggestions, Ms. Know It All?" He retorted.

"Talk to Paschal. His dinner will make him very ill, requiring his immediate departure. Capiche?" Charlie piped.

Rafe eyed his petite accomplice. Her curly red hair highlighted demanding green eyes. Disinclined to allow Charlie to think she was in control, Rafe growled, "We'll see."

The Vitamin Sea's chef's bolstering summons called the crowd to attention. Hungry mumbles accompanied the famished group to the expansive dining room table. After a grueling day, the delectable smells of Jerk Chicken, conch fritters, and the like made their mouths water.

Rafe watched in awe as Paschal shoveled food into his mouth at a record pace, barely pausing to chew. Paschal's sudden cupping of his lips signaled Rafe's success with the plan. Pleased with himself, Rafe looked at Charlie and tipped his glass. Her broad, satisfied smile caught Rafe's notice before he continued.

"Buddy, you good?"

Covering a spontaneous gag, Paschal grimaced. "I don't feel so well. I shouldn't have doubled my medication tonight." Moans and belly clutches reinforced Paschal's plight. "I need to go home. NOW. Jaden, can you take me?"

Jaden's restrained irritation fell on Rafe. "Guess I'll have to miss the important stuff. I was hoping to find out a couple of secrets about ya this evening." She winked.

Rafe ignored her flirtation and rose to assist his friend. Rhonda's firm tone returned him to his seat. "I'm perfectly capable of helping him to the car, Rafe. My poor Paschal needs a tender touch." She smiled.

Seemingly angered by Rafe's rejection, Jaden declared, "Uh, ya forget who's taking him home, blondie."

"I'm sorry; what did you just say?" Rhonda spouted, tugging Paschal to her. Jaden responded with a yank of her own as a battle ensued.

Paschal moaned louder, "Oww, careful, ladies." The two women hauled his hunched frame out the door, each jerking the man from side to side.

"Shouldn't one of you guys go out with them?" Leah asked. "He doesn't look very stable."

Rafe smiled. "It's not Paschal I'm worried about." No sooner than the words left his mouth, Rhonda stormed back into the villa.

"The nerve of that woman. If she thinks I'll give up Paschal that easy, she's wrong." Rhonda stomped, tapping her toe furiously against the tile squares. "She doesn't know Rhonda Wright."

"Rhonda, you can calm down. Paschal's illness was a self-induced fake." Charlie laughed. "We needed Jaden to leave." Charlie yielded to Rafe with a swipe of her hand, "Your turn."

Rafe surveyed the room, landing his focus on Brent.

"My time is almost up. To fill you in on all the details

at this late hour will increase your risk of harm and jeopardize my mission. Charlie and I will move forward working as a team for reasons I cannot and dare not explain. The rest of you still have a choice." Rafe's gloomy stare converged on the group.

"We know most of the story, Rafe. To say I'm curious about how deep Charlie's connection runs would be an understatement. As I've told you before, we are with you. Tell us what you want us to do." Brent's suspicious look moved to Charlie.

"Like he said, for reasons we can't explain," Charlie said. "Just know I'd never betray any of you."

"Tomorrow, we move. And this is how it will work…" Rafe informed.

Over the next hour, Rafe outlined the plan, awe-struck by the grit and courage of his new comrades, especially Charlie. With only a few days to fulfill, Rafe prayed his strategy was foolproof. Charlie's zealous cooperation had surprised him. She accepted her role with little complaint. Of course, he knew he would need to keep her close and protected. Her welfare wasn't only important to her sisters; it was also pertinent to their "mutual friends," who regarded her in high esteem. Important enough to share top-secret information.

Conflicting emotions ravaged his heart. While he was elated that Amber would be safe and secure with Evan, Rafe mourned the loss of that protective position, like the death of a friend. Surviving this mission hinged on his ability to handle the role reversal.

~

Shades of bronze and orange glimmered on the horizon, offering a new day's bright outlook. Sunshine poured through the Vitamin Sea's glass panes with golden promises of success. Amber lounged across the cushioned window seat, her ankles crossed, staring serenely at the soothing Caribbean waters. Prayers of thankfulness and protection flowed from her. Creases pinched the outer corners of her eyes, spurred by a broad smile. Her body tingled with a wonderous sense of joy. While her day lay chocked full of the unknown, she remained unafraid with Evan by her side.

Amber giggled softly, amazed at how the short island getaway had turned her world upside down. Her life had been riddled with old demons and ill-gotten feelings. Now, hopes of a new beginning embraced the day. Happiness engulfed her even as danger nipped at her heels.

She rose from the bench, stretching her arms high above her head. A lengthy bend to sweep a touch upon her toes elongated her tall frame. Crackles and pops provided ample relief to any lingering tightness in her spine. Deep cleansing breaths before her rise released a pleasured puff. Her observation of the essence of masculinity standing in her doorway filled her life with purpose. Elevated pulsing sensations dispelled her former tranquil mindset. Met with Evan's mischievous grin, Amber continued her stretches, struggling to remain unfazed. She leaned left, arm perched above her, toe pointed.

"Hello." Her perky response preceded a sudden swing to touch her calves.

Evan bent over, head flipped upside down, "Having fun?"

"You should try it sometime. Relax your muscles and tone your core." She spouted, lifting and bending to her right.

Evan hiked up his shirttail, exposing rippled abs. "You know, I think I'm good. I'll just watch you." Impish eyes stared into hers, urging her to respond.

Wise to his game, Amber rolled her eyes. All the while fighting to control the urge to run to him. "Suit yourself." Evan's deep chuckle steeled her restraint.

I'll show him.

Amber's long limbs twisted into a new pose, returning

her gaze to the blue waters over her shoulder.

"Today, please do what I tell you. As I recall, you completely disregarded my instructions the last time. I can't protect you if you don't." Nervousness replaced the prior twinkle in his eyes.

"I promise to do that only if I feel it's in OUR best interest. I worry just as much about your safety as you do mine, Evan Holcomb. And I see no reason to stand by the wayside if you're in danger." Amber huffed, pulling at the bands holding her lengthy strands in a ponytail.

"I can handle myself. Look at me. I'm not defenseless." Taut muscular arms crossed his chest.

"I'll have to trust you since Leah and Brent will be right behind us," Amber replied.

"I'm impressed." His devilish smile working its magic.

Amber's resilience softened. Evan's comment expressed his belief in her ability to protect them. "So, you admit I can help today?"

"No, not that." He coaxed.

"What, then?" Amber twirled a golden strand of hair through her fingers, toying with him as much as he was with her.

"Such dedication to your morning exercise routine. I'm going to head downstairs. Continue." He whisked a hand in her direction. Evan's turtle-paced turn revealed his motives to her.

Amber's gleeful steps carried her to him in seconds. "Where do you think you're going?" She asked, jumping in front of him. No longer able to withstand the irresistible gleam in his eyes, she squeezed both cheeks and melded her lips to his. Her pleased moan stifled his satisfied chuckle. Amber raised her mouth slowly, savoring the moment. She coiled his dark tendrils around her fingers in satisfaction.

"Proud of yourself, aren't you?" She teased, nuzzling

the tip of her nose against his cheek.

"I was starting to think I'd lost my charm." His ragged, raspy answer was proof of her hold on him.

"Au contraire. You, Mr. Holcomb, will never lose your charm." Short pecks grazed along his chiseled jawline. Moist imprints lingered there while Amber made a path to his agreeable lips. Evan swallowed hard, a low growl of pleasure stuck in his throat. Limber hands gently massaged his neck before she entwined them behind his head. Plump lips hovered over Evan's, reassuring him she'd cooperate in today's tasks. Melting him in her grasp, Amber felt Evan's knees bend as he drew her closer. Her playful mood pulled them both into the danger zone. And there was no time for that.

Time to stop!

Her small backstep led to his unhappy moan. "You should know," Evan groaned, "You can try your charms on me anytime you like." Curved lips rose into a sexy grin.

"Evan Holcomb, you are impossible!" She cried. "I'll see you downstairs." Her steady push sent him through the threshold into the hall. Amber blew him a kiss and eased the door closed. Releasing a sigh, she laid her head back against the door frame and listened to the disgruntled mumbling that preceded heavy footsteps down the stairs.

I love that man.

~

In search of new scenery, Rafe ventured into the brightly lit sunroom. Gauzy curtain panels billowed in the morning breeze that whisked through rows of windows. Refreshed instantly by the salt air, he paused for a moment to inhale. He was happy to cleanse his body of the troubles that gnawed at his insides. Life, death, victory, defeat, and his career all rested on the success of his strategy.

Clutching his cup of "joe," Rafe walked up and back, spanning the room. Filled with astonishment, he pondered why one man needed an estate as vast as the Vitamin Sea.

His stride relaxed and slow as he perused the room's furnishings, lingering on three paintings. Neatly lined in a row, the scenes of everything from rainbow cottages and yacht-laden harbors to vibrant coastlines called to him. Colorful watercolors portrayed the island's tropical splendor from very different perspectives. The artist's renditions intended to draw the observer into an unimaginable paradise. Rafe studied each one as the sun's rays spilled onto the canvases. Reflections of their radiant strokes bounced off the glass enclosure. Eyeing their beauty, Rafe could understand how the local modest sidewalk artist had become so famous. World-renowned for his paintings, the celebrity hid among the townspeople. Protected by the islanders, Rafe only learned of his notoriety from Paschal.

Special as the renderings were, Rafe found himself fixated on one. Bending his knees, he slid back against the rattan sofa. Sipping his coffee, he scrutinized the vivid blue canvas markings. Unconcerned with Charlie's entry, his focus remained intact.

"Someone said you might be in here." Silence encompassed them. "Mesmerizing, aren't they?" She asked.

"Umm, hmm."

"I can tell you where to get one, if you like. Of course, no two are identical. Which one has you so enthralled?"

"The coastline."

"Funny, that one is mine. Amber bought the harbor print and Leah the other."

Rafe's eyebrows furrowed. "Any reason you purchased that one?"

"Oh no, I know that tone. No, Culliver, there's no particular reason. Not that you believe me." She snapped. "I liked the serenity. The vendor was having a sale. Amber insisted we get one. If you must know."

"Don't get testy. It was just a question." Rafe's nonchalant response contrasted with Charlie's.

"One never knows with you," Charlie tossed.

"Notice anything in the background?" Rafe's hazel eyes never parted from the canvas.

"Like…?"

"The cliff walls." He raked his forefinger back and forth on his lip.

"No." Charlie moved to within a foot of the painting. Squinting before stepping backward and up again. "I would say you amaze me, but I know it would go to your head." She chimed.

"So, you do see it!?"

"Barely, but it's there. Isn't it strange how the location vaguely resembles the area we marked?" Her uptick of excitement was evident.

"Strange indeed. I'd venture to say you were not the intended buyer for this print."

"Perhaps…" Charlie stared into the depths of the canvas. "Who then?"

"No clue. You ready?" He questioned, anxious to get moving.

"As I'll ever be." She extended her hand. Rafe grabbed ahold and pulled himself up.

"Let's go," he muttered, nudging her arm.

Spurred by fate, their unlikely partnership sparked a flame for newfound friendship. Smiling, Rafe followed Charlie out the door into the unknown. For now, they remained on task.

THIRTY-ONE

Crushed stone crackled underneath the wheels of the sporty cherry-red two-seater. Evan's dark mane blended in with the Porche's lush black interior. Tinted windows lowered, creating a cross breeze that whipped Amber's lengthy strands about her face. Slow rolling to a halt, Evan scanned right then left before he veered the Carrera toward town. Amber placed her hand on his atop the shiny stick shift. Fluid motions changed their speed, quickly moving them away from the estate.

Perfectly timed, Brent eased the Ranger Rover to a stop at the drive's end. Laughing, singing, and lofty giggles billowed from the three women inside. In stark contrast to the red Porsche, the white Rover entered the roadway, leaving a "party vibe" in the air. Cooper sat sandwiched between Carol and Rhonda. His chin, sporting a small bandage, angled sideways from his skirmish on the beach. Brent's eyes floated to the rearview mirror, then to Leah, and he stepped on the gas.

In flawless execution, Steve steered the van onto the blacktop two-lane. Precise fulfillment of the plan placed the occupants in motion, maneuvering their puzzle piece down the paved surface. Kimberly traveled shotgun with Suzanne seated behind her. Charlie's petite frame bounced in the center section. Rafe peered out the windows, searching for his former trackers. Because of his irresponsible actions, those "shadows" now only focused on him. He had drawn their attention elsewhere, endangering his new acquaintances. He prayed today would initiate steps to right that wrong.

With no indications of being followed, Rafe urged Steve onward. Each car's controlled speed placed the vehicles at a perfect pace with the other. The oversized van rolled on toward the marina where Paschal would be waiting. Rafe drew in a deep breath of apprehension.

"This is going to work, you know," Charlie said with assurance.

"True, if we find what we're searching for."

"We will. Keep the faith," she encouraged.

"The Rover's just ahead. No tail." Steve reported, adjusting his acceleration. Anxiety flowed through the van's riders as each watched the Ranger Rover split off, making a sharp left. Rafe sighed.

So far, so good

Combing his fingers through tousled hair, Rafe reviewed every calculated step like scenes from a movie. Unlike the "happy-go-lucky" façade traveling in front of them, his vehicle sat silent. Possibly burdened by "what ifs."

"We're here," Steve announced.

A blur in an endless cycle, the trip passed without notice for Rafe. Twenty minutes felt like two. Steve eased to a stop.

"Ready?" Rafe's hazel eyes sought agreement from each.

Anxious nods followed as the group exited the van. Pretentious smiles and senseless chatter accompanied the party into the marina office.

"What's up, good people?" Paschal greeted. He pointed to Rafe and teased, "You're late for work, dude."

"Yeah, whatever." Rafe tossed. "Has Jenkins arrived yet?"

Paschal's shoulders stiffened. "No, dude, and I hope

he doesn't before you get out of here."

Steve laughed. "I can't wait to meet this Mr. Jenkins. Paschal, you look terrified."

"He's a stern old dude. I'm not keen on straying from his policies. He weirds me out."

Kimberly tilted forward, staring out the aged, sea-sprayed window. Her troublesome question startled everyone. "Would this Mr. Jenkins drive a white GMC, perchance?"

Paschal jumped to attention. Fear contorted his expression. "He wasn't in the plan."

"So, we'll wing it." Charlie confidently chimed, patting Paschal's back.

Rafe heard the familiar clicking approach the door. His cane swung in the bend of his elbow as Jenkins strolled into the office. "How are you, sir?" Rafe's warm, cordial greeting made the elder man smile.

"Well… young man, it seems we have a full house. Always good for business, I say."

"You remember Charlie Ashby?"

"Of course. Glad to see you've recovered."

"This is Steve Alexander, Kimberly Vega, and Suzanne Harper."

Friendly greetings fell upon the man's curious expression.

"Lovely to see you all. What's brought you into my little slice of heaven today?"

"Those three," Rafe nodded in Steve's direction, "are interested in renting jet skis. And I'd like to accompany Charlie on her charter. That is if you don't mind, sir?

Paschal remained stoic and motionless.

"Good grief, Paschal, you look as though you've seen a ghost. Is there something I missed?" Jenkins' lips pressed firm, questioning.

Paschal wiped his forehead. "No. No. I'm going to get the equipment ready. You guys follow me." And he was off, leaving Rafe and Charlie to contend with Jenkins.

"Paschal is quite skittish today. Any idea why?" Jenkins asked, placing his cane on the worn wooden desktop.

"His incident with a ski's kill switch has made him leery of the things."

"What? Why wasn't I told?" His face enflamed, Jenkins threw his hat across the desk.

"We fixed the issue. No need to worry you. About Ms. Ashby's charter, do you have cause for me to remain here?"

Jenkins' slanted stare froze on Charlie. Met with her gracious smile, Jenkins mumbled, "By all means, accompany her. I don't want one of my guests out alone, especially Ms. Ashby."

Charlie's hesitant response resonated with Rafe. "How kind of you to be so concerned about my welfare. I appreciate your willingness to allow Mr. Culliver to come along." Her green eyes lingered on Jenkins.

"Don't trouble yourself, my dear. Today will provide you with a better experience than your last." Jenkins spouted, shuffling his desktop contents to and fro.

"Is there a problem?" Rafe knew the answer before he questioned the man.

"Just looking for something I thought was here. You two hurry on." Jenkins shooed them toward the door. "And tell Paschal he'll be in charge of the office."

"Any particular vessel you prefer we use?"

"No, take whichever you like." His tone escalated as nervous hands lifted rumpled papers.

"Okay. We won't be gone long." Rafe urged Charlie out the door. Turning back, Rafe paused, "Oh, sir. Would this happen to be what you're searching for?" Rafe reached behind his waistband.

The sly smile that crossed the older man's lips placed Rafe on notice. Reaching for the *Island News* neatly folded in Rafe's hand, the senior muttered, "Well played, young man."

"I thought so too, sir." Rafe spun about and headed out the door, only stopping to exhale when the familiar bell's clanging ceased.

Charlie squeezed Rafe's arm. "You good? Did I miss something?"

Rafe's monotone response sent chills over them both. "He knows that we know."

Rafe felt a slender clasp on his clammy palm. "We have a job to do." Charlie smiled.

An eerie quiet accompanied them down the boardwalk. Charlie's hasty wave to Paschal initiated their plan. Rafe now had to contend with the latest burrow in their bum – Jenkins. Pointing toward the dock's end, Rafe decided to pour salt on the wound and moved toward the Savannah Jane.

"We're taking this one?" Charlie exclaimed.

"Yup. Let's see how Jenkins reacts when we take his prized possession."

"But…"

"Don't worry, we'll take care of her." Rafe cast off the lines, leaving them splayed along the planking, and pulled Charlie aboard. He revved the engine and headed the vessel out the inlet, bound for the cliffs.

"Think Evan and Amber are okay?"

"Positive," Rafe responded with a grimace.

Charlie tapped her index finger on his shoulder, "How about we focus on handling our part."

He shoved the boat into full throttle, chuckling when Charlie lost her footing and careened onto the captain's seat.

Today should be interesting.

~

The Porsche's motor hummed with precision as Evan guided the red Carerra along the island road, speeding up, then slowing down. Amber's arm fluttered outside the window. Her hand motions pointed out the island's historical markers, mimicking typical sightseers. Evan's curved smile confirmed phase one's success. He had spotted the black sedan in his mirror within minutes of departure from the Vitamin Sea. The other two vehicles were free and clear if Charlie's assumptions were correct. Keeping rhythm two car lengths behind the Porsche, he eyed the pursuer following them around the curvy roads. A casual check of his watch prompted Evan's sharp turn toward the vista's shops. His thumb gently massaged Amber's open palm.

"This isn't the ideal way to get some private time, but I'll take it." Her measured lean across the console graced his temple with a kiss.

Amber's infectious smile reminded him of how much he loved her. "Me too." He lifted her hand and adorned it with a peck.

"They're still behind us, aren't they?" She asked, tugging on her bottom lip.

"Yes. We need them to be."

"I know." Amber anxiously twirled a strand of hair around her finger.

"As long as we keep them busy, Charlie and Rafe have more time. I won't let anything happen to you." His statement was intended to assure her of his present and future protection.

"True." Amber's answer yielded wisdom. "Let's shop!" She exclaimed. "We can lead those two hoodlums on a wild goose chase, darting in and out of stores. Plus, it'll be fun."

"Maybe we're better off driving."

"Oh, come on." Nimble fingers toyed with his dark locks. "Brent and his crew are close by if we need them." Her playful, moist lips skimmed across his cheekbone, coercing his agreement.

"You win." Piercing blue eyes crinkled in amusement. Evan knew his capability to deny Amber anything was grossly inadequate.

A fast glance in his rearview confirmed his suspicions. The black sedan remained in tow. Evan squeezed the sporty two-seater into the only available space. Left with no options, his trackers breezed by him and Amber. Positive the two henchmen would double back, Evan reached for Amber's arm, stopping her exit. "Wait. We need to make sure they return."

"Didn't think of that one." She scrunched her nose before a giggle. "And that is why you are the boss, Mr. Holcomb."

"I'm going to remind you of that statement one day." Restricted by the small car's limited size, his muscular frame shifted against the black leather to face her.

"One day! No, I only meant you're the boss today." She teased, her long eyelashes fluttering over blue pools of wonder. Her subtle allure tested his willpower beyond all measure.

They need time to catch up, right?...

Unable to resist the desire that seized him, Evan gently lifted her chin as her lips parted in wait. Held in bondage by the unfathomable joy gripping his heart, the question flowed from him without hesitation. "Amber Scott, will you marry me?"

Sputtered gasps fell from stunned lips. Her rapid blinking led to an astonished stare. "Are you serious?"

"Do you realize how much enjoyment you bring to my life?" Steady hands brushed her windblown strands of hair aside. "You consume me – heart, body, and soul. You have blessed me with a love I never thought possible. As I said before, our lives will be hectic. My company obligations are daunting, and you will be in the spotlight more often than not." Aware his life was and would always be under someone's microscope, ragged breathing stalled his progression.

Her expressive nods encouraged him to continue. "Holcomb Industries will only prosper with you by my side because I could never live without you." Evan leaned his head into her shoulder and uttered a small prayer. Raising, he cupped her flushed cheeks. "Say yes."

Amber placed a hand atop each of his shoulders and yanked him closer. "Yes. Yes." She yelled enthusiastically.

Satisfaction flooded his soul. His lungs collapsed in relief as he devoured her full lips. His kiss was met head-on with every bit of assurance she could muster. Their mutual passion turned to something more in that moment – the promise of a lifetime.

Evan eased his mouth from hers. His kisses trailed to her earlobe. With a gentle nibble, his husky whisper relinquished a vow, "You won't be sorry."

"Neither will you." Her breathy reply coursed through his veins, elevating his pulse. His heart galloped like a racehorse when another of her raspy exhales assuaged his senses. He drank in the succulence her soft lips offered. Evan reeled in a world of contentment until he was interrupted by Amber's sudden tug against his arm. He slowly cracked open one eye. Unwilling to release her, he rallied every ounce of restraint and leaned back. Amber's erratic breathing spawned one word. "Look!"

Parked beside the opposing curb sat a black sedan - empty. Terror filled Amber's eyes. "Where do you think they went?"

Anger inundated Evan's tall frame as he opened his car door and moved to Amber's. Alert eyes swept the length of the sidewalk. Neither man was in sight. "I don't see them, but you can bet they see us." Evan's firm grasp on Amber's elbow conveyed his concern.

"Follow me," Amber whispered and slipped her hand into his. Obnoxious laughter roared between them. "Stop teasing me. I don't have that many dresses." She exclaimed, dragging Evan into the first boutique they approached. Inside, he released her and stood guard by the door as Amber shuffled clothing along the racks. Sweat lined his forehead.

Where did they go…?

"You ready? I don't see anything interesting." Amber's thin smile worried him.

"Hungry?" Evan scanned the walk again, calculating his next move.

"Yes. How about Paschal's favorite place?"

"Sounds good to me." Evan wrapped an arm through hers.

Once outside, he drew her close while guarding the curb streetside. Each moved in a rhythmic pattern toward the bustling restaurant. Hand in hand, the two entered into an atmosphere chiming with music and roaring conversation.

Tucked within the crowds of spirited laughter, Evan felt a small sense of comfort. Amber stilled beside him. Her chair inches from his. Her eyes constantly scanned the room.

"We're okay in here." He squeezed her knee in reassurance.

Accustomed to Jaden, their previous spunky server, Evan was disappointed when an unfamiliar face appeared. Jaden's rambunctious approach to life would have been a welcome refreshment to their current waitress. Of course, remembering her interactions with Paschal, he couldn't help but believe she had a late night with their new friend.

"Hey, is Jaden around?" Evan's eyebrows arched in curiosity.

"I wish she were." The exasperated woman grumbled, wiping sweat from her brow. "Seems she had quite a time last night. Very unlike her not to show up at work if you ask me."

"Really…" Amber smiled at Evan.

The server tucked the menus under her belt, shoved a pencil behind an ear, and chirped, "I'll be back when I can." Pages of orders flopped from the pad stuffed in her back pocket as she rushed to the kitchen.

Amber's giggles brought a refreshing smile to his face. Never tired of her magical laugh, Evan parked a kiss on the tip of her nose. "Looks like this island has become infested with a very contagious illness."

"Illness? I'd call it a blessing," she professed, dragging a soft graze of her fingertips up and down his forearm.

"Then, madam, the two of us and our friends are indeed blessed beyond measure. Who would have thought all those sparks would fly in two short weeks?" A deep chuckle brightened his cobalt eyes. Her timeless beauty and smile at that moment engrained the scene in his heart. Forever more to be the cornerstone of his new life sat the most loving, generous woman he'd ever met.

Loud moans preceded the slam of sizzling plates onto the table. "You two lovebirds think you can find a minute to detach from each other to eat? There has to be a full moon tonight or something." She huffed, clearly ill by the abundance of patrons, and stomped away.

Hungrier than imagined, the couple, void of conversation, inhaled their meal. Fueled and ready to return to the task they were assigned, Evan hailed the waitress, smothering a chuckle with his hand.

"Something else you need?" The woman's flat lips groaned over the filled-to-capacity room.

"Our bill, please?" Evan's amusement ended with Amber's swift kick of his ankle.

"No worries. He paid your tab." Her index finger directed Evan to the slender man smirking on the opposite side of the room. "Said he'd catch up with you outside. Have a good one." Their overworked server tossed as she stumbled away, arms piled with dirty plates.

Amber's terrified inhale made Evan's spine tingle before he shoved his seat backward. A strenuous yank of her hand instantly elevated her long-legged frame, sending her chair sprawling across the floor. Evan seized the opportunity to outmaneuver his pursuers, thankful for the chaos that unfolded from their quick departure.

Within seconds, he pulled Amber into the street and headed for the narrow alleyways. Keeping her in tow, Evan weaved a path between the pastel walls. Rushed hollow clicks of their heels echoed off the cobblestone walk. He listened intently to the hurried steps that scurried around them in pursuit of prey.

In full flight to the sun-drenched, busy sidewalk ahead, Amber paused, jerking Evan backward. Puzzled by her reasoning, he scanned their perimeter. Sure she was doing the same, he watched Amber closely. Her focus remained not on the street but on the tiny storefront window. Front and center sat an exquisite stone, glistening against the white velvet draping.

Motionless, she exclaimed, "Just look at this. Isn't it gorgeous?" Evan's finger flew to her lips.

"Quiet." He whispered.

Angry shouts approached from the opposite end of the alley. The unsettling "ping" and spraying of concrete shards fell feet from them. Gunfire echoed in succession behind them. Escalating their need for escape, Evan shoved Amber forward and pressed redial.

On the first ring, a fierce "yeah" greeted him.

"We're in trouble. Back alleys around from the bistro. They're firing on us."

"On my way. Evan, get to the open." Brent ordered.

Amber covered her head with her free arm, "Tell Rhonda it's where she found me the other day."

Rhonda shouted, "Hang on, Amber, I remember."

"Hurry," Evan yelled and tossed the phone into his pocket.

"Run, now!" He commanded. Amber leaped into a full sprint. His palm pressed into the center of her back, propelling her forward. Evan protected her back while she watched their path ahead.

He heard her mutter in true "Amberism" style, "At least we're giving Charlie and Rafe the time they need."

Misfires struck all around them as bits of cobbles and cement sailed through the air.

No professional is this bad of a shot.

Convinced the two men preferred them alive, Evan inwardly cursed the lack of details he'd received from Rafe as to the attackers' motives.

"Evan, come on." Amber's check on his safety slowed her pace just long enough for disaster. High-pitched screams pierced his ears as she crumpled to the cobblestone walk. Hit by the ricochet of a stray bullet, she wailed in pain, feet from the busy sidewalk exit.

Enraged by her injury, Evan's elevated pulse sent his endorphins into overdrive, "Amber! Hold on, love. This will hurt." In one hurried sweep, his masculine arms cradled her bleeding body against his chest. Gut-wrenching cries assaulted his senses, infusing his powerful legs with inhuman speed. One final check over his shoulder showed him the skinny man's bobbing fist. Shouts of deadly promises bounced off the narrow alley walls. Bursting into the open square, Evan scanned the street for Brent. Bright red spots saturated his shirt's midsection. Blood oozed from Amber's thigh and streamed down her leg.

"Hold on. I've got you." Curious shoppers gasped as the couple emerged. Other bystanders clutched their mouths in horror at the sight. Evan moved to the curb, nervously pacing along the edge. Horn blowing, the Rover screeched to a stop before the duo.

Evan leaped into the passenger seat and angled Amber's bleeding frame onto his lap. "Go now." Tears trickled from his eyes when Amber buried her mouth into his shoulder, stifling her anguished cries.

"Bloody demons," Carol cried. "Amber, hang on."

"Evan…." Brent clenched his jaw.

"Brent, it wasn't his fault," Leah said, brushing hair from Amber's eye. "Take a left here," she shouted. "We have to get her to the hospital."

"Contact Culliver, now." Evan bellowed. "Warn him. They're no longer with us."

Brent snatched up the phone, his call paused by Evan's grim warning.

"If she dies, I'll kill him. Make sure he knows that." Evan nuzzled his chin against Amber's head and whispered prayers into her ear.

THIRTY-TWO

Rafe barreled the Savannah Jane into the deep blue Caribbean Sea using every bit of the power within her. A churning wide wake was all that lingered, leaving a tell-tale message for Jenkins visible from the marina windows. Laughing, he couldn't help himself. Rafe knew Jenkins was watching them. If he disapproved of Rafe's vessel choice, he made no attempt to let them know. The radio remained silent.

Calmer waters graced their mission today. Shorter, slower tidal intervals sloshed against the hull, a welcome change to the bow-beating nightmare they experienced two days ago. Moving skillfully along the sea walls, he angled the SJ into an unexposed nook, invisible from any passing vessels.

Rafe watched from the helm as Charlie roamed about the Savannah Jane, proficiently exhibiting her abilities. Lined across the decking was their dive equipment, prepped and ready before he could even secure the anchor. For whatever it was worth, Rafe felt a strange sense of comfort in Charlie's hidden talents.

Who knew…?

Rafe chucked the satellite phone into the high-back chair and shoved one leg into the cool neoprene suit. Lowering his right shoulder, he slid the black sleeve up his arm. Immersed in his thoughts, he calculated and recalculated the plan's potential, all the while knowing it was their only option. Jolted by the unexpected sound, Rafe reached for the vibrating phone. In a split second, he moved from positivity to apprehension. Rafe knew the incoming call meant one thing. Something had gone awry.

A hesitant "yeah" flowed from his lips.

Screams and shouts rumbled from the receiver. "Rafe, Amber's been shot. Evan and Amber narrowly escaped." Squealing tires roared in the background. Tears welled in his hazel eyes. Barely audible, he mumbled, "How bad?"

"She's losing a lot of blood. Evan has tried to stop the bleeding. We're taking her to the hospital now." Brent uttered between gut-wrenching sobs.

"No!" Rafe shouted. "Take her to Jenkins as fast as you can. He'll be ready. Or he'll rue the day I met him." Rafe's promises rang clear.

"Or me." Brent's threat solidified the breadth of Amber's injury. "We're headed to the marina. Rafe, you and Charlie need to move quickly. They could head your way."

"We'll handle our end. Just get Amber to Jenkins. And, Brent, I never meant for any of this to happen." Sorrow hung over the helm as Rafe slid down to his knees. Grief and anger brewed deep within his bowels. Tears poured down his cheeks, dripping onto the neoprene collar. Riding an emotional rollercoaster, Rafe snatched the phone from the floor and dialed.

The man's tenacious bellow greeted Rafe. "Who is this?"

"Jenkins, this is Culliver."

"I thought I told you…"

"Just listen," Rafe warned. "To say I'm aware of your involvement in this game of cat and mouse is an understatement. I don't give a crap where your allegiance lies." Rafe inhaled deeply, fortifying his resolve. "Amber Scott is on her way to the marina with a gunshot wound. She's hurt because of me and, probably, you also. You better move heaven and earth to ensure that she lives."

"See here, boy…" Jenkins' interruption served little consequence to Rafe

"You need to pray Amber doesn't die because if she does, I will hunt you down, and you will pay. Do you understand?!" He didn't wait for the elder's answer. He threw the phone on the floor and beat a path down the stairs.

"Charlie." He called as he wiped salted moisture trails from his cheekbones. Tears filled his eyes again when he saw Charlie's worried expression.

"I'll get a boat ready." His sniffles subsided as he turned his attention to business. Alerted by Charlie's concerned stare, he felt compelled to share the news. Rafe raked his long fingers through course locks. His tanned skin appeared marred with a stark paleness when his eyes fixed on hers. "We have to hurry. Slim and his cohort vanished after one of them shot Amber."

Charlie's shocked gasp and partial collapse sent Rafe rushing to her side. Lost in sorrow, the two paused. Their height difference offered little challenge to their steadfast hold on the other. Charlie's head skimmed the top of Rafe's shoulder. He locked her petite frame in a bear hug, relaying the phone conversation to her. Whispered vows of retribution poured from their lips on Amber's behalf. Moments later, Rafe released his grasp and focused on Charlie. "We need to lower the dinghy."

Charlie chewed on her bottom lip and whisked a tear from her eye. "Let's handle this so we can check on Amber."

Rafe's timid grin ushered in a new sense of purpose as they readied the small craft and climbed in. Pushing his worry aside, he started the motor and guided the boat toward the marked cavern.

"I didn't think you would remember the way." Her weak smile teased.

"Oh, ye of little faith."

"Think those thugs will know we're here?" Skepticism rang in her voice.

"There's no way they could know where we are. They were too focused on Evan and Amber." Rafe bowed, stroking his brow in anguish.

Charlie nudged his knee and tied the dinghy to the familiar sharp-edged rock. Their planning and preparation were evident as they donned ankle-high swim boots and stepped into the recessed hollow. LED rods surged to a bright glow with a simple shake, illuminating the narrow corridor.

"Take it slow. I'll go first. If there's any indication of trouble, get back to the boat and call the CG." Rafe turned to Charlie, questioning, "Capiche?" Charlie's swift kick in his rear pushed him forward. Her irritated moan followed short shuffles along the uneven cave bottom.

Rafe slid his open palm along the slick sidewall, inch by inch. Trickles of water dripped from above, marking their crown with damp hair strands. Crevices etched from flooding surges of the sea's angry wrath shimmered in the bright light. Moss and dampness clung to the swim shoe bottoms as the two cautiously moved deeper into the darkness.

"Did you and Amber make it this far in last time?" Rafe questioned.

"Yes. Just ahead is where the rocky flooring turns from rough to smooth." Charlie touched his waist, measuring her distance.

Rafe extended his arm and thrust the luminous stick into the pitch-black before him. Limited by the light's lack of depth, he scanned the immediate perimeter. Moisture-laden walls expanded into a larger hollow. How large, he couldn't tell.

Charlie pulled at the back of his wetsuit. "Do you feel the change?" She asked, her foot nudging against Rafe's heel.

Squatting down, he lowered his light to the cavern bottom. Nylon parachute material lay strewn about. Met with resistance to his tug on the corded lines, Rafe yanked harder to no avail. "Wait here," he ordered.

"But…" Charlie stuttered.

His glaring reprimand made its mark when Charlie replied, "Don't be gone long."

Crouched on all fours, Rafe crawled forward. Rocky abutments poked through the neoprene into his knees. Trailing his hand along the tangled cording, he followed a path to the mysterious heaviness opposing his powerful yank.

Weary of the beating his kneecaps and legs suffered from the jagged rocks, Rafe carefully rose to his feet. A breathy inhale singed his nostrils as the air noticeably thickened. Hurriedly, illuminating the cavern with a wave of light, Rafe located the opposition to his unsuccessful tugs. Tethered to the corded parachute lines sat a massive crate. Military-grade steel concealed the chest's contents. Rafe guarded his flank and edged closer. He ran his long fingers along the cool steel's sides prepared for trip wires. Nothing… His slow, calculated reach for the lid to peer inside was interrupted by familiar slang echoing from behind. "Now, why ya wanna go and open Pandora's box, handsome?"

In disbelief, he spun around, "Jaden?"

"Ya sound surprised." Her petite frame emerged from the cave's dark recesses. "Couldn't risk those two halfwits killin' ya. Someone with some brains had to step in."

"How are you involved in all this?" Stunned, he planted his feet, ready for an attack.

"Oh, it's just a hobby. The opportunity kinda fell in my lap. This island harbors quite a few secrets and important people. And like I told them, ya just too cute to kill."

Rafe gritted his teeth, "Jaden, you know I won't let that happen."

"True… exactly the reason why my employers have instructed me to allow ya to join our side. Ya got skills, Culliver. Something desperately needed if ya haven't noticed." Her sinister tone made his skin crawl.

"People like your 'employers' leave a very bad taste in my mouth. And those two idiots of yours critically wounded someone important to me. For which they'll pay. So, thanks, but no thanks." Rafe snapped, inching nearer to the island beauty.

"Ah, yeah, I found out about poor Amber. I sensed a history between the two of ya since that day at the bar. It's unfortunate they got her to Jenkins before we could intercept. Elimination of the competition might've brought ya to my door." Her flirty, malicious giggle reverberated through the cavern.

"Any way… what's ya answer, Rafe? I can't wait forever." Jaden reached behind her back and pulled a handgun from the dive belt.

"You heard my answer," Rafe growled. His LED flashed, spattering slivers of light. The wand grew dimmer by the minute.

"So ya gonna make me kill ya! Such a waste, but ya must know I have no choice."

"Jaden, don't make me do this. I don't want to hurt you."

"Hurt me? How ya figure?" Her laughter clung to the saturated cave walls in the dense air.

Rafe squinted to see. Racking the gun's slide, Jaden leveled the handgun. A nonchalant apology fell from the blackhearted islander, "Well, I'm sorry, handsome."

Defenseless, he launched his makeshift weapon into midair and prayed for a strike. The dimming light stick instead thudded into the black wall behind Jaden. Total darkness enveloped the cavern. Rafe dropped to the cavern floor, dodging the rapid succession of shots when he heard a disgruntled, "No, I'm sorry."

Jaden's surprised gasp preceded a loud whack that spiraled the empty handgun onto the black ground. An eerie silence foreshadowed the heavy thump of her limp form collapsing to the ground. Rafe snagged the opaque device shoved toward him. Emerging from behind Jaden, Charlie chucked the large stone aside and pulled a fresh light stick from inside her wetsuit.

Filled with anger and awe, Rafe lectured, "I thought I told you to stay put."

"Um, a simple thank you might be in order." Charlie spouted, brushing the damp moss from her hands.

Humbled lips whispered, "Thank you," as Rafe moved to Jaden's side. Two firm fingers pressed against her slim neck.

"Is she dead?" Charlie hesitantly asked.

"Not yet. She needs medical attention."

"How do you propose we resolve that issue since we're not supposed to be here? From a professional perspective, I don't think she deserves help." Charlie huffed. "But my conscience will not allow me just to leave her here."

Rafe scratched his head, "Give me a minute to think."

Charlie clasped Jaden's petite wrist. "A minute might be all you have. Her pulse is weak."

"Hold on." Torn between duty and morals, rapid pacing back and forth veered him toward the sturdy steel box. Charlie stepped in behind him. Rafe squatted down. Determination drove him forward. His muscular arms created a sizeable wingspan covering the cold steel's breadth. Rafe gripped the locker's lid. Exhaling slowly, he raised the heavy steel. Charlie crept closer and angled the light for a better view.

Enthralled with the sight before them, Rafe thumbed through the encrypted five-page manifesto.

"Why such a large chest for that?" Charlie asked.

"Because there was more. Jaden or her accomplices must've removed something." Jarred by the sound of her name, Rafe shoved the pages under the wet suit, pulled the zipper tight, and clinched Charlie's hand. As they neared Jaden's listless body, a painful moan escaped her lips.

As she lifted the woman's head, sticky red blotches clung to Charlie's fingers. "You figure out what we should do with her, hotshot? She needs help."

"It may not be the best idea, but it's the only one I have right now."

Rafe scooped up the woman and followed Charlie's lighted path. Inching along, they made their way to the tiny cavern opening. The two maneuvered Jaden's body into the raft. Shallow breaths of crisp, clean air filled her lungs, giving way to sputtered coughs. Rafe yanked the pull cord and roared the small engine to a start. He hastily guided the three back to the Savannah Jane. Jumping from the free-floating craft, Rafe dragged Charlie onto the SJ's decking and beelined for the radio.

Charlie's insistent tugs on Rafe's hand spun him around.

"The boat's floating away. We didn't tie it off." Charlie's anxious shouts appeared to go ignored until his finger flew upward to quiet her cry.

"Coast Guard, Coast Guard, this is the Savannah Jane."

Silenced by an incoming chopper's whirr, Rafe dropped the mic as he watched three divers launch from the open doors. Two were already aboard the dinghy before he could blink. Brisk arm strokes propelled the third to the SJ's swim platform and ladder. Rafe interlocked his fingers behind his head and waited with a smile.

"Hello, sir." Bright, shining eyes rose over the stern and peeped back at him.

"Wilder." Rafe grinned. "Thanks for the assist."

"No problem, sir. Been here all the time." The young man beamed and shrugged off the wetsuit's hood.

"You?" Charlie's eyebrows lifted.

"Yes, ma'am. You know some very powerful people, Ms. Ashby." Wilder's boyish grin spoke volumes.

"True." Rafe chuckled. "If it makes you feel any better, James, I learned that fact the hard way." His teasing shove of Charlie's arm gleaned a soft giggle from her pursed lips.

"Then I should offer my thanks, James, for your protection. And your service." Charlie's extended hand brought forth his cheerful acceptance.

"You're welcome, ma'am." Wilder's proud nod made Rafe's heart leap. He remembered those early days when missions fueled your every purpose in life. Nothing else mattered but success. It's the reason his pulse still raced, even now.

Wilder cleared his throat. "Uhmm. Sir, did you locate what we've been searching for?"

"I did." Rafe eased his hand inside the neoprene suit's chest cavity and withdrew the objective of their entire mission. "Unfortunately, the young woman aboard that dinghy may have one of the most important pieces hidden somewhere. It's imperative she remain alive. Or we could lose our chance of ever finding the thing."

"What piece would that be?" Charlie interjected, nudging her way closer to the two men.

"The map." Rafe moaned, reminded of his failure to complete his orders and keep Amber safe.

"I think we're good, sir. I've had possession of the map for some days now. Our adversaries' hands remained tied without it. Your manifest is only useful if correlated to that chart. Strategic defenses lie submerged between the two, not to mention the lives of some skilled patriots."

"You mean…" Rafe stammered.

"Yes, sir, I do. The 'Dozen' sent you in to locate and

retrieve the chest while our island contact kept the map secure." Wilder James tossed a wave to the chopper's pilot. "I have to go now. If I may say so, sir, it's an honor to be a member of the 'Dozen' serving alongside you." The young man offered a salute and dove into the water. His head broke through the crystal waters, and Wilder hoisted his body into the dangling basket. "And, sir." He shouted, riding the winched carrier up to the copter. "The Scott woman is going to be fine. Talk to Jenkins." Stowed inside, Rafe watched Wilder toss a final salute before the chopper whipped about and headed out to sea.

Charlie's comforting squeeze of his fingertips accompanied her encouraging smile. Amber would live, thanks to Jenkins, it appeared. Rafe draped his arm around her shoulders and stared into the radiant horizon. "I think it's time we see what Old Man Jenkins has to say."

"Agreed," Charlie murmured. "And we should probably say a prayer for Paschal."

"He has good reason to be terrified of Jenkins." Rafe's comment started with a chuckle and rolled into hysterical laughter.

Charlie's spontaneous giggles joined in his amusement. "Ready?" She asked.

"Ready." Rafe led the way to the helm. He pushed the Savannah Jane to her max, to which she responded as expected – brilliantly.

~

Jenkins stood silently at the end of the marina boardwalk. His hat sat anchored at just the perfect angle to compliment the proud tilt of his head. Soft inlet breezes whistled through the gray hair wisps protruding from underneath. He had vowed never to step aboard the Savannah Jane again. The namesake belonged to the same woman who stole his heart all those years ago. His fixation on the Savannah Jane as the craft entered the marina stirred vivid memories of the beautiful redhead. Her flaming curls adorned the bow many a day in stark contrast to the lush white leather cushions surrounding her. The older man winced at the pain his career choice had cost him.

Unwilling to linger in the past and love lost, he breathed deep. Today's events rekindled the fire he felt in his belly for live action. The "Dozen" was his band of brothers, and forever would remain so.

Jenkins watched the unlikely pair. Rafe had repeatedly docked the SJ with a precision that made the man beam. Charlie leaped onto the gray planking and secured the cleat ties. Jenkins strolled to the SJ's slip. His stiff posture portrayed him as evermore the captain and boss.

Rafe moved toward the man, "Sir, thank you for saving Ms. Scott." His head lowered in humility.

"You're welcome. The Dozen's members always protect their own." Jenkins bellowed.

Rafe jumped to attention. His expression seized with shock.

"Well, don't look so surprised, my boy. Being older doesn't mean I can't still be useful." Old Man Jenkins laughed. "Oh, of course, I won't be in the thick of the hunt, but I can still help. Recruits like Wilder take our place as we age and move on."

"But, why didn't you tell me, sir?" Rafe questioned.

"Now, why would I expose myself to anyone and everyone? You had a job to do, just like I did."

Clearing his throat, Rafe threw a head toss to his right side. Rafe's attempt to remind him of Charlie's presence stirred Jenkins' loud chuckle. Charlie rushed to join their huddle. "Oh, you needn't worry about Ms. Ashby. From what I hear, she's held in very high esteem. My clearance level can't touch her friends, my boy. Nor yours, I might add."

This time, it was Rafe's turn to laugh. "How well, I know, sir."

"I'd appreciate it if you two would stop talking about me like I'm not here." Charlie piped, a hand astride each hip.

Jenkins slapped Rafe on his back. "Be careful, my boy. This one has the fire that my Savannah Jane had, along with her red locks." The old man paused and looked to Rafe, "I'll let you two say your goodbyes. Come to the office as soon as possible. I have something for you from your friend Brent. Ms. Ashby, meeting you and your friends has been a true pleasure. Come see me if you visit my paradise again."

Water puddled in his tear ducts. Jenkins knew the anguish Rafe would experience leaving his rekindled relationships with his friends. And Charlie, whether he'd admit it or not.

"Sir," Rafe called.

Jenkins turned around. Admiration curved his mouth into a thin smile as he was greeted with Rafe's formal salute and a "Thank you." He smiled and strolled down the old boardwalk, clicking his cane tip.

~

Rafe and Charlie lingered motionless, shocked by Jenkins' admissions. Each watched the elder return to his usual position inside the marina office.

Charlie pitched the toe of her sandal into Rafe's calf. "The 'Dozen,' huh?"

"Um, hum. Surprised?" Rafe teased.

"Nope. Not all. I know you have skills, Culliver." Charlie giggled.

"I don't suppose you want to tell me who our mutual friends are?"

"Afraid I can't. Who knows, we may need their help again." Charlie paused. "You leaving soon?"

"I presume so. Must be what Jenkins wants to see me about." Rafe surveyed Charlie's reaction. Did he see a hint of disappointment? Her eyes misted over. "It's for the best.

They call us 'ghosts' for a reason." His reply made him sadder than he expected.

"What should I tell Amber?" Charlie's inquisitive nature was on point again.

"Tell her to be happy."

"Okay," Charlie scrubbed her toe on the weathered planks, staring down.

Rafe knew the look. If honesty prevailed, he was feeling the same emotions. He wanted to rid them of the sad atmosphere surrounding the moment. Rafe tilted Charlie's chin and looked into her eyes. "Hey, if the 'Dozen' needs a backup, I'll pass along your name. Capiche?" He grinned, brushed her red curls from her face, and kissed her cheek. Then Rafe spun her around, nudging her forward.

Charlie laughed. Posed for a rebuttal, she whirled back around to find an empty dock.

Concealed from Charlie's view, Rafe listened to her irritated complaints as she walked away.

That was much harder than it should have been...

THIRTY-THREE

Mumbled, frantic voices rolled around in her head. Threats and arguments, then orders, preceded her descent into a nightmare. Her leg throbbed in pain. She thrust her hand toward the tightness that pierced her thigh. Pulling against the bound leather, she screamed to whoever would listen, "Make it stop." Evan's words no longer calmed her. They infused her with anger. He promised that she would be okay. She wasn't. Continuous piercing stabs shot through her nerve endings, causing her head to ache. A warm liquid spilled onto her fingers as her screams gave way to sobs.

Her body was lifted from Evan's lap. An older man's voice roared, "They've got her. Let them help her."

She felt as though she were floating upward. Amber fought to cry out, "Evan…." Suddenly, hollow sounds of air swishing above her head ushered her into blackness. Further attempts to control the circumstances that unfolded around her were useless.

Bright lights blinded her as a woman patted her shoulder. "Breathe deep, honey." The woman's soothing voice said. Amber experienced a numbness shoot up her leg, followed by deep, grunted murmurs surrounding her. Then, nothing…until she felt a soft touch on her hand.

Amber willed her eyes to open, but they were too heavy. It took too much effort. Closed, she wouldn't have to see any unpleasantry if things were bad—no grim expressions upon Evan's or her friends' faces. Closed, yes, she preferred them that way. Closed, she was at peace: no pain, no worries, no problems.

Raspy pleas fell against her ear before she traveled on to blessed darkness. "Amber, please wake up. Remember your vow. You would never make me sorry." Amber squinched her eyelids when cool, moist droplets fell on her cheekbone.

She felt a warm tug on her finger and then a sudden weightiness. Soft strokes across the center of her palm created an inviting welcome. Tear-saturated lips brushed hers, drawing and guiding her back to the one place she'd never freely leave – Evan's love.

Amber willed herself back. They had so much to do together—decades of love to share. Fluttering eyelashes initiated a rise in numbers on the hospital monitor. Her pulse rate quickened.

"Amber, come on, little one. I'm waiting for you." Strong, sturdy arms clung to her.

A tiny sputtered breath filled her lungs, bringing her body to attention. Rapid blinks gave way to slivers of light fragments infiltrating her pupils. Her lids batted, adjusting to the fluorescent tube's brightness.

"Thank God," Evan rained kisses on her forehead.

Her blue eyes, weak from the anesthetic, continued to flutter. "Where am I?" Amber gingerly rotated her head to each side of the pillow.

"Military base. Seems Mr. Jenkins knows some people." Evan's low chuckle brought forth a helpless smile.

"My leg?" Too frail to move quickly, she tried to lift the sheet for a look.

Evan smoothed the covers down. "You and Paschal may be moving at the same speed for a while, but you'll be fine. Jenkins saved your life." A single tear rolled down his face.

"Remind me to thank him." Amber's breath hitched

as she raised her hand to Evan's cheek. Sitting upon her ring finger was the small island store's prized possession. "Am I dreaming?" She choked. Her hand twitched in awe of the vibrant stone nestled on her hand instead of on the velvet display.

Evan's affectionate gaze warmed her heart. "That's the one, right?"

Her head gently bobbed yes. "But how?"

"A bit of memory, but mostly Rhonda. She knew the exact one. Things were a little chaotic when I saw the window showcase. Remember?"

"I definitely remember." Amber jested and then winced in pain when she tried to move.

"Lie still. I'll get someone to help you."

"Evan, I'm okay. Are you sure about this?" Light glistened off the diamond-encrusted ring.

"I told you. I won't do life without you. Besides, you do recall promising to marry me, don't you?" His forehead creased in concern.

"I do." She whispered. "Now come here." She kissed him softly.

"Looks like you have a wedding to plan, Ms. Scott." He brushed the hair away from her face.

"That's going to take a little while." As the effects of the anesthetic wore off, hesitancy and apprehension seized her. "Brent, Leah, is everyone safe? Rafe and Charlie?

"Everyone's fine. And yes, Rafe and Charlie were successful. There's a lot I need to fill you in on."

"I want to go to the Vitamin Sea. Can I?" Her mouth formed a thin smile.

"Let's ask!" Evan replied.

EPILOGUE

Ripples of excitement sent the group into spontaneous cheers. Their weeks of pleasure, drama, and danger spent at the Vitamin Sea could not compare to the giddy emotions that enveloped the gang when Amber and Evan walked through the villa doors. Amber, assisted by Evan's sturdy grasp and a single crutch, hobbled along, sporting a bright smile. Hugs and thankful prayers echoed about the familiar foyer.

Evan released Amber's arm and tossed her a smile. "You good?" Forever concerned for her welfare. With a short nod of her approval, Evan moved toward his buddies and away from the chattering women.

"Fellows, I've never been so glad to return to the Vitamin Sea in my life. From the stiff recliner my carcass sat in for hours upon end to the bland food, two days seemed like a year."

Shrill, ear-splitting screams had the four men clutching their ears for relief as they saw the sisters pawing at Amber's finger. The diamond-encrusted engagement ring gleamed in the light. Tears flowed like a spigot spraying water.

"You didn't!" Brent exclaimed. Nervous hands kneaded the back of his neck. "Do you realize what you've done?"

Evan's deep chuckle preceded his proud grin. "I do. And your sister said yes."

"Leah is going to drive me crazy. She'll expect a proposal, too." Brent's sweaty palms rubbed against his denim pant legs.

The tight clasp of their mouth stifled Steve and Cooper's laughter.

"Oh sure, go ahead and laugh. Look over there…Carol and Kimberly have spun their web of allure around you two. I wouldn't find my situation too humorous if I were you." Brent's anxious stare hit home with the two men, sending them into wild-eyed wonderment.

Finally able to relax, Evan leaned against the foyer table, allowing him time to observe the wonderful splendor coursing through the room. If his friends were this excited, how would his siblings react?

Guess it's time they met Amber…

That introduction would be the first item on his agenda when they arrived in Charlotte two days from now.

Amber limped over to join him, cozying up beside him. Her radiant smile filled with delight, and he couldn't have been happier. Pushing the crutch to her side, she teased, "I think we caused a ruckus."

"I'd say we did. Your brother's freaking out, if you can't tell." He laughed.

"Oh, believe me, I know. So are they." Amber's swift point toward her sisters spelled trouble. "We're going to have our hands full trying to keep this wedding manageable. Kimberly is already designing the gown in her head and wants us to fly to LA."

Evan leaned over and graced her lips with a tender kiss. "Your wish is my command," he replied with a bow.

Suzanne's shout sent Brent to his knees, "We can have a double wedding! Leah, you and Brent should get married, too."

Steve reached down and drew his friend's limber frame upward. Brent's expression paled before he choked, "I knew it."

More squealing sounds from the sisters induced worried stares from Brent, Steve, and Cooper.

Evan could only smile. Amber would soon be his bride, and if his instincts were correct, he'd be granting his beloved co-worker plenty of time off, too.

Amber leaned to whisper in his ear. "I love you, Evan Holcomb. Now and forever."

A blissful aura surrounded the couple. "Remember, I said it first." He beamed. "Now, let's see about this LA trip."

~

Scornful slanted eyes peered through the Vitamin Sea's window as he watched the energetic group with disdain. Plans of marriage, trips, and endless love made his stomach lurch. Anger over how the failure of his agenda had cost him millions of dollars coursed through his veins. Not to mention, he was also the center of ire for some very resourceful people. Their vow to extract justice and vengeance would not go unfulfilled.

The slim man concealed by the shrubbery listened intently as he clutched his side, mumbling a vow to enact his revenge. Like a snake in the grass, he slithered away from the happy cries of the seven women inside. His lips curved in a sinister grin.

"Time to book a flight to California," he mumbled.

T C (Terri) Wilson was born in Augusta, Georgia. Crossing the Savannah River and moving a mere thirteen miles away at age five, she resides in the quaint equestrian town of Aiken, South Carolina, with her husband, Randy. The retired mother of two welcomed her first grandchild in January. She enjoys watching her favorite NHL teams pass the puck surrounded by her rambunctious granddogs when she is not spoiling baby Wilson. A member of the SCWA and RWO, her first novel in the Sisters Seven series, *Finding a Stranger*, debuted in 2023. *A Stranger's Protection* is the second release from the series.
Connect with Terri online at www.tcwilsonauthor.net
Facebook:@tcwilsonauthor
Goodreads: @tcwilson